Praise for **The**

'Heart-wrenchingly funny, bitter-sweetly romantic, Mendelson is rapidly becoming the English Nicholas Sparks'

Paul Harrison, BAFTA-winning director.

'A beautifully written and deeply touching love story, with an elegant plot, and an engaging protagonist'

Leigh Russell,
bestselling author of the *Geraldine Steel* series.

'A real page-turner. Paul A. Mendelson weaves a compelling tale across 20 years full of romance, comedy and great one-liners. I was both amused and engrossed.'

David Lister, *The Independent*.

'Paul A. Mendelson's hugely entertaining tale of a Scotsman's attempts to come to terms with a formative incident from his youth that is also the biggest unresolved regret is a winning mix of romance, wistfulness and laugh-out-loud comedy that flips intriguingly (and unpredictably) between past and present.'

Paul Alexander. Screenwriter. *Staggered. Red Dwarf*.

'A page-turner of a story about an intoxicating teenage romance and the long shadow it casts over our life, written with Paul A Mendelson's trademark warmth, wit and honesty. A joy to read that made me laugh and cry!'

Hayley McKenzie,
script editor, founder & CEO of *Script Angel*

'What a wonderful story. I was sucked smoothly into this rites of passage tale. From a shy youth who embarks on a brief teenage love affair, on an exchange trip to America, Charles emerges as a confident writer of novels who finds himself revisiting his past and finding that part of him had stayed in the USA forever.'

Roy Gould, TV producer and writer.

'I loved this book! It is warm and engaging from the start - the characters and situation both funny and believable. A delightful and moving page-turner, with some unexpected laugh-out-loud moments!'

Rebecca Lacey. Actor.

'A thought-provoking tale, which doesn't always take you in the direction you think it will. It captures perfectly the longing, awkwardness and thrills of a first love. And crystallises a time before mobile phones, WhatsApp and FaceTime when we actually waited for a letter, making that longing even more poignant.'

Francine White, show-business journalist.

'A beautifully written coming-of-age story. The vivid writing and brilliant non-linear structure made reading it so cinematically alive that I had to make myself a bowl of popcorn while I read it!'

Susan Denaker. American actor.

The Forever Moment

Paul A. Mendelson

The Book Guild Ltd

First published in Great Britain in 2023 by
The Book Guild Ltd
Unit E2 Airfield Business Park,
Harrison Road, Market Harborough,
Leicestershire. LE16 7UL
Tel: 0116 2792299
www.bookguild.co.uk
Email: info@bookguild.co.uk
Twitter: @bookguild

Typeset in 11pt Minion Pro

Printed and bound by CPI Group (UK) Ltd, Croydon, CR0 4YY

ISBN 978 1915603 852

British Library Cataloguing in Publication Data.
A catalogue record for this book is available from the British Library.

To M.
Forever.

This book is dedicated to all the kind people of Lexington, Kentucky, who welcomed and hosted a group of Scottish schoolchildren so graciously many decades ago.

And with apologies to the elderly lady in the record store who sweetly asked us if we spoke English and we told her that we had learned it on the plane coming over.

The truth brings the past into the present
and prepares us for the future.
That's what truth does.

MAYA ANGELOU

The airport is hoaching with schoolchildren.

'Hoaching' isn't a word with which the locals are particularly familiar, although several of those attending this departure day have become far more familiar with this and other such arcane words over the preceding three and a half weeks.

The teenage girls or, as they prefer to think of themselves, young women (especially those visitors who are concluding somewhat reluctantly a very first long-distance trip on their own) are unashamedly sobbing. The young men stick to manfully shaking hands. Or – if forced/ gently encouraged – hugging bravely.

It isn't a large airport, as airports in this massive country can be, but the noise levels this particular Sunday defy such modest description. Even more so when the parents of the host children, together with whatever other offspring or elders they have dragged along with them, rally together to scream what has now become almost a mantra, in raucous but genuinely heartfelt unison.

"Y'all come back now, weans!"

Even amidst all these painful separations, one young man appears notably more unwilling to break free than his fellows.

Whilst he cannot permit himself to be quite as uninhibited in demonstrations of anguish as he might wish, his quivering face – and that of the equally desolate young person staying behind – tell the story with utmost clarity to any observer. (Of which at least three, it must be said, are looking far more relieved than saddened.)

And, in some special way, it is stories that have brought this young couple together. It is what they have been all about.

When the customary farewells are politely and properly delivered (with expressions of gratitude sufficiently eloquent to make the departing fellow's parents back home justifiably proud), it is left to the teary young woman to utter the final words.

Words with so much meaning that they will resonate for far longer than even the boy might imagine.

"Don't forget to write."

All he can do is nod. And turn away before he fragments.

THE REUNION

ONE

Charles can't recall exactly which town he is in.

He realises – or at least devoutly hopes – that this is a purely temporary lapse. It is more likely brought on by the fact that he is standing in yet another well-stocked but currently almost deserted bookstore, in one more attractive university locale, channelling all available energies into charming the bookstore manager, an elegant woman in her late fifties, and her younger, more overtly enthusiastic assistants. All this whilst awaiting the doors to be opened once more on the evening's special event, and for those devout book lovers already gathering outside, on this thankfully balmy spring evening, to stroll excitedly in.

Charles doesn't consider himself by nature an arrogant man. At least not as arrogant as he believes he could justifiably be in the current clement circumstances, leaning as he is on a display table brandishing review-

3

splattered showcards and gleaming hardback copies of *The Forever Moment* by C.D. MacNaughtan, his latest and potentially most successful novel. It's not *The Da Vinci Code*, which is still topping the bestsellers list here and surrounds him even now like a curse, but it should help him to pay his bills for a while longer.

There is a term that he is fumbling for, the go-to buzzword to nail the relationship between this particular book and the recent happy trajectory of his career, but he can't quite grasp it. At least not while he's enchanting the staff with one of his well-worn stories. An anecdote related, as ever, in his gentle but distinctive – and hopefully not too impenetrable – Glasgow brogue. Glasgow, Scotland he has to keep explaining, in case there might be another one closer to home. Like Paris, Texas, or London, Ontario.

"...And I'm forever chastened by that story of the author Monica Dickens signing her books in Australia," he begins, and notices with appreciation the rapt faces of his younger listeners. "A wee lady comes up to her, novel in hand and asks—"

"C.D.…."

"No, she doesn't ask 'C.D.'" He smiles, turning to his interrupter. "Kevin, you're killing my charm offensive here."

"Mea culpa," says Kevin Roberts, a tall, urbane African American in his early thirties, with an amiable smile to rival that of his author, only with better teeth, yet invested with a sense of purpose and punctuality of a far higher order. Unlike Charles, the younger man is wearing a serious tie, because despite preconceptions

4

– at least those of this particular Brit, whose first such transatlantic book tour this is – Americans can often be surprisingly formal.

"Excuse my publisher," continues the guest of honour, "where was I? Oh, aye… so the wee Australian lady says to Monica, 'Emma Chisit'. And the famous writer duly takes her pen and scribbles on the book '*to Emma Chisit, from…*' But the wee lady yelps in horror: 'No! EMMA CHISIT?'"

Three looks of utter bafflement confront him. And he can't even see that of Kevin, whose head is swiftly turning towards the front entrance. "It's '*how much is it?*' in Australian," explains Charles, his patience wearing just a tad thin. "Emma… chis?" He finally turns to Kevin. "Maybe we'd better—"

"…stick to the book readings," agrees Kevin Roberts, nodding to the store manager, who gratefully accepts the nod and passes it discreetly on to her youngest assistant.

"Let battle commence," says Charles, running a hand through his thick, well-cut hair, deep brown and wavy with a premature but hopefully distinguished hint of grey, as he tries yet again to recall the name of this bloody town.

*

He is well into his reading when he first notices her.

Or, at least, when she attracts the earliest sliver of a glance that is still focussed more earnestly on the volume in his hand, although by now he could almost quote the relevant passages unaided. It must be when he raises his eyes a fraction, unusually dark, hooded eyes in an almost olive, quite un-Scottish face, to acknowledge the gratifying smiles from his audience, that the young woman first truly begins to impinge.

> *"'...Oliver supposed that the painful act of recollection, even decades before his inevitable decrepitude, must already be a little like drowning,"* he reads, *"that time when they say your past life flashes so swiftly before you. Yet surely, he mused, a whole lot of people would have had to have survived such profound immersion and reported back for this particular theory to hold water."'*

She is just strolling in through the narrow doorway, a straggler, a latecomer, although seeming not in the least contrite or sheepish. In fact, looking almost surprised that this visiting author from over the pond should have dared to commence his one-night-only event without her. But then she shrugs a sort of apology into the air, as if this is something one is supposed to do rather than anything particularly heartfelt.

> *"'And exactly what episodes of your past life are meant to spring to mind, as you're going under for the accepted and conclusive third time?'" He pauses for a self-deprecating smile. "'The pivotal moments or the trivial, the ecstatic or the sad? The birth of your first child or where you left those keys you'd been looking for over the ages. Damn, wouldn't that be annoying?'"*

It is on this next, more deliberate glance, as he acknowledges the appreciative and always appreciated laughter, that Charles suddenly finds himself unable to breathe. He is not certain which will come first – the heart attack or the release of the entire contents of his stomach. The cold perspiration forming on his brow and less available parts of his anatomy could presage either eventuality.

As his eyes connect with hers – almond-shaped eyes which impossibly are still so familiar to him, in a fetching face whose features he believes are by now almost etched into his feverish brain – the stammering begins. Not a good look in an author whose delivery should remain proprietorially fluid. Nor indeed is the accompanying, verging on rabid, stare over the attentive heads of almost everyone else in the room.

> *"'Yet – er – yet what still comes cascading back – er – to him today, on this his 'big' birthday – yes – as he sits surrounded by glittery, shop-bought cards announcing cruelly that people will have to shout at him from now on or – or – made-to-order items from similarly ageing cousins, showing them both as half-naked toddlers – is – is…'"*

Despite his obvious distraction, he can sense that certain members of his audience are just beginning to grow restless or, at the very least, vaguely disconcerted. When a few turn to follow his slightly mad gaze towards the back of the bookstore, C.D. MacNaughtan, author not in residence, concludes that he had better make some serious attempt at getting through the task at hand.

Curiously, this slowed down yet oddly staccato manner of delivery actually serves to make the final paragraph of his reading even more resonant.

"Er – 'the one brief yet evanescent moment in his young life that truly affected everything from that time onwards. For better or indeed for worse. What he calls – with an ex-adman's glib turn of phrase – his... er... his "forever moment"!"'

Charles makes to bestow a disarming smile on the gathering, graciously acknowledging this recent brief fugue, as he continues to read.

Yet Kevin, who has been scanning the room with professional acumen, in order to gauge the prevailing levels of attention and propensity to buy, is starting to notice how his author's eyes appear to be continuously swerving back, like rifle sights, to lock on to one particular and far from unattractive young listener. Most probably a student, he surmises, in a room which assumedly boasts more than the average share of temporary or tenured academics. (Although even this evening's featured author would grant that his latest opus, whilst apparently compelling and acceptably well wrought, is far from a literary heavyweight.)

After offering a few more hopefully enticing paragraphs, Charles finally closes his by now well-thumbed and much-annotated copy. The immediate response, to his and his supporters' relief, tips towards the enthusiastic rather than the merely polite. Which happy outcome is noisily endorsed by the manager of the bookstore, grateful not to have to lead the way, as she occasionally must, with some firm, *pour encourager* claps.

As the rolling wave of appreciation gradually subsides to a ripple, the older woman edges towards its recipient, still clapping. "Thank you so much, Mr MacNaughtan – or 'C.D.' – for such an enticing nugget of *The Forever Moment*. Which I for one cannot wait to devour, when I get some rare 'moments' on my own. But first of all – would you please tell us what these intriguing initials stand for?"

"Eh?" says Charles, manfully wrenching his gaze away from its semi-permanent perch on back row centre of his audience. "Oh, well, I would. Gladly. But then I would have to kill you."

The older woman appears shocked, until she realises that this is simply a further example of her esteemed guest's rather curious and probably British attempt at humour. Taking her cue, however, from the welcome laughter of those who she trusts are about to become her customers, she happily chortles along with them.

Charles notices with some gratification that the young person as yet unknown, who has now become the only audience that matters, is also laughing unreservedly.

This makes her already alluring face, shrouded in long, swishable, ash-blonde hair, suddenly glow, as if his gaze has become a powerful spotlight in the otherwise subtly lit room. Yet, even more significantly, it also causes her own disarmingly open eyes to crinkle in delighted amusement until they almost disappear, as if all these elements, finding themselves supported by some impressive bone structure, are working faultlessly as a team. Somehow he knew that this would be exactly how her distinctive features would collaborate, whilst also pondering that this is a face he would define as unmistakably American, without having the slightest notion as to precisely why. Unless, of course…

Sensing that the bookstore manager is staring at him, Charles reluctantly drags himself back to his duties.

"Yes. Well. I'm sure we have a whole barrel of questions to fire at 'C.D'," says the bemused woman. "So – who would like to start?"

As a Scot, Charles is only too aware of that natural reluctance to be the 'tall poppy' in a crowd, any crowd. It is a recognised syndrome of his clan, despite having so much as a nation about which to feel tall. He has already observed, over these few hectic days, that folk on this side of the pond do tend to be rather more forthcoming, yet he suspects that tonight's lot might require at least some gentle prodding. So he is quite surprised when the one person with whom he most wants to engage is the very first to speak.

"Hey," says the young woman. "Thanks for the read, Mr MacNaughtan. Book sounds great. Did you… did you have a 'forever moment'?"

It is only when he hears Kevin whispering his name with some urgency, from a seat right at the front, that Charles realises he has been staring at the questioner a mite too intensely and processing what she has just enquired of him perhaps that wee bit too long.

"Eh? Er, yes. Sorry. Great question. Thanks. Aye, I did. Have a… 'forever moment'. Not the exact one my older guy, my fifty-year-old – *I'm not quite there yet!* – not the one that he remembers." Once again he appears to go into himself, as if he is thinking out loud rather than addressing an audience. "But without it... well, I truly doubt I could have written this novel."

To his surprise, the young woman continues to interrogate him. "Are you pleased you had it? Sorry, that was two questions."

"I'll forgive you," says Charles, with a smile, "and offer you two answers. As a writer, yes. Yes, I am pleased. Our lives are the well we draw from. And then we... y'know, we embellish. We reconfigure. We 'what if...?'" He shakes his head, as his expression for a moment loses its professional patina and becomes almost uncomfortably real. "But, as a human being – that's a far longer story."

"I've got all evening," says the young woman.

Charles can almost hear the audience raise its collective eyebrows.

"Next question, please?" says the bookstore manager hurriedly.

As more hands begin to rise, Charles rips his attention away from the still-smiling questioner. He manages, with a supreme act of will, not to stare at her again – or at least not too overtly – until she is standing patiently at the table to which he has finally shifted, all questions answered, in order to sign copies of his book.

Those behind her in the line are already sensing they might be waiting some time for their own brief, semi-private audience with the tall, darkly interesting author from way over the ocean.

"Thanks for the questions," says Charles.

He covers what could be an unnerving upwards gawp from his bookstore stool with a smile that he is hoping approaches natural. If he has found this person's appearance perturbing from a distance, he is feeling even more disconcerted now that her innocent yet curiously knowing face is only inches away from his own.

"Kinda obvious," she replies, with a grin. "But you're welcome. Hey, I really loved your other books."

"*So you're the one!*" says Charles, still scrambling for that lightness of tone which could be the exact counterpoint to the way he is currently feeling. "Well, this is the fella that's supposed to be what they call my – what's the term – aye, my 'break-out'. Words that hitherto I'd only heard employed when talking about Colditz or rampaging acne." Who still says 'hitherto', he wonders, even as she grins. And who knows from Colditz?

"I'm sure it's wonderful." She pauses for a moment, not moving, and Charles is certain that he can hear a communal sigh from the line rapidly backing up behind her. "I'm a writer too. Well, trying to be. Actually… er…" He registers her hesitation and nods her on. "See, I run the college writers' group. This college. Are you still here tomorrow night?"

"Well…" says Charles, seemingly thrown by such an incisive question. Fortunately, his trusty publisher is at hand with a cough and a brisk shake of the head, both of which Charles seems to hear at equal volume. "Sorry." The author shrugs, with what appears to be genuine regret. "If it's Tuesday, it must be Connecticut! Or somewhere."

He pauses for a moment, simply to stare at her, wondering whether to take just that one step – or, more accurately, Olympian leap – beyond propriety. And knowing that he really has no choice, even while he senses Kevin breathing Ivy League frustration into his writer's overly taut neck. "But we could have a coffee or something after this. To... discuss your writing. If you're..."

"I'll be in the place across the road," says the young woman, immediately. "No rush." She taps her copy of the book, as the sighs behind her morph into despairing moans. "It's Abi. A-b-i. Short for Abigail. Abigail Chadwick."

"Abi," repeats Charles, as if it is the lost chord or some other enchanting sound his ears had never expected the sublime pleasure of hearing. He signs: '*To Abi – and thanks for the curiosity. Good luck with the writing. Best wishes, C.D.*', then adds the 'MacNaughtan', just in case she forgets.

He is certain that he hears someone in the line mutter, "*Is he writing another frickin' novel?*" but chooses to ignore it. An attitude he maintains even after Kevin has whispered, "*What the fuck?*" in his ear. Until, of course, he realises that, in this case, he has to come clean. Or at least not appear quite so dirty.

As Abi moves out of his orbit, temporarily, in order to complete her purchase, Charles turns to the younger man. "I'd love to explain," he apologises quietly, "but I can't. Because honestly, Kevin, I don't even bloody understand it myself."

They both notice that his hand is shaking, as the next open book is slammed down in front of him.

"Is this cheaper on Amazon?" comes a voice from the crowd.

"Quicker," comes another.

TWO

Charles has never, of course, frequented this particular crowded Main Street bar/café/restaurant, yet it feels utterly familiar to him. As he had almost expected that it would, déjà vu clearly being the specialty of the season.

Perhaps it is the dim lighting and exposed brickwork, the classic forties movie posters on the walls alternating with framed vinyl covers, an over-equipped bar (brimming with product nobody drinks or can even pronounce) running the entire left side of the room. Inevitable candles in tinted glass flicker and melt on the grainy wooden tables, contemporary yet inoffensive music blends with well-tempered air-conditioning and excitedly upmarket, liberal chatter. TV screens spread around the room show muted sports, soundless MTV or the latest incredible images from Mars, courtesy of Nasa's latest, much-travelled Rover.

Charles reckons that anyone visiting here, even from a distant planet, would discern within seconds that this is a popular, mid-level hostelry in a college-dominated town. The uniting factor of denim alone sends out its unmistakeable signals, providing the uniform for a student population striving ceaselessly for individuality and, for the town's academics, what is seen as right-on agelessness, as they attempt to blend in unshowily with an eternally youthful crowd.

There are also the obvious tourists, who aren't quite certain whether to dress up or dress down and so compromise with an uneasy mix of both.

The venue's most recent arrival reckons that he has the visiting-Scottish-author-in-random-New-England-university-town look firmly nailed. And the casually glancing around, for someone who already has a table and is most probably a habitué, gives him an air of unforced confidence, with permission to smile. Especially when he notices Abi, the amiable young woman from the bookstore and object of his recent, unresolved fixation. She is ensconced at a corner table, busily tapping her phone, and already has an unsipped coffee beside her. He swiftly orders a beer for himself.

Before joining her and in advance of her glancing up, Charles takes some time out just to watch this Abi person for a moment. He knows that he is still quite shaken by their encounter and that he has to strive a bit more earnestly for insouciance, eminence grise and any other French stuff that won't simply unsettle her. Yet he can't help wondering if she is writing or texting a friend about him or maybe even looking him up on that new Wikipedia thing.

It is only when his latest fan raises her head to check

out the bar area for recent arrivals that he is prompted to move in her direction.

"Hey!" she says, which he knows is simply American for 'hi' and not the instinctive expression of outrage that it is back home.

Charles wonders briefly if he will ever stop thinking of this country as the world's biggest outlet for getting English so intriguingly and delectably wrong and knows immediately that this is just another symptom of his 'problem'. Something dating way back to a previous century, a more innocent time, memories of which the unanticipated advent of this young woman has stirred up sufficiently to send him reeling.

He sits down, saying nothing, and simply smiles unblinkingly at her. After some moments of this, the young woman thinks enough already, and decides to take the lead. "Do you like do this a lot?"

"What," he replies, slightly shaken, "invite young American women for coffee?"

"I meant book events. But this too."

"No. No, I don't. Invite…" She wonders why Charles should appear quite so flustered. This is what she might have expected, and indeed has occasionally experienced, in guys her own age, not someone older and more formed, with all the cards firmly in his hand. "It's just…"

Abi waits until the silence becomes uncomfortable and then a bit longer. "Just…?" she says finally, fascinated by what this increasingly bemusing foreigner might have to say.

Aware of her gaze and his own jarring hesitancy,

Charles makes a stirring effort to come across as at least semi-normal. "So – Abi. Short for Abigail. Tell me about yourself."

"About myself – or my writing?"

"Don't you think they're one and the same?" suggests Charles, now on firmer ground. He senses that in the throes of an ongoing, semi-professional conversation, his staring into her open and clearly engaged face and possibly her very soul has regained at least some modicum of legitimacy. Surely it even verges on respect. "There's nothing more plumbable than our own depths, Abi."

The young woman appears to afford this nugget, hardly earth-shattering in writer-world, more mind space than Charles might have deemed it deserves. "Sure. I suppose," she says, but then adds, looking almost morose, "if a person's got depths there to plumb."

When she notices that this curiously self-deprecating admission is confusing the older man and is even in danger of railroading what might clearly be a pivotal conversation, at least for her, she immediately offers him her best and hopefully most cheery smile. "Okay, I shall reveal myself in all my profoundness or maybe profundity – if you tell me what C.D. stands for."

"Well…"

"But hey, if it's a state secret…"

For a few seconds Charles says nothing and simply sips his beer. Abi wonders genuinely whether it represents a name so mortifying or dorky that the poor man's credibility will be demolished at a stroke. Clarice would do it.

"My first name is Charles," he reveals, which is hardly mind-blowing. "MacNaughtan was my mum's maiden name. So far, so good, I see you thinking. Well, here's what you might call the kicker. My real surname is Dickens."

For a moment, Abi says nothing. And then she almost snorts. "Oh. Oh, Jesus! *Was that a joke?* I mean... your parents..."

"They thought it was hilarious." He shakes his head. "Why am I telling you this? I don't tell anyone this. So schtum. Omertà! Writers' code! O-kay, moving swiftly on. Where are you from, Abi?"

She senses, from the interrogatory nature of the question and the surprising intensity of his stare, that Charles is looking to her to provide critical information rather than simple background detail. Although God knows why.

"Surinam," she says.

"You're making that up."

Abi smiles mischievously. "You got me! I'm from New Paltz. It's in boring upstate New York. Which, as you may not know, is absolutely nothing like scintillating downtown New York."

Charles looks deflated. "Oh. New York State. Aye. Okay then."

"See!" says Abi, almost exultantly. "Now you're disappointed! And the way you've been like looking at me..."

Charles sighs. Wasn't she bound to notice? "Oh, sorry. Do I seem... creepy?"

Abi shakes her head vehemently. You probably do

not want the guy who could possibly further your writing career thinking you regard him as a total scumbag. "More like, y'know, weird. But not, y'know, like in a serial-killer way," she explains reassuringly. "Not even in a hitting-on-me way. It's like… well, it's like you already knew me. But you just can't recall from where. Hey – maybe if you drowned a little!"

"You're very perceptive," says Charles, permitting himself a laugh. "Which is kind of mandatory, for a writer! I'm sorry, Abi, but yes, you're absolutely right. You do truly remind me of someone. Uncannily so. Someone from so very long ago."

"Is *that* why you asked me here?" He doesn't deny it or at least not swiftly enough. "Well, just thank her from me, whoever she is. Now – can I quiz you on how you got your big break in writing?"

"You can indeed. But I doubt it'll help and right now your life is more interesting. At least to me." He rests his head on his hand, bestowing on the young woman the garland of his full attention. "Just give me a wee bit more about Abi. I dunno – something *you* could write a book about. Or maybe you already have. Like I said, and I'm sure you already know, we writers are our own best subject."

Abi stares right back at him, looking thoughtful. Their faces are now inches apart at the small table, in the flickering candlelight. Her voice lowers, as if she wants no one else around to hear.

"O-kay. I suppose you mean like… oh, I dunno. Well yes, like me being adopted at birth by fundamentalist Christian missionaries?"

Charles looks as if he has been struck. Abi is certain that, even with all the music and the chatter, she has heard the man gasp.

And so she carries on. "Hence the biblical name. Abigail was one of David's wives. His second to be precise. Doubt he called her Abi, though." After a few more seconds of silence, when the author still isn't responding and it looks like temporary paralysis might have set in, with a dash of lockjaw on the side, she dares to touch his wrist. "Mr... MacNaughtan? Charles? Er... C.D.? You okay? You seem a little... I dunno... shocked. Was it the Christian mom and dad bit?"

Charles finds himself still unable to speak. The thoughts are coming too fast, none of them shareable. He simply swigs his beer and waits.

"So. Who's your favourite author?" asks Abigail Chadwick, clutching at straws.

THREE

The hotel that Kevin has selected for Charles and himself in this attractive little town could have been located anywhere in the state or even the entire country. Possibly anywhere in the world. So whilst Charles has in fact recalled the name of the place in which he has briefly but far from uneventfully found himself, the lodgings haven't exactly been throwing out many definitive clues.

He feels relieved that by the time he descends for breakfast he has his bearings geographically, because everything else in his life over the past twelve hours has been sucker-punched off its axis. And the sight of a large, florid man at the next table pouring a local forest's worth of maple syrup onto a pile of breakfast pancakes the size of a well-sprung mattress isn't helping much to settle him.

"Good morning, Braveheart."

Charles hasn't even noticed his publisher's approach, so he is certainly not prepared for the shit-eating grin on his face. A face still flushed with pride from what Charles now recognises as the super-fit New Yorker's ridiculously early jog.

"On your own, I see." The standing man smiles.

"Excuse me?" says Charles, before he absorbs the full implication. "Och, man, you didn't think…?" He notices that Kevin is holding a large manila envelope.

"Hey, she was cute," says Kevin, sitting down for a moment before the breakfast buffet calls. "You're single. Roguish. Okay, old enough to be her—"

"I'm thirty-nine, Kevin!" protests the author. "Not… fifty. And FYI, all that we exchanged were addresses. I said that she could send me some of her stuff. Y'know, her writing."

"An oldie but a goody," says the younger man, offering him the envelope. "And I'm guessing she didn't waste much time. Reception asked me to give you this. It was handed over early this morning, apparently." He stares at Charles, unwilling to let this go. "Charles, something else was going on last night. You even said so yourself."

Charles pauses for a moment. Yet even Kevin can discern that, in the pantheon of human pauses, this is less of the having nothing-much-to-say variety and slanted far more towards the this-is-something-*way*-too-important-with-which-to-come-right-out. "Kevin," he says, eventually, "I want you to change our itinerary. Please."

"Do what?" says Kevin. Understandably. He has worked good and hard on every tiny facet of this itinerary, spreadsheets to the fore. It is what he does. He also does it for holidays, which drives his wife crazy.

"Kevin, I can't explain," continues Charles, looking as mystifyingly apologetic as he is able. "It doesn't have to be today or tomorrow."

"Oh, good," says Kevin, but he doesn't really mean it.

"But I need you to set up another reading." Charles opens the bulging envelope and slides out a thick sheaf of typewritten pages. An inexpensively printed business card is paper-clipped onto the covering letter.

"The schedule's pretty tight, Charles," protests the bemused publisher. "We've got Cambridge, Georgetown, New Haven… Where were you thinking?"

"Lexington."

Kevin appears somewhat relieved. "Well, at least that's in Massachusetts, so—"

"Lexington, Kentucky," corrects Charles.

"Shit!" says Kevin Roberts.

FOUR

En route to Lexington, Kentucky. May 1982.

"CHARLIE DICKENS?!"

The plane belongs to Pan-Am and is a 747-100 from Prestwick, Scotland, to the Worldport Terminal at Kennedy Airport, New York.

The incredulity belongs to the seventeen-year-old passenger sitting next to a similarly teenaged Charlie Dickens.

The boys are just two of almost one hundred spirited ambassadors for Scottish youth bound for a handful of ultimate destinations in the USA, most of them towns and cities of which they have barely heard in their lives. Courtesy of the renowned English-Speaking Union, although to many English speakers around the world some of these fortunate delegates would barely qualify.

Indeed, the accent of the lad sitting next to Charlie, a young Scot who is proudly and perhaps even defiantly wearing a kilt, is one of the strongest Charlie has encountered for some while. And coming from Glasgow, as the young Dickens does, this is saying something.

"It was my dad's idea of a joke," explains Charlie, not for the first time. He has a brand-new spiral notepad on his knee, in which he is determined to record every aspect, observation, phrase, saying and experience over the ensuing three and a half weeks, whilst also secretly hoping that his days will be so filled with wonders and surprises he will hardly have time to put newly purchased Parker pen to paper.

"Ha bloody ha!" says the other boy, shaking his head in disbelief.

"I wouldn't care," says Charlie, who clearly does. "Dickens wasn't even his family's real name."

"What was it – Shakespeare?" The boy, who is one of the blondest people Charlie has ever encountered, with the palest of skin and eyebrows, is laughing at his own repartee.

"I wish." Charlie laughs, because right now he is in a state of such overwhelming excitement that he would laugh at a sick bag or a safety drill. "I dunno – Dershowitz, Dishowisky. Something. When my dad's family came here from Poland, they chose a name they knew was very English. They were – they are – Jewish."

After this revelation the other boy can do nothing other than simply stare, wide-eyed and white eyebrows raised, at his new travelling companion. As if searching for what – horns? Charlie is unused to such scrutiny, especially from someone so ridiculously Aryan, but the other guy appears so very affable and genuinely curious that it would be impossible to take offence.

"Away ye go!" exclaims the boy. "I've never met a Jew. Never even seen one, except maybe on telly. Definitely not in Falkirk. Nobody has. I'm Norman, by the way. Norman Gemmell. Presbyterian."

"Away ye go! Actually, there's a fair few Jews in Glasgow. When they got off the boat from Russia, they were told it was New York! But really I'm only half-Jewish." He can immediately sense this Norman Gemmell guy checking him out, as if to determine which half is the more Semitic and deciding, on the limited scrutiny permitted, that it could well be the upper. "You ever been to America before?" asks Charlie, hoping that spiritual discussion and pursuant examination have run their course.

"Never been on a fuckin' plane before," admits Norman Gemmell, shaking his head. "And now look where our schools are sending us – us and half the kids here. Kentucky, for Christ's sake! Not New York or LA. Not even Chicago. *Where the hell is Kentucky?*"

Charlie realises that he has been so beside himself at being selected by his school to make this trip, a voyage supported financially (in part) and emotionally (in spades) by his devoted but far from wealthy parents, that he hasn't really bothered to check out his actual destination in much detail. Which even he would admit is an egregious lapse, especially in someone who calls himself a writer and has hitherto assumed that he is fully possessed of a writer's perpetually burning curiosity.

"Sort of south, I think," he ventures, uncertainly. "Or middle. Aye, middle. Actually I'm not entirely sure. It's where the fried chickens roam. Has your 'family' been in touch?"

"Well, the guy has. He's called Robbie. Sounds nice. Friendly. I think most Yanks are, aren't they? Well, friendlier than us. What about yours?"

"I got a very short letter. From 'Brian'. He lives by some sort of a military hospital. His dad's a top man there, apparently. He has a mum who doesn't work and a twin sister."

Norman's face breaks out in a huge grin. "Lucky you!" Charlie just shrugs, a little shyly. He hadn't thought of it this way. "Got a girlfriend back in Glasgow then?"

"Aye. Sort of!" says Charlie, who hasn't anything remotely resembling a girlfriend. He has been out on the odd date and seen the occasional girl a few not very satisfactory times. With a home-by-eleven ground rule.

He is firmly convinced that he's not that much of a looker yet reckons that coming from a boys' school, one of the best in Glasgow but certainly not for dating or easy intimacy, his romantic life has been unjustly stifled. There are probably far less prepossessing boys, 'hacket', as his pals would say, who are in the city's populous mixed schools enjoying unbridled sex from the moment they enter the playground. Still, he'll be at university in October and everyone knows what goes on there. "What about you?"

"Off and on." Norman shrugs, adding somewhat obscurely, "but I'm no sooner on than I'm off." Surely he's just being wry, thinks Charlie, and hopefully not talking about premature ejaculation. "But if I don't get to shag an American lassie in the next four weeks," he adds, with a new note of determination. "I'm no' coming back at all!"

As if to amplify his resolve, the kilted seventeen-year-old fishes into his small but appropriately positioned leather sporran and brings out an imaginatively varied hoard of condoms.

"Got these in a pub lavvy. Well, quite a few pub lavvies." Charlie just stares at them, never having seen so many such items in his life. Extra-fine, ribbed, flavoured. Suddenly Norman scatters a few onto Charlie's notepad. "Here, have some on me, Mr *Dick*-ens!"

It is at this crucial dispensing point that a fresh-faced, full-bodied female flight attendant, with the biggest, stiffest, unBritishest head of blonde hair that Charlie has ever seen, reaches their seats. Charlie thinks that the young woman, whom he finds unbelievably erotic, embodies in one infinitely capable, tightly uniformed frame, everything he has ever imagined about America and especially female America. Even the utterly disapproving look she throws their way does little to dispel the allure.

"After-dinner mints," explains Norman, unhelpfully.

FIVE

Lexington, Kentucky. May 1982.

Having seen precious little of New York, save for some admittedly breathtaking views out of the descending plane and less exciting ones from the airport windows, a diminished but hugely overstimulated group of Scottish teenagers is now on an internal flight to Louisville, Ky.

Their fellow transatlantic passengers, those not on any sort of exchange and way beyond school age, are truly thankful to have seen the back of them and already wondering whether echoes of that shrill and raucous chatter, to which they have so recently been subjected, will ever quite leave their heads.

Young people who were virtual strangers just a few hours ago are now, on this smaller aircraft, the very best of friends, already planning to see each other when they finally return back home and at every opportunity in-between. They all appear to entertain two overriding cultural ambitions for this trip. To have one hundred per cent American burgers and fifty per cent American sex.

The descent into Louisville is marked by a distinct change in atmospherics. Not simply inside the aircraft but in the hearts and minds of those onboard. It suddenly hits them, like a shockwave of turbulence, that they are about to meet the families who will be their *in loco* parents for the next few weeks, responsible for their safety, well-being and, most important of all, entertainment. In its broadest and hopefully most exciting sense.

Not one of these young people, all of whom are at state schools, some in fairly deprived areas, has been to the United States before. It was an unwritten prerequisite of the trip. The farthest a few of them have travelled is to the Costa Brava with their parents. So the extravagantly technicolour images in their heads and snappy, wisecracking dialogue that they firmly anticipate as a matter of course, have all been downloaded courtesy of Hollywood.

Drugstores, diners, stampedes and drive-by shootings figure quite prominently, as do big bikes, even bigger cars and trucks, all loomed over by buildings that disappear way up into the clouds. They all know for a fact that high schools have homerooms and proms and bleachers but aren't one hundred per cent certain what any of these exotic facilities actually are. All they are certain of is that they will return home far worldlier and more sophisticated, infinitely more experienced and much the wiser.

Charlie Dickens and Norman Gemmell are already a small but solid friendship group, as they finally and rather exhaustedly enter the Louisville arrivals hall with their bags.

Charlie can tell that his new pal is enjoying to the full the attention that a fit young man clad in a kilt of the Gemmell tartan can attract outside of his own proud country. The darker lad in the newly purchased and well-pressed fawn corduroy trousers is himself no stranger to kilts – in every class at his school there have always been at least two or three lads who regularly wear them. He might even consider wearing one himself, were they ever to uncover or create a Dershowitz or Dishowisky tartan.

Although there are salaried representatives here from the organisation responsible for such visits, fearless grown-ups who have been accompanying the school kids on the flights and shepherding them through the various barriers and onto assorted modes of transportation, continuously checking their names off against lists and feverishly counting heads (losing even one Scottish teenager can really count against you job-wise), they and the kids themselves are expecting the host families to do most of the heavy lifting from now on.

In this respect they are almost totally correct.

The Scottish party emerges from the long but relatively sedate airport corridor, like infants leaving the womb, into a noisy hallway awash and bursting with excited adults, even more excited teenagers, confused younger siblings and dozens of huge, handwritten signs displaying a variety of mostly Scottish names. Anyone not in the know might assume that it was a bring-your-family-to-work day for the cab drivers of Kentucky.

Happily apprehensive, Charlie and Norman scour the ranks just beyond the barrier, searching for their own names. They can already hear elated yelps of '*He's wearing a kilt!*', with 'skirt' substituted in the mouths of the youngest observers. Suddenly Charlie feels a nudge in his side and turns to see Rob Roy beside him, gleefully pointing into a section of the crowd.

"Could they be yours, I wonder?" he says.

As Charlie turns to gaze in the direction of his new friend's finger, he notices a lot more than his own distinctive name writ large. The exceptionally tall and broad young man with the crewcut, who appears congenitally unable to stay still, is assumedly Brian-of-few-words, his putative host. He is dressed typically for the summer, which just beyond the air-conditioning it now surely is in these parts, at least judging by the visual assault from all around him of vivid, short-sleeved shirts and shorts in clashing checks. This obviously sporty guy – don't they call them 'jocks' or something here? – is also looking more than a little embarrassed. And the reasons for this are not hard to discern.

Standing next to him is a beaming, fresh-faced lady in her early forties, who Charlie assumes has to be Brian's mother, Mrs Sherman. The petite and rather pretty young woman beside her, with flowing, ash-blonde hair and smiling eyes, would be her daughter, the twin whom Brian mentioned in his rather monosyllabic introductory note.

The exact source of this male twin's acute embarrassment is all too obvious; behind the large card they are holding, which screams out 'Charles Dickens' in black sharpie for all to read, both ladies are wearing highly elaborate and most probably stifling crinolines and bonnets from an era long gone by.

"What do you reckon?" asks Norman, disingenuously.

"It's a mystery," muses Charlie. "Well, I'd better go introduce myself. See you at school or something, Norman."

"Aye. Have fun with the weirdos. ...*Anyone here for GEMMELL?*"

"Up yer kilt!" says Charlie amiably, and drags his suitcase, which is packed tight with all the outfits a dutiful mum can wash 'n' iron and gifts of a particularly Scottish nature – from tinned shortbread to medium-priced malt whiskey, tartan place mats to woolly tam o' shanters. With some lily of the valley thrown in but hopefully not too violently.

"At least yon sister's no' ugly," he hears Norman say, perhaps a fraction too loudly.

Charlie can't help checking out that stark but perceptive observation, as he trundles towards the Victorian brandishers of his name. He also can't help noticing that the trio are clearly observing his approach with some surprise, almost as if they had been desperately hoping to receive the more overtly Scottish-looking one in the fabulous swirling kilt, rather than the darker, vaguely Slavic specimen making his tentative way towards them.

"Charles?" asks the older woman, barely disguising the suspicion in her voice.

Charlie simply nods and smiles, trying hard to dispense friendly eye contact equally between the three of them but knowing already where it is most likely to devote its precious time.

"Aye," he says finally. And then adds, "Hello… er… Mrs Sherman. Good to meet you."

"Likewise. And these are our twins. Laura and Brian."

"Welcome to Kentucky, Charles," says Laura, somewhat shyly.

"Thanks," says Charlie, wishing he could think of something more to say but suddenly finding himself almost totally overwhelmed by the occasion. "Laura," he adds, which isn't much but it's better than nothing.

Brian just smiles and grabs his new guest's bulging suitcase as if it is a pebble off the beach.

*

America is smacking Charlie Dickens in his windswept face.

Sitting gratefully upfront next to the driver, the enthralled foreigner has shoved his entire, freshly trimmed and sun-deprived head out of the window, mouth open, eyes straining, taking in everything, including fumes, as if he is going to be quizzed on it later for some pelmanistic test or brutal interrogation.

He still can't quite believe that he is really here and not watching a movie about a teenage boy hotrodding the busy highway from the airport in Louisville to Lexington, Ky. He checks out the iconic cars and ogles the equally mind-blowing American faces within, all colours and ethnicities included (he is certain he spotted a Native American, which he recently learned is what you are supposed to call them), reading half-aloud every green and white road sign along the way.

Unsurprisingly, in the airport car park, Charlie did the usual Brit tourist thing of entering the Sherman station wagon on the driver's side. And, of course, the vehicle owner, in this case Mrs Sherman, made the customary response of asking her new passenger if he intended to drive them home. At least this broke the ice, although it wasn't exactly perma in the first place, as the friendly Americans had been all over him like a rash, firing a load of questions from the moment he had first said hello in that wonderful, almost intelligible, accent of his.

Questions mostly, of course, about the flight but at least a couple on the Scottish weather, which they had heard was terrible and which he hadn't felt at this early stage in the relationship was worth defending. And, anyway, it usually was pretty terrible and had actually been tipping it down this morning when he left. His mother had told him to say that this was why British complexions were the envy of the world, but he thought he might let this observation pass for the time being.

As they were driving away from Louisville and because he hadn't asked, either out of politeness or a surprising lack of curiosity, Mrs Sherman had felt duty-bound to explain. "We borrowed the costumes, Charles, from our church theatre group. And it is so *hot* inside of them!"

"The things we do for our guests." Laura had chuckled in the back. Unselfconsciously and possibly even unconsciously, she had undone a couple of the delicate buttons at her throat.

"Laura thought it would be kinda funny," Brian had said, dismissively.

Charlie realises now that this was almost the first time he had heard his actual 'host' form a sentence and even more surprisingly discovers that this hadn't really bothered him. He did notice, however, that the boy, clearly the same age and school year as himself, has a far deeper voice than his own. Hardly unexpected, considering the guy's bulk, but Charlie instantly resolved to let his own voice descend just a bit, whenever he could remember to do so and without it sounding like he is doing a crass imitation or had gone inexplicably mental. He also noticed that the young man's arms appeared to hang down pretty low but he wasn't going there for the moment.

"Brian thought it would kinda piss you off," says Laura, after a while.

"*Language*, Laura!" Mrs Sherman throws her a sharp, maternal glare via the mirror.

Charlie wrenches his head away from peering into one of those magnificent, yellow school buses, which he can't quite believe is almost within scraping distance of their car, and swivels round in his seat to catch Laura's eye. The swift but open smile she offers tells him that it was worth the effort. It is one of those all-systems smiles, the sort that features the eyes as much as the mouth, that he tells himself should be encouraged at the very slightest opportunity. He is already looking forward to its next appearance.

"So, Charles. What do you plan to do?" The splendid voice beside him swiftly steers him back.

"Er... have some genuine Kentucky Fried Chicken, Mrs Sherman," he says, hoping that he is not appearing too forward or coming across too pushy this early in his stay. He notices the older woman, who seems a kindly enough sort, if just possibly of the type who might well suit the stiffness of Victorian crinoline, begin a tight little smile.

"I meant as a career," she says. "But okay, KFC it is."

"Oh, sorry." Charlie winces apologetically, feeling a bit foolish. "I thought... er... I'm going to study law at uni. University. In Glasgow."

He feels a thump on his shoulder, as if someone has randomly assaulted him with a meat pounder.

"So, you wanna be a lawyer, Chuck," says Brian, astutely.

"No," says Charlie.

There is silence in the car and he realises that his new family must already be thinking that he is being either rude or sarcastic. Or both. Yet before he can qualify his negativity, Laura, perhaps tactfully, changes the subject.

"Are you looking forward to getting a taste of our beautiful Blue Grass State, Charles – above and beyond KFC?"

Charlie turns round once more and gives her one of his best, full-on beams, which he can only hope registers the way hers are already resonating with him.

"I have Great Expectations, Laura," he says, resolving to use her name whenever he can, a verbal trick which his father has told him is the best way to curry favour and win approval on both business and social occasions. Not that his dad, who is in lower-level management for a major Scottish department store chain, has done much of either over the years.

"My very favourite of your works, sir." Laura laughs. "I adore Master Pip." That open but eye-closing smile again.

"And I have a burning passion for Miss Havisham," he responds, and is rewarded with a charming giggle.

Deciding that he can't just keep on turning round and grinning at the young woman, let alone lobbing what he considers seriously witty banter, Charlie digs into his duffle bag for his new camera – a holiday gift from his maternal grandma – and proceeds to snap everything and anything visible out of his open window. He follows this up with some off-guard portraits of the Americans within, as he knows that his parents are bound to ask.

Brian and his mother exchange a look via the driving mirror. Perhaps they should have insisted on that one in the kilt.

SIX

"You actually *live* in a hospital!"

Charlie has understood, since deciphering Brian's handwritten and fairly curt introductory letter, clearly penned with some reluctance, that his father is someone important in the city of Lexington medical system. But he hasn't fully appreciated, until the station wagon turns in through the massive open gates, that the Sherman family actually lives on the grounds.

When he is informed that this is a Veterans Administration Hospital, serving the medical needs, both physical and psychological, of past and present US servicemen and women, his mind immediately leaps to images of deranged warriors in uniform escaping sealed wards with bloody bandannas and fully loaded weapons, primed by instinct and trauma to slaughter everyone within sight. Charlie wonders if everyone sees the world in stories, sometimes romantic, occasionally comic or even farcical, but worryingly often action-packed, artery-spurting and destined not to end well, or if this is just his own particular curse.

Mrs Sherman simply nods as the station wagon approaches the largest garage Charlie has ever seen. When the doors glide open at the feathery touch of a remote control, he thinks all his birthdays have come at once.

The house itself, in the short time he has to appreciate its exterior before the car enters its hangar, is like nothing he has ever encountered in real life and everything he has imagined.

Coming from a relatively small tenement flat in a large grey sandstone block on the south side of Glasgow, this is Charlie's first time staying in a home that isn't attached to someone else's and certainly in a house where wood has any part to play other than to keep the ceilings from falling down. The spaciousness and grandeur is almost overwhelming.

There is not a hedge in sight, nor indeed another house – the remaining buildings, which are even larger although less individual, must clearly be designated for patients and possibly the 'live-in help'. The house has balconies, for heaven's sake, and a front porch with columns! He bets there are even porticos and a widow's walk, although he is not entirely certain what these are, because when he sees such words in books he tends to gloss over them, without recourse to a dictionary, as they're rarely integral to the plot and it is plot that sets his juices flowing.

As Mrs Sherman opens the side door into the house itself, Charlie feels almost sick with anticipation, yet senses instinctively that he has to play it just a tiny bit cool. Especially if he doesn't want to look and sound like a rather tall and overexcited eight-year-old.

Whilst the air-conditioning, already a splendid feature of his car journey (despite his persistent opening and closing of the automatic passenger window), continues its unfamiliar dominance inside the home, his hands are feeling quite warm from the massive bucket of Kentucky Fried Chicken he has been allowed to hold.

Meantime, Brian is hefting his case from the boot (or trunk) of the car like a sack of coal. Charlie prays that none of the precious gifts inside, which his mother had spent literally days listing, considering, paring down and then sourcing all over Glasgow and beyond, are now in pieces and dripping on his underwear, but he doesn't as yet feel able to tell new 'friend' Brian to be just a wee bit bloody careful.

The kitchen he finally enters is around the size of Hampden Park Stadium, or at least a good half of his parents' entire apartment, with one of those islands/breakfast bars marking what in any normal house would be an outer limit of the room and not its halfway point. There are boxes of cereals that he has never heard of but look brilliant, all neatly lined up like a row of tower blocks, alongside preserves that he knows he has to call jelly, as in peanut butter jelly, although he is not entirely certain if this latter is itself a particular type of jam or a do-it-yourself combination that would make his parents retch just to look at it.

Whilst most of the items dotted around are pretty familiar, albeit in their more compact European versions, Charlie is not prepared for the military memorabilia displayed in frames on the walls and extending out into the hallway. Regimental swords and banners, ragged fragments of blood-tinged uniforms, ancient sepia-tinted photographs of miserable-looking bearded men in military gear. As the only superfluous objects in his kitchen at home are drawings he did when he was around six and a Mother's Day poem he composed at nine, all of which he dearly wishes his parents would shove in a cupboard somewhere, he finds the selection around him, whilst a little sombre, at least not embarrassing.

"And *here* we are!" says Mrs Sherman, a bit unnecessarily, but Charlie soon realises, when he hears some heavy footsteps, that her words are as much an announcement as an observation.

"*Welcome!*" booms the man, who has instantly filled the entire doorway. "I'm Doctor Sherman."

The man looks unlike any doctor Charlie has ever encountered or indeed might wish to, as his sheer bulk is an intimidation. To be fair, the good doctor doesn't appear at first glance to be in any way cruel or threatening and Charlie imagines that if you were lying on the battlefield with your guts spilling out, you might indeed find his presence moderately reassuring. Yet standing tall and square in the kitchen, with eyes of the steeliest blue and a military haircut that makes Brian look like Mick Jagger, he seems to dominate the room and those in it without even trying.

Before Charlie can answer or attempt to shake hands, which wouldn't itself be the easiest of endeavours, considering how his upper limbs are currently occupied, the man is nodding his enormous head towards him and his load.

"I see you're being initiated into this region's culinary wonderland."

Displaying not just a massive set of teeth but most of his gums, the older man offers a cordial but also slightly scary smile, which Charlie gratefully accepts and returns, again in the economy version. Whilst by no means an expert on American accents, he can detect that the one currently on offer is what you'd call southern. Perhaps even more southern than those he has thus far encountered on the journey.

It is at this point that the visitor suddenly realises exactly how much the manner in which he has been hearing Laura Sherman speak, these soft, almost undulating tones, the way certain words are totally mispronounced, with a quality of genteel slowness, even languor, built-in, has only added to her already unarguable charms. And how much he wants to hear her speak some more, almost regardless of content. She could say 'I' as 'Ah' all night and he would sleep content.

"Pleased to meet you, Dr Sherman. I'm Charlie."

"Well, come right in, why don't you, Charlie? And make yourself at home." He beckons him onwards with a mighty hand. "How long is it you're going to be our guest?"

The man asks this latter question on the move, with the clear indication that Charlie et al should follow him. The newly arrived guest believes that he can detect a sense of weary apprehension rather than overweening excitement in his host's impossibly deep voice, but this could just be because Charlie is still new to the territory.

On his way to the next magical location, in this new

domestic wonderland, he takes a look at the garden, which is predictably vast, filled with colourful plants and stuff he couldn't identify if you paid him. Charlie assumes that it is all professionally well maintained.

Right at the far end, surrounded by shrubbery, he thinks that he glimpses an open-air swimming pool. *Jesus!* Not only has he never swum in anyone's private pool, he has never swum in the open air anywhere. Not even in the sea itself, as he has never holidayed in foreign resorts and, in his opinion, anyone swimming in the seas around Scotland would have to be certifiably insane.

Charlie Dickens suddenly feels like one of those poor children who are given a final trip to Disneyland before they expire, which is a horrible thought that he is not going to share with anyone right now. Or ever. Except possibly in his journal, which as yet is looking rather sparse.

Realising that there is a question left hanging and unanswered in the rarefied southern air, Charlie belatedly responds, "Oh. Er… three and a bit weeks, Doctor. But I think I'll be at Brian's school most of the time."

"Poor guy." Brian chuckles, thumping him again on the back, which rattles the chicken limbs Charlie hasn't yet found the opportunity or a suitable location to set down. "Hey, your English is pretty good, Chuck. Where'd you learn?"

"They speak English in Scotland, Brian!" says Laura, in that glorious accent again. Charlie loves the way she says 'Scot-Land' as if it is two separate words, each meriting equal respect. She shakes her head in their guest's direction, as she gently takes the KFC from him, her fingers just lightly brushing his and sending warmer thrills through his body than Colonel Sanders ever could. "It won't just be school, Charlie. We've got picnics arranged for you guys... dance... parties..."

"*Sports!*" adds Brian, with unnecessary finality, before his sister can bring up something ridiculous. "Hey, what do you play, Chuck? Bet you like soccer."

"Not much. In Glasgow it's reckoned a blood sport. I do a bit of curling." His hosts look mystified and he decides that explaining a peculiarly Scottish game played on ice and using forty-four pounds of granite and a broom on a stick is maybe a weirdness too far. "But I'd love to see a baseball match. Oh, and it's Charlie. My pals call me Charlie."

The teenagers start to walk up the staircase, leaving the older generation in the lobby.

"Charlie he's ma darlin'," pipes Laura.

"*Laura!*" booms a suddenly outraged physician, from the foot of the stairs.

"Dad, it's a song!" protests Laura, with a light if slightly nervous chuckle. "We're learning them at school – to welcome the Scots kids. It's by 'Rabbie Burns'."

Charlie stares down at Dr and Mrs Sherman, who don't look totally convinced. He wants to tell them that he knows far worse songs than this but instead attempts to lighten the mood by saying, "We call him *Rabbi* Burns in our family."

If you can feel a chill in the heart of Kentucky in May, this is what now whistles through the Sherman house. Charlie catches the parents exchanging a look, which they then shoot back up to the twins, as if their kids have been concealing some sort of classified information from them.

"So you're a Jew, Charles?" says Mrs Sherman, with a deliberate lightness of tone. The same tone, thinks Charlie, as she might have said 'so you're a vegetarian', as if this is nothing more than a casual making of conversation. Charlie, trying to be fair, reckons that perhaps it genuinely is. "Isn't that funny, dear?" she says to her husband. "I never knew they had Scotch Jews. Bless my heart!"

"Mom!" says Laura, who clearly senses an offence Charlie has yet to take. He's still in Paradise and it would need far more than this to cloud his skies.

"I'm interested, Laura, is all. We have some very nice Jewish families here in town, I believe, Charlie."

Charlie just nods. He never knew there were Jews in Kentucky but has no reason to doubt his hosts nor to care. It's reassuring that they're nice ones.

"Perhaps you should have specified," says Dr Sherman.

If Charlie is just beginning to feel slightly uncomfortable, it is worth every wince just to receive the bonding glances with which Laura is virtually bombarding him right now.

"Charlie will be totally fine here," she insists.

"Aye," agrees Charlie, adding, "Nae worries," which is not something he normally says but he thinks they'll like the colour of it. "Anyway," he adds, for reassurance, "I'm only half – can I use your toilet, please? Or the 'john', as I think you say."

This calls for another affectionate pile driver from Brian, which makes Charlie's need all the more pressing.

"'John's' this way," he says, barging past his exchangee with the suitcase and a chuckle.

The final, softly spoken words from downstairs just catch Charlie as he is heading for the bathroom.

"Maybe he'd like to visit our temple?" says Mrs Sherman. Which Charlie thinks is a rather gracious suggestion but one on which this tourist will happily pass for now, thank you very much.

SEVEN

There is an inordinate number of kilts on display this bright Monday morning, in the main auditorium of Lexington's largest and most prestigious high school.

Tartan is not totally unknown here. Unlike in the majority of schools attended by today's very welcome overseas guests, modesty and respect are the only specifications for a daily uniform and the length of a skirt is far more of an issue than the material from which it is made or the pattern imprinted thereon. But kilts with sporrans and socks to match, young men's pale but solid legs encased firmly within – this is way more than Kentucky expected.

And the Kentuckians here this morning, or more specifically the Lexingtonians, cannot take their eyes off them.

It is not only a select number of the visiting boys, however, who have chosen to wear their celebrated national dress. Some of the girls, many of whom wouldn't be seen dead in a tartan skirt at home, have rummaged about and struggled into their richly checked and distinctively patterned ambassadorial wardrobes, or been handed some by patriotic relatives, and are putting on quite a show.

The school principal, a small but stocky man in his mid-fifties, with a dwindling amount of auburn hair combed over his rather large head but a fine, well-trimmed beard to compensate, is addressing the entire school. Behind him sit his staff, listening attentively and looking perhaps a touch more involved than might be usual on these occasions.

"And school, we'd like to give a fine Kentucky welcome this morning to our new guests all the way from Bonnie Scot-Land. Would they kindly stand up, please, and could their host students stand up with them?"

Charlie is still so enthralled by the unfamiliar accent and by actually being here, at a real American high school, alongside real and super-friendly American kids, who are being really American as if just for his benefit, that he fails to stand up quickly enough. Or at least sufficiently quick for Brian, who gives him a dig in the ribs that sends most of the air inside him flying out.

As he rises, in some discomfort, he gazes around and sees a kilted Norman with his own genial host, another big guy who looks, in that colourful phrase from home, as if he is built like a brick shit-house. The wimpier exchangees swap friendly smiles and shrugs, diminutive brothers-in-arms.

Other young men and women scattered around the hall rise to the occasion, some proudly but a larger number with some diffidence, uneasy with being stared at and feted.

Charlie realises that he is barely more familiar with the Scottish contingent than he is with the rest of the assembly, as aside from a couple of guys from his school, neither of whom are his pals, the group hails from all over that small country. Yet he already knows that the American kids will have assumed only too readily that these guys are all the closest of friends from home and possibly even related. In the schoolyard, even before he and Brian had registered, someone had approached him with the news that their own second cousin was living somewhere in Scotland and did Charlie know him? Somewhat to his own regret, Charlie had replied that he did but only in passing.

The young Scot is already resisting, albeit with some considerable difficulty, the impulse to turn and stare hard and repeatedly at Laura Sherman, who is sitting a couple of rows behind with her friends.

Charlie had in fact chatted with her earlier this first morning on their way to the school, which happily is a fairly long but leafy and, at least for him, interesting stroll from the hospital. She had informed him, in that lush yet fetchingly crackled southern voice, that whilst most of the kids here either drive to school (there is even a car park for pupils!) or are driven, her father has always insisted that his twins start their day with a brisk walk, for the good of their health and mental well-being. Brian obviously takes this daily jaunt as a training exercise and finds plenty of overhanging branches to swing on or even roll fully over along the way.

"School, please make our guests feel right at home when they join you in your classes today and over these next few weeks. And meantime, let us all give them a huge round of applause as they sit down – I imagine somewhat gratefully! – once more."

As Charlie takes his seat, grateful indeed but also heartened by the genuineness of the long and almost ecstatic responses all around him, he assumes that it will now be business as usual. Announcements, timings, sports fixtures and perhaps a toilet out of action. (More probably in this venue the result of a simple plumbing glitch rather than the wanton destruction that can happen with monotonous regularity on his home turf.)

What he is most definitely not expecting is for a tall black gentleman to enter from the wings, in full Highland dress – in fact, almost excessively Highland, as there is barely an inch of flesh left untartanned – carrying and playing the bagpipes. Before Charlie can even turn instinctively to someone, anyone, to share the gobsmacking shock of this, another quite different sound registers above the cacophony. One with which he is not quite so excruciatingly familiar.

From the other side of the stage emerges a small woman in what he thinks might be called buckskin but wouldn't swear to it, playing – or is it plunking? – a rather beautiful banjo. When he finally gets his head around this, he realises that the piper and the plunker are playing – or attempting to play – what could well be the same tune. And this is confirmed to him when the entire school, save for the bemused guests, begin to sing:

"*Hark when the night is fallin'*
Hear! Hear the pipes are callin'

Loudly and proudly callin'
Down through the glen..."

As 'Scotland the Brave' continues, learned faithfully and possibly painfully by heart, Charlie understands why there are so few bagpipe 'n' banjo combos treading the boards in either of their respective countries.

He can't resist turning to check out Laura's reaction. He assumes it will be as rapt as that of her fellow Lexingtonians all around her, who do indeed, as did she on this first morning's 'walking tour', seem inordinately proud at what their fair city can offer its foreign guests. There is also, so far as he can ascertain, not a single atom of cynicism in her slight but entrancing frame.

So it is to his delight, as she catches Charlie glancing at her with obvious bemusement, that Laura Sherman very sweetly yet unmistakably rolls her eyes. It is a moment, brief but potent, that they are joyfully sharing together, two tickled and not totally unsceptical minds reacting as one, in this vast hall. And if his heart is beating out of rhythm with that being blown and strummed or plunked or whatever onstage, then he is just going to go along for the ride.

"Land of mah heart forever,
Scot-Land the brave."

*

As she is taking a package of curriculum subjects that are for the most part quite different, in both kind and energy, to those of his host, Laura Sherman has few opportunities to elide with Charlie's pre-arranged academic schedule. Should she indeed even wish to.

For his part, Charlie has no idea whether the twin sister of his designated pairing is being especially friendly towards him because of the heady Caledonian charm he is exuding from every pore, or is simply being herself and behaving as she would to any guest, however gauche or noxious. And, indeed, as any of her friends or acquaintances might behave in this relatively small, hospitable southern town. He suspects this latter is more the case but whatever, he is prepared to enjoy it for exactly what it is.

It is not until lunchtime that he has the opportunity to run into her again.

Meantime he has sat through a science class, which was sort of interesting, except that it brought back memories of his own physics and chemistry O-Grades, which were some of the worst times in his life, and a math session that was baffling for much the same reason.

This did not prevent the current teachers in both subjects from asking him and any of his fellow visitors to tell the class about Scottish schooling and the differences between the two systems. Charlie thinks he acquitted himself quite well, with just the right balance of informed wisdom and native wit. Although one young woman's telling the class that she could listen to him all night long, even if he were just reading the names off the walls of remembrance, sort of brought him down to earth.

Charlie Dickens wishes he could take a look at how his own favourite subjects are being taught over here; English, French, Latin, history and maybe even geography at a pinch, as clearly quite a few of the regular students have absolutely no idea where Scotland actually is. But then he reminds himself that he hadn't a clue where Kentucky was until yesterday, so he's not one of the world's great cosmopolites either.

To Brian's delight, the morning ends with a basketball session.

Charlie has played basketball exactly once in his entire life yet manages to convince his new American teammates and opponents that he is a complete novice.

He has always considered himself reasonably tall for his age, but in this particular crowd he feels like a Scottish leprechaun. Fortunately he has Brian on his side, but the efforts the guy is making to appear kind and considerate towards his guest only serve to exaggerate how pathetic Charlie is at this. Had Brian Sherman actually lifted him up with the ball clutched in his hands and dropped him feet-first through the basket, he couldn't have felt more inept.

The school cafeteria is the one place Charlie Dickens feels quite at home. The atmosphere and menu are noticeably different and admittedly superior to the bill of fare to which he is accustomed, Glasgow being the gastronomic hub for chip butties and deep-fried Mars Bars, but food is food. You don't need special skills, a sportsman's body or advance knowledge of the syllabus; you just need to know how to eat. An arena in which Charlie, with Jewish grandparents on one side and a proud and nurturing Scottish family on the other, has absolutely no problems.

He is sitting with Brian and some of his classmates, all of whom are being incredibly gracious and appreciative, even about his basketball. Charlie seriously doubts, should the positions be reversed, whether he or his own fellows back in Glasgow would offer their guests quite the same warmth and interest. But perhaps he is being ungenerous. He suspects that a person like Norman, who is now approaching the table with his Kentucky counterpart, would lay out the tartan carpet for all and sundry.

Charlie is surprised that Robbie, given his stature, wasn't a party to his recent humiliation, but he supposes that height isn't the only requirement for a basketball team. He doesn't afford the matter much thought, however, as right behind Robbie, obscured until now by his sheer bulk, is Laura Sherman, tray in hand.

Coming from a boys' school, where stuffing your face with chips and sausages or maybe a lukewarm pie is the order of the day, any day, Charlie is fascinated to observe that Laura, and indeed every other young female in sight, is settling down to a modest plate of fresh salad, with perhaps a yoghurt on the side. Who does that, for fuck's sake? he thinks uncharitably. He assumes that it has something to do with maintaining their figures and he really isn't going to protest on that score. But don't they get hungry just a few minutes later, when all their best intentions battle with fatigue and noisily empty stomachs?

"Hey, you guys!" she says, greeting them with a huge smile. Charlie finds himself fascinated by the way she instinctively avoids dipping her long, ash-blonde hair into her coleslaw, as she sits herself down so gracefully at their table. He reckons that if he was proud owner of such lavishly flowing hair, by the end of a day like this you'd know exactly what he had been eating just by checking the strands. "How's your first day at a real American high school?"

"A whole lot better than my place," says Charlie.

"Yeah?" says Brian, showing an unexpected sliver of interest. "What we got that yours don't?"

To which Charlie and Norman respond in unrehearsed but heartfelt unison, "*Lassies!*"

Brian and Robbie look puzzled for a moment then Robbie smiles. "Oh, like girls? Well, you can take some of ours back with you, if you want."

"Especially the dogs," adds Brian, charitably.

Instinctively Charlie looks at Laura. He is rewarded with a tiny but heartfelt sigh, which he does his best, without maligning his host, to endorse with just the slightest raise of his eyebrows.

"Hey, Scots," continues Brian, obliviously, "Robbie and I, we got football practice tonight and coach won't give us a free pass. Wanna come watch us? It's different from your football – y'know, soccer – and we're pretty good."

"Aye. That'll be interesting," says Norman, checking it out with his new pal. "Eh, Charlie?"

Charlie can't think of anything he would enjoy less, especially if, heaven forbid, they ask him to have a go. And there's no way he could produce a credible 'please excuse Charlie' note from his mum at this late stage. He finds himself glancing towards Laura for salvation.

To his delight and eternal gratitude, Laura is immediately on the case. Although she wisely keeps the tone casual rather than flinging the lifeline too publicly out there.

"Or, I dunno, you could come to our creative writing group."

Brian and Robbie moan theatrically. Brian adds to the subtlety by shoving a ketchup-enhanced finger halfway down his throat.

"*You're a writer?*" says Charlie, ignoring the sound effects. How come he didn't know this? And why should he? He only arrived yesterday.

Brian fills in some of the blanks, but she won't be hiring him as a publicist any time soon. "She does 'poetry'," he explains, in the same tone as if she ate her own toe clippings.

"I *adore* poetry!" exclaims Charlie, which comes as news to him as much as to anyone, poetry being fairly mid-range in the pantheon of his literary passions. It is Norman who now does the 'vomiting' gesture, which makes them all laugh, as it would be churlish not to.

"You do?" says Laura, with a palpable excitement that surprises and even alarms Charlie himself. "Are you a poet? What do you write? Do you have your poems with you?"

"…Never without them," lies Charlie. "But, to be honest, I'm into prose mostly. Y'know, stories. I'm particularly proud of my *Little Dorritt*."

"Disna sound like much to be proud of!" chimes Norman, as Charlie has thought and indeed hoped that he might.

"Boom boom!" cry Charlie and Norman together, causing students at adjoining tables to check them out. And sneak a look at Norman's kilt again.

"You guys," Laura laughs, "you're like a double act!" She stares at Charlie, with a gaze of mock intensity. "So, Mr Dickens, do you have something you could read for us? A work-in-progress?"

"Och, I don't think so." Charlie shrugs, slightly scared now and backtracking for all he is worth. "I'm no' that good, Laura."

"We'll be the judges of that, sir," says Laura Sherman, staring into his eyes with some gravity. For a moment the rest of the cafeteria, the other students, even his lunch, appear to fade away.

"Do you need a spade to dig yersel oot?" asks Norman Gemmell, either leavening or screwing up the moment. Even Charlie isn't quite certain.

EIGHT

New England, April 2004

"It was as if she already knew him better than he knew himself. Yet how could this be, when they had only just met?"

As he reads yet another extract from his book, choosing a different passage from those he has shared on previous occasions, just in order to keep himself from going slowly insane, Charles is aware of one particular set of eyes focussed almost unblinkingly onto his.

These are not this time the familiar, almond-shaped eyes of an innocent young woman, bearing an impossible resemblance to someone he knew briefly but quite magically so long ago. This evening's quizzical gaze is far more explicable. It belongs to the good-looking guy who is here with him, representing his North American publisher. A man who is currently piecing together fact and fiction to compose his own story of what is taking place. Someone who right now, to his own clear frustration, doesn't have all the facts at his disposal – and perhaps never will.

Yet, even as he reads aloud in what he knows is his still distinctive Scottish brogue, despite its maybe inevitable mellowing after some years away down south, Charles's own mind is being dragged uneasily back to that very time, those singular events, that spurred on and inspired the writing of this book in his hand, however fictionalised a rendering it might protest to be.

> *"Much later on he was to wonder fancifully if they had encountered each other before, perhaps in another life. Right now he was simply hoping that the hormonally adolescent sweat he had felt just starting to gush some seconds ago didn't yet show on his face, under the harsh school lights. And that he wouldn't say something to blow the moment totally.*
>
> *""'I'd sell my mother for a fag," is what he said.*
> *"'One moment totally blown.'"*

Charles raises his head from the book and smiles at the audience in this attractive bookstore, in the historic heart of a town whose name he has thankfully remembered.

"Where I come from, 'fag' means cigarette," he explains, for clarity. The audience nod as if they knew, which, to be fair, the majority did. But now they laugh and applaud, just to show that they did.

C.D. MacNaughtan ceremoniously closes the book that bears his made-up name but not his photograph.

Hovering beside him the evening's grateful bookseller ushers his overseas guest to the signing table, whilst encouraging his more local patrons to follow.

Before Charles can reach the ambitious pile of still-virgin books, he feels a firm hand on his arm.

"Hey, mystery man," says a smiling and just slightly smug Kevin. "Some grossly overworked but criminally underpaid publishing wizard just scored you a slot next Saturday. Ask me where." Charles knows that he doesn't need to ask because the younger man is practically drooling to tell him. "Glad you did. Only the famed BlueGrass Books in 'dahntahn' Lexington, Ky. Right next to the even more famous Cheapside slave-auction block."

He waits for Charles to both sigh and look impressed, and is duly rewarded.

"I'm getting a picture here, Charles," continues Kevin Roberts, his air of self-congratulation transforming itself, as if on a dime, into one of almost fraternal concern. He taps the uppermost book on the unsullied pile. "But when Art goes *mano a mano* with Life, Life don't always win."

A hand suddenly grasps the book and flicks it open to the title page. "Sign it 'to Delphine'?" says the customer. "It's French. Like you."

NINE

Lexington, Kentucky. May 1982.

"'...and nothing was left of her that fatal morn,
save the sound of the shimmering sea.'"

The young African American woman is reciting a homegrown and only slightly derivative poem with some passion. Charlie Dickens can't fail to notice that her audience, this small group of mostly female high-school students, sitting in a circle in the dusty classroom and listening politely, are staring with far greater intensity at him.

There is one other guy there, a skinny, redheaded fellow, who right now looks almost as uncomfortable as Charlie. Possibly because he fears the foreign interloper could be wondering in silent amusement why he is a regular member of a patently female-oriented creative-writing circle.

In a country that has produced such literary giants as Poe and Hemingway, in the very state that gave the world Robert Penn Warren, whose *All the King's Men* rates as one of Charlie's all-time favourite books, even if it does tend to veer off into the poetic a mite too often for his tastes, this serious gender bias does appear a little disconcerting. But Charlie is not complaining, as he knows all too well why he himself is there, and it is not in the interests of literature or equality. Perhaps the redheaded guy has had the same idea. Good luck to him.

As she is already sitting down, the only way the by now fully spent reader of the poem can indicate that her work, like her heroine, has finally reached its sad conclusion is to look incredibly sheepish and almost bury her face in her blouse.

Fortunately, muted but polite applause is forthcoming. The young woman nods shyly, with a gratitude verging on relief.

"That was so beautiful, Nancy. And moving. *And* dramatic. Thank you so much," says Laura Sherman, whose group this clearly is.

She now shifts her gaze so abruptly and unswervingly towards Charlie that he can swear he sees her eyes flash. He feels himself jolting back instinctively into his sturdy school chair. "And now," she says, with a welcoming and possibly even proprietorial smile, "I reckon it's the turn of our own very special guest from over the 'shimmering sea'. The guy with the unbelievably magical name – Charles Dickens. Yeah, I'm serious. Kid you not. And he's a writer himself! Isn't that cool! A good one, I'll bet. ... *Charlie?*"

Charlie senses that after this introduction he should appear rather diffident, which isn't that tricky, as it is exactly how he is feeling, alongside hugely intimidated and practically spotlit. He is aware of at least eight pairs of kindly but laser-like southern eyes on him, including those of the redheaded boy, although he can't discern as yet whether his fellow male wants him to play a blinder for their side or fall flat on his ass.

Stalling for time and the better to still his embarrassing breathiness, Charlie makes a big deal out of rummaging for the trusty notepad in his duffle bag, then searching assiduously through it to find exactly the right page. For some obscure reason he suddenly recalls the French 'Higher' he just took back home, his final school exam, and the way that irritating Flaubert guy was always seeking '*le mot juste*'. He mulls on whether he can throw this in and, if so, will it just land with a thud? He does mutter something mid-scour about finding '*le page juste*' but of course it goes for nothing.

He can almost smell the anticipation in the small, musty classroom, so disappointingly similar to the ones at home (save for the piercing shafts of sunlight), and wonders if Laura, on absolutely no evidence and from an innate but surely misguided graciousness, has built him up out of all proportion.

"Thank you," he begins, "and hi... y'all... er... as you say here. Ha! Aye... well, appropriately, after Nancy's lovely poem, this one that I'm going to... to render for you... is called 'The Tay Bridge Disaster.'"

He takes in his audience, with some solemnity, as befits the subject. They can already sense that this is going to be a work – an epic – of the utmost seriousness. Suck on that, Nancy and your shimmering sea. And in order to give full weight and indeed gravity to the words, Charlie Dickens of Pollockshields, Glasgow, Scotland, stands up and addresses the room.

The mode of delivery he chooses, one that he has adjudged most appropriate for the sombre piece he is about to share, is heightened, declamatory, loud. And very, very Scots. Yet easily within the bounds of comprehensibility for a foreign audience, as he wants and needs every word to count. Words he knows – or hopes he knows – from memory, as the notepad page itself is as blank as a hermit's address book.

"'*Beautiful Railway Bridge of the Silv'ry Tay!*'" he exclaims.

He pauses to ensure that everybody – and he means everybody – is listening. Nancy, skinny ginger lad, this includes you. He can tell by their eyes that they are all ears. So, without resting any overlong glances at this early stage on anyone in particular, he continues at full volume.

"'*Alas! I am very sorry to say*
That ninety lives have been taken away
On the last Sabbath day of 1879,
Which will be remembered for a very long time.'"

Even as he is emoting, Charlie can make out the expressions on the faces of the young group, as these appear to glide from an initial, almost excited anticipation to a courteous but genuine interest and then inexorably onwards to something else. Almost as one, save for the redheaded guy, who is still rapt, they gradually begin to evince the first vague signs of unease.

Undaunted, Charlie Dickens allows the full tragedy of that fateful eve to unfold.

> *""Twas about seven o'clock at night,*
> *And the wind blew with all its might*
> *And the rain came pouring down*
> *And the dark clouds seem'd to frown*
> *And the Demon of the air seem'd to say –*
> *"I'll blow down the Bridge of Tay.""""*

Charlie can just make out Laura's face. He realises that he has never yet seen her frown or look suspicious, not that he has exactly been swamped with opportunities, as they haven't actually known each other for much more than a day or two. (Dear Lord, is that all!) Now that he has, this doesn't diminish her attraction in the least. Yet he still experiences the first stirrings of unease. Nevertheless, onwards to disaster…

> *"'When the train left Edinburgh,*
> *The passengers' hearts were light and felt no sorrow,*
> *But Boreas blew a terrific gale,*
> *Which made their hearts for to quail.*
> *And many of the passengers with fear did say,*
> *"I hope God will send us safe across the Bridge of Tay.""""*

Suddenly a shriek of laughter that can probably be heard in Dundee itself rends the hitherto placid Kentucky air like a siren.

Charlie stops.

He can sense the shock all too vividly on the faces

circled all around him but has no idea whether this has been elicited by his own stirring performance or by the recent shrieker. A shrieker who turns out, not unexpectedly, to be the convener of the group herself.

He swivels round to glare down at Laura, an expression of the deepest hurt clouding his long, slightly lopsided face and sensitive brown eyes. "Is this how you treat your visiting poets?" he says.

Even though his eyes are fixed on Laura, he can tell that the other members of the group are struggling with whether to feel utterly mortified or really quite relieved.

"Oh, come on, Charlie." She chuckles. "That was total crap – and I'm kinda guessin' it wasn't your own, home-reared total crap."

Charlie looks completely broken. Tears begin to well up in his eyes. The other writers are starting to wish they were somewhere else.

"I thought it was pretty good," says the redheaded boy, which Charlie so hopes is out of simple solidarity.

The interrupted reader allows a few more excruciating seconds to creak by, before his face bursts into a massive grin.

"*You got me, Laura!*" he admits, to everyone's delight, save perhaps that of his fellow schoolboy. "That wee gem was, in fact, the magnum opus – or magnum hopeless – of the late, great William McGonagall, a fellow countryman and generally regarded as the very worstest poet ever in the English language."

Now the group laughs. Almost too uninhibitedly.

"Thought so," says the redhead.

"It's sort of my… party piece," continues Charlie. "I don't really have anything of my own worth reading."

"Charlie's being modest," says Laura to the group but with a smile Charlie hopes is his alone. "Brits do that a lot. He told me coming here just now that he writes short stories. He's even started a novel. *And* I saw a journal – in your room."

"What were you doing in his room, Laura?" asks one of the group.

"Ironing his kilt!" says Laura, with a speed that Charlie finds invigorating.

"Maybe next time I'll read something of my own," says Charlie. "When I get to know you all better."

Again he and Laura exchange a smile. This time the other members of the group register its passage. And mull quietly to themselves on how strange the potency of terrible poetry can be.

TEN

The girl can hear the sharp, staccato knocking on her door but chooses to ignore it.

When you're thirteen you choose to ignore a lot of things but your mother tends to be the main one. Especially when there's no dad around to add the weight of numbers and a deeper voice. Wearing in-ear headphones and holding an mp3 also helps in this endeavour but sadly won't always drown out entirely the more persistent knocker.

"*What y'all doin' in there?*"

The girl recognises the tone as one of exasperation rather than undiluted anger, so she knows that she has a slice of flexibility before the door is finally flung open.

The door is finally flung open. Perhaps she got that one slightly wrong this morning.

"*Mom!* Can't you like knock?" protests the girl. She can't help feeling that, despite her conviction that she is an individual, with an individual style and with thoughts that are entirely her own, she is working to a pre-arranged script.

"Er, like I did. And like I yelled a bit," says the intruder, who is well aware that she is working to the same script but feels powerless to demand a rewrite.

The mother character looks around the room and tries to recall, as she often does, whether her own teenage years were as equally devoted to squalor, chaos and an almost total lack of self-esteem. She doubts it. Not because she was a better or more mature human being, although there are indeed times when she fears that she might have been, but because she had a father who was in the military and a mother who listened to her husband.

The older woman catches a glimpse of herself and her daughter in those portions of the full-length mirror that aren't obscured by multi-coloured post-its and wacky group pictures from the Photo-Me booth. Sometimes she can't see any resemblance between the two of them whatsoever. Of course, the daughter is of mixed ethnicity, so she was hardly likely to have inherited her mother's blondness, nor would Mom have wished this. But just a little similarity in bone structure or the shape of the eyes or the set of the jaw, this would have been, well, reassuring. Yet there are likenesses, she believes, geared more to personality than those superficial, outwardly charms.

For example, the two females in the household clearly share the same sense of humour. Which, interestingly, causes them to clash just as regularly as it leads to a meeting of minds.

"C'mon, Jess, you've got a test today," encourages her mother. Even as she says it, she knows that this is hardly the carrot she seeks.

"Like it's only English," says the girl. "No offence."

"Why should I be offended? Oh yeah, I'm an English teacher."

"Not mine, thank God," says Jess, knowing with some satisfaction that in this particular conversational round, she has had the crucial last word.

"Ditto," says Laura Griffin, somewhat feebly. "And your dad's picking you and Henry up right after school."

"Yayy!" says Jess, grabbing her pre-packed schoolbag and trotting out of the door.

As she hears the girl, who is relatively slight in build, thumping down the stairs of the small suburban house, the older woman sneaks a look at herself in the mirror, as if wanting to check out just for a moment what a single mom looks like, one whose daughter is so delighted to spend a weekend away from her and with her now-separated dad.

Laura removes her glasses, which are one of her best features, being large and bright yellow and – well – fun. But they have the disadvantage of allowing her to see, with brutal clarity, exactly what she likes less about herself. The plumpness around her middle, which is a family feature on the Sherman side but one she had hoped she would avoid. And the weariness, particularly around the eyes. Even her hair is tired, although it isn't that bad. Shorter than it was but still sort of blonde, a darker blonde, albeit with a little help from her friend Julie in downtown Lexington, where she has been going for don't ask how long. She would like to move on, re-model herself, but in a town like this and being who she is, that really isn't an option. Julie would have to die and hopefully this won't happen any time soon.

She hears footsteps on the stairs, moving back towards her. What has the kid forgotten this time?

"Sorry, Mom," says Jess from the doorway.

Laura puts her glasses back on, so that she can look even more quizzically at her daughter. When does Jess ever say sorry?

"Sorry? What for, hon? What did you do that I don't know about yet?"

"*Nothing!* I just like didn't ask what you're gonna do with yourself. Y'know, this weekend. All weekend. Like on your own?"

"Oh, Jess, that's sweet of you," says a touched Laura, who has absolutely no problem being on her own for a weekend, as she is already worn out and exhausted by lunchtime Thursday, but would always be happier to do it in the knowledge that her kids are missing her desperately. Which she kind of suspects they really aren't, as being with their dad is a treat and, let's face it, a respite for them too.

"Oh, I dunno," she says, with a profound sigh. "I suppose I'll just have to go down to Kroger Field." She turns to look at her puzzled daughter. "SoulDecision are doing a concert and somebody gave me tickets. Think they're some sorta like Canadian band..."

Jess suddenly freezes, as Laura knew or at least hoped that she would.

"I *know* who they are, Mom!" yells Jess. She can't keep still and has to walk around the room, which isn't actually that easy as they are both almost knee-deep in TJ Maxx. "Oh my God! *You're going to see SoulDecision!* You're forty! SoulDecision? Oh my God!"

Laura Griffin's tired face suddenly lifts and the broad smile that even her daughter would have to admit lights up her mom's face is back in town. "Kidding!" She laughs, loudly. "I'm kidding. And by the way, I'm thirty-nine! For the next five years." Jess starts to smile too, relieved that she won't be missing anything important or fun this weekend and that her mom won't be too desolate without her. (Although a bit of desolation wouldn't hurt.) "I'll probably just go see Grandma. Oh, and one of my students, the one who reads, is working part-time at the bookshop. She's asked me to come to another author visit."

Jess tries gamely for enthusiasm, although this is clearly her idea of hell. She hopes she never gets to a stage in life when hearing some guy or woman read aloud like someone in first grade is her idea of a good time. "Oh, that's nice," she says, encouragingly. "You like those."

With this she turns and goes down the stairs.

Taking one final, infinitely depressing look at the Pearl Harbor bedroom, Laura follows, still talking. "I just hope it's not another southern serial-killer book. Might give me ideas."

"LOL," says Jess.

"I have no idea what that means."

Henry, who is eleven, knows what LOL means and is still reasonably malleable, is just finishing his Cheerios at the breakfast bar.

"See you're ahead of the game, hon," enthuses Laura, stroking him gently on the head, which you can still do before they have a teen to their name. "You all packed? Got your inhaler?"

On his nod, she turns to Jess. "Eat a healthy breakfast. It'll be junk food all weekend."

"I hope," says Jess Griffin.

*

Lexington, Kentucky. May 1982

Twenty-two years earlier, in a far larger kitchen just a few miles away, a young man recognises the smell of bacon as he strolls in after another great night's sleep. This is not a smell he knows from his own home, but he is familiar with it from cafés and the homes of his friends.

The family are sitting quietly at the breakfast bar. Or maybe they have just grown silent when they heard his step on the stair. Charlie has to pause for a second, at least in his head, just for reorientation and to remind himself once again that he is living for a few glorious weeks in a splendidly luxurious home almost four thousand miles away from his own, having been temporarily adopted by a pleasant but completely different family. Differing not only from the one he has just left but from any family he has ever known.

In America, for fuck's sake!

The very room appears to be touched by light in a manner far removed from any room Charlie has ever seen or visited. Perhaps it is simply because they are in the warmer, sunnier south of the United States rather than the often grey, western side of Scotland, yet right now it feels like he has just strolled onto a film set, where everything is gleaming, art-directed and blemish-free. Larger than life itself or at least life as he knows it.

Dear Lord, even the cast appear well honed and starry! He feels almost disloyal to his own parents, as if they have been found wanting and lacklustre, unable to provide for him in such a manner, affording little special by way of illumination or design, but the feeling soon passes.

Charlie knows instinctively that he must devote equal and assiduous attention to all four members of this new and generous family, even though there is one particular Sherman for whom he is starting to feel an only slightly disturbing affinity. This is especially crucial as he is sensing, even after a few short days, that the male members of this new grouping already have their suspicions about him.

"Well, good morning, Charlie," greets Mrs Sherman, pleasantly. "Did you sleep well?" Before he can answer (although he is hardly likely to say no, even if the bed had been lumpy and bug-ridden, rather than his most luxurious ever), his hostess continues. "I'm just doing some bacon. Oh, but maybe you don't…"

For some reason he looks to Laura, who is wincing, even though Charlie can't recognise anything other than sensitivity in the question. "It's okay, Mrs Sherman," he assures her. The woman's concerned face immediately loses its frown. "Bacon would be fine. Lovely. I really adore bacon. Yum. Thank you." He can't help feeling he might be overdoing it a bit here.

"I had an attorney who was a Jew," says Dr Sherman. "Good man. Shrewd. Said he had no head for figures and got sick at the sight of blood, so the law was his only option."

Brian laughs at this but again Charlie senses Laura turning to him to check out whether the observation has cut him to the quick. Right now Charlie doesn't think anything could puncture the euphoria he is feeling or dial down the warmth of just being here in this brave new world. "My dad feels very much the same," he tells the man, as he sits down next to Brian. "I mean, about me and the law. He's not a... a professional himself."

"But Charlie's going to be a writer, one day," says Laura swiftly, perhaps before Charlie can elaborate uncomfortably on the lowly position his own parent occupies on the employment ladder. Parents, in fact, because his mum helps out with the kids at a local nursery. "I'm reading his work. It's quite fine."

When he hears it, this writer thing, spoken aloud by somebody other than himself, somebody who hardly knows him, it comes as a bit of a shock. A dream, or perhaps even a woolly ambition, has suddenly been elevated into a career choice, a profession. A calling. And, if he were to be brutally honest, as he assumes a writer must forever be, it scares him shitless.

"Och, well, I don't know..." he says, a bit feebly. He is grateful to receive some bacon at this point, as he now has something to shove into his mouth other than his foot.

"Not something you can make a living at," decides Dr Sherman.

It is Brian who comes unexpectedly to Charlie's aid. "TV writers do okay."

Before Charlie can endorse this undoubtedly true observation, not that he has ever met any writers for television, Laura slips in once more and cuts him off at the knees. "Charlie wants to write novels. Sweeping, romantic novels."

He tries to recall exactly when he told Laura this. He also wonders if he ever did, but she is hardly likely to have made it up, so he must have mentioned it on their way back from the writers' group, when he was on some sort of high from having made her and her friends laugh. He realises that he can't wait to make her laugh again.

Meantime, Dr Sherman is just shaking his head and sighing volubly. Charlie wants to tell the man that whilst he may currently be *in loco parentis*, this is more about keeping his young charge safe from forest fires and doesn't quite extend to crapping all over his dreams.

"Bless your heart!" says Mrs Sherman. "I do hope you won't write about us."

Charlie laughs heartily at this. As he would at anything that a friendly local has said, when they clearly expect a positive response in return. "Don't worry, Mrs Sherman. You're safe!"

"Too boring, I suppose," grunts the good doctor. "Not very... exotic."

"I wouldn't say that," says Charlie. "Everything's pretty exotic after Pollockshields."

He knows that this will baffle them and thus enable him to get on with the scrambled egg and something a bit fried, that looks a little like the latkes his paternal grandma makes but clearly isn't, which has just come gliding onto his plate from afar.

"I hope you like hash browns," says the short-order cook.

"I hope so too," says Charlie, which isn't exactly the appropriate response, but he is too fascinated by what just landed.

"Charlie, our school senior play this year is *Pygmalion*," announces Laura, out of nowhere. "You know, by George Bern-ard Shaw. Wanna come see it tonight and hear the terrible British accents?"

Before he can respond, her father is in there. "Laura, as I recall, Charlie's exchange is meant to be with Brian."

"It's okay, Dad," says Brian, charitably. "He doesn't like sports."

Charlie thinks that the taller boy says it as he would were he to be announcing their new guest's homosexuality, whilst simultaneously letting it be known that it's really no big deal.

"I'm a fiend at curling," says Charlie, once again, although he really isn't, but they're hardly likely to test him. "You do it wi' big brooms and stones and ice. In... er... Scotland." Their bafflement forces their eyes back down to the safety of their breakfast. "I don't mind what I do. Honest, guys. Sport. Culture. Lessons. It's all really interesting."

"For a writer," adds Laura.

They all smile, as Mrs Sherman finally joins them at the breakfast bar with her rashers.

"Shalom, y'all!" she says, spreading the joy.

ELEVEN

Approaching Lexington, Kentucky. April 2004

"…And what makes you think she'll even *be* there?" asks a mystified Kevin Roberts, for what Charles reckons must be around the umpteenth time.

Charles is still wondering why they didn't all fly directly into Lexington so many years ago, as he and Kevin are doing right now, but assumes that life and aviation have moved on in two decades. It might also have been simpler for the kids billeted all over the state to be collected by their respective hosts in the Louisville hub and then deposited back there three and a half weeks later, for that operatically tear-ridden farewell he can still recall so well.

He tells himself that he has thought more about this brief, long-ago visit over the past few days – in fact, since he first set startled eyes on Abi, the young woman in the bookshop and heard her jolting story – than he has in years. He tries not to wonder if this is anywhere remotely near the truth.

"In the damn city, leave alone the reading!" adds Kevin, as if his frustration had not already made itself sufficiently clear.

"I really don't *know* if she'll be there, Kevin," sighs Charles, who has been doing a fair amount of sighing over the last few days. "But Laura did love her books." He realises that this sounds on the very cusp of pathetic. He recalls that she was also pretty fond of fish, but he could hardly hang around the local fishmongers.

Turning to stare at the man, as if to add weight to his uncertainty, Charles notices again how very handsome the guy is. Somewhere, in the blank pages he stores in his head, he wants to write about him. Knowing shamefully little about the African American experience, he is all too aware that what he would be writing would at best derive from what he has observed secondhand, via movies and books. And he did enough of that sort of writing as a teenager. Isn't he always telling himself and indeed everyone else, begin with what you know?

"Worth a shot, don't you think?" he says, hoping that this will be taken as rhetorical.

"No," says Kevin Roberts, who is not big on rhetoric. The man can feel his Brit author's eyes almost boiling the airline Diet Coke in his hand. "All this because you happened to meet a young woman who looks a bit like her? No – a bit like how you *remember* her looking."

"A *lot* like," corrects Charles, insistently. "That young woman, whose name is Abi... Abigail, by the way... she just brought some old stuff back." He appears to go into himself and half-mumbles a different, far more troubling thought. One that totally bemuses his travelling companion. "And maybe threw up some bloody unbelievable new stuff."

Kevin detects a clear change of tone in the older man, a definite tremor of what could almost be perceived as fear. His writer is, at the very least, seriously rattled, and Kevin Roberts has no idea why. This most probably isn't the time to delve. Not that his curiosity is exactly boundless.

"Well, I got news for you, C.D.," he says, trying somewhat desperately to lighten the mood and – who knows? – possibly even move on, otherwise it's going to be a long few days. "Your schoolboy crush ain't gonna look so much like that sweet young lady now. And what is more, my romantic Scottish friend, even if – *big if* – this gal of yours still is in town, she might barely remember you and your fleeting visit, after twenty-two long years! Or, dare I say it, *want* to. Ever think of that?"

Charles fails to respond, which curiously irritates Kevin Roberts even more than when the guy couldn't stop banging on about it.

"Shoot, this a first," says Kevin, shaking his head. "Never been with an author who's reliving his own damn book."

"*That was fiction, Kevin!*" corrects the author, sternly.

To which his publisher just laughs. "Okay. So you're *not* still obsessed with something that happened to you as a teenager. And it hasn't screwed up your entire friggin' life."

"Absolutely not," insists the Scotsman, deriding the very idea. "My life is fine, thank you. More than fine. I've moved on – clearly. Just like my guy in the book does.

Eventually." Charles doesn't see the look of scepticism on Kevin's face, yet he could still describe it for a police artist. "*I'm a writer, Kevin!*" He laughs, taking a sip of his own drink. "We just cannot abide dangling threads."

He only half hears the other man muttering, "Don't come runnin' to me if her husband beats the shit out of you."

TWELVE

*"'You fahnd me cold, unfeelin', selfish, don't you?
Verry well: be off with you to the sorta people you
lahk. Marry some sentimental hog or other with
lotsa money, and a thick pair o' lips to kiss you
with and a thick pair of boots to kick you with. If
you cain't appreciate what you got, you'd better get
what you kin appreciate.'"*

Charlie can't fault Lexington Central High School
Theatre Department for ambition. He has never actually
seen *Pygmalion* on stage or screen, but his parents made
him sit through *My Fair Lady* on the TV one Christmas,
so he has a pretty good idea of the context.

He has a distinct feeling that he and possibly the
extremely bright young woman sitting close beside him
in the darkened auditorium might be the only members
of the large audience who can see the irony of a young

Kentucky schoolboy, firmly buttoned into what must be a stifling three-piece woollen suit on a sweltering weeknight, attempting to instruct a very pretty and equally enthusiastic schoolgirl on how to speak proper English. A young woman whose mastery of her 'native' Cockney over the past couple of hours has led her into a fascinating spectrum of accents Charlie doesn't believe exist.

Despite the more overt drama on the other side of the footlights, Charlie finds that he can't stop shifting his gaze to his closest neighbour in the stalls (or 'orchestra'), in the hope that she is equally tempted to do the same. The advantage of being seated so close together in the darkness is that few others can detect what is going on. The disadvantage is that he himself can barely see that face on which his eyes would happily linger for the entire duration of the performance. (Which does indeed appear to be interminable.)

Charlie has no idea whether the glistening pools of perspiration on the brows of the beleaguered actors, clad for more temperate English climes, is what is causing his own face to break out in sympathy or whether this is a direct result of the major supercharge his whole body is experiencing right now. The same feverish rush that is making his heart pump so fast and hard that he fears it will become audible any minute.

Their eyes meet this time and they share a smile. Not the first this evening but for Charlie one of the best. And most encouraging. He decides he will dare a whisper.

"I shouldn't judge. We did an American play *The Crucible* and I bet our accents were just as awful."

"What part did you play?" asks Laura, so quietly he can hardly hear.

"Mary Warren."

"That is rough." She giggles.

"No. What's rough is that we did it with the local girls' school."

Laura looks at Charlie, catches the mischief in his eyes and just manages to stifle a roaring laugh. Unfortunately, it comes out as a honking snort, which some might consider even worse. She diverts her attention sharply back to the play.

> *"'That's done you, Henreh Higgins, it has. Now ah don't care that for your bullyin' and your big talk. Ah'll advertise it in the papers that your duchess is only a flower gal that you taught, and that she'll teach anybody to be a duchess just the same in six months for a thausand guineas. Oh, when ah think of mahself...'"*

Charlie resolves that before the lights go up, he will attempt to hold Laura's hand. What can she do? Well, she can wrench it away, that's what. Or gently but firmly slide it back to its safe harbour well away from him, which in its own way might be worse. She could also keep her distance and not talk to him all the way home or even the next day and beyond. Basically, in one crass juvenile misstep, he could blow everything and screw up what has surely become, even in such a short time, a genuine meeting of minds and a truly rewarding friendship. Why bollix it up now?

Their bodies are already so close that he can smell the delicious freshness of her skin and hair and catch whatever scent she is wearing. He has no idea if it is perfume or soap or hairspray, or possibly even something she exudes unaided; he is no expert in these matters. But he does know that it isn't sweat, which is what he can sense on himself. He is certain that his hand will also feel sweaty. Perhaps hers will too but it still doesn't mean she'll go a bundle on his own clammy fingers.

"'...you little fool. Fahve minutes ago you were like a millstone round mah neck. Now you're a tahr of strength: a consort battleship. You and ah and Pickerin' will be three old bachelors together instead of only two men and a silly gal.'"

Now or never.

Very slowly, in the Shavian darkness, Charlie Dickens leans forward in his restricted space, at the same time tilting leftwards towards the adjoining seat. After a tiny bit of exploration, he sets his trembling hand gently down onto his companion's.

When Laura Sherman doesn't leap back in shock, or vomit into her own lap, he grips the small hand more firmly. He notices that it is delightfully soft yet quite firm. How does she do that? It is also far drier than his own. He senses a sharp movement and fears for an ugly moment that his quarry is shifting brusquely away. Yet, to his relief and surprise, and with an echoing tilt, she turns her hand around quite deliberately, so that it is soon clasping his own with equal vigour.

Their eyes remain firmly on the stage, as if any slight acknowledgement of what is going on in the darkness might allow reality to intrude and kill the moment stone dead.

Charlie realises that Laura has far more to lose than he this evening. After all, she is surrounded by friends and classmates. So far as he can tell, only a couple of his compatriots are in the audience, neither of whom he knows, save for a vague nod at lesson time or in the Lexington streets.

The faintest rush of scented air and a delicate shift in the darkness tell him that the head beside him is slowly moving closer to his own. So close that he can feel her hair – that lustrous, ash-blonde hair – as it just glances his (assumedly) reddening cheeks and tickles his (definitely) burning ear.

Charlie is firmly convinced that he has stopped breathing.

He has this bizarre notion that if he dies this minute, screams will be heard, the lights will immediately go up and this audience will never know what happens at the very end of the play, which he is almost certain must be at hand. The English Speaking Union will be blamed and the special relationship will suffer. Yet despite the palpable lack of magic onstage, he really doesn't want stark reality and endless curtain calls to intrude just yet. He wishes now that the long-winded George Bernard Shaw had just a bit more wind left in him.

"I don't want this to end," breathes Charlie Dickens.

"Neither do I," murmurs Laura Sherman.

And, for all each of them knows, the other might

simply be talking of the Lexington Central High School Theatre Department's seminal production of George Bernard Shaw's classic play about a meeting of opposites.

*

Charlie Dickens wishes that the Americans were more into hedges.

Back in Glasgow there always seemed an available hedge to sink into, when you were walking a girl home and fancied a good and decent snog. Not that, if Charlie were being truly honest, this has happened to him as often as he might have wished, even where hedges were in abundance. But he has enjoyed the odd dalliance, with lassies from his sister school, although almost inevitably the young ladies in question would move on after a couple of dates to older and better game. Usually with a car.

Guys with a car were known to have it made. His dad had promised to take him out for lessons, but so far none have been forthcoming. In America he firmly believes that everyone his age has a car or access to one, almost by divine right, and they all go to drive-in movies to 'make out' (where, apparently, the quality of the film is irrelevant) or curiously deserted beauty spots, with views of the Hollywood sign in the distance, or another valleyed city with lights twinkling obliviously below and rain never entering the picture.

So he is finding it rather frustrating that he can't source anywhere between the school and the Sherman house to take things just that bit further, with the special person who is now gripping his hand so hard that he doesn't know which will go first – the bones in his fingers or whatever it is that keeps your heart pumping. He is also feeling the inevitable stirrings down below, which are premature but far from unpleasant.

Finally, he spots an opening between two stone pillars, which may be a rather posh footpath or an alley or just the start of someone's drive. He really doesn't care. With Laura's slim body nudging his own more often and with more vigour than you might expect on a simple friendly walk, even of the handholding variety, and conversation being at an all-time low, considering how much they have found to talk about over the past few days, he reckons that if he doesn't make some sort of move now, however clumsy and inept, the moment may pass, never to present itself again.

In a sequence of manoeuvres with which even he is impressed, Charlie manages to ease his apparently willing companion towards the darkness of the pillars, whilst simultaneously attaching his already primed and puckered lips onto hers. The response is immediately encouraging, and even the fact that Laura immediately trips over his outstretched foot and he has to grab her to prevent her from smashing her head on a stone lion doesn't detract from the beauty and excitement of the moment. In fact, her wrapping her arms around him, if only for self-preservation, offers him all the encouragement he needs.

It seems like just a few seconds, but could have been far longer, until Laura's soft and velvety lips part and a more frenzied lingual exploration can begin. He feels that even as he is ceasing to breathe, he is somehow inhaling her.

Charlie can sense the heady warmth of her cheeks as they mould softly onto his own, which instantly feel as if they're on fire. Even in the darkness he can tell that her strikingly expressive eyes, eyes that seem to define their owner with a clarity he has never known, are gently closing, as if of their own accord, as she savours and contains the moment. He wonders why his own eyes are still open but then tells himself it has to be so in order for them to enjoy the look on her face and also to keep himself alert to unwanted predators. Man the protector.

Suddenly, to his immense frustration, Laura breaks free. "My dad will be wondering why we're so late…"

Charlie knows that he has to respond but wonders if he can do it while they're still kissing. Maybe he can give his answer straight into her mouth. "Tell him we got caught up discussing the play," he suggests to her tonsils.

"Like he'll believe that!" More kissing. "Do you have a girlfriend, Charlie?"

Charlie decides to respond as Henry Higgins in a recent, magical production of *Pygmalion*. "Ah do now, Ma'yaam. What about you and… gentlemen callers? Ah cannot imagine a… a dame so lovely not…"

When Laura responds, Charlie is gratified to observe that the delivery is equally as muted and breathless as his own, although perhaps less jokey. "There've been boys. Sure. Kids I've grown up with. But nothing like… Jeez… this is happenin' so fast."

"We've only got three weeks," explains Charlie.

She kisses him even harder. "I know," she gasps, managing to sound urgent and desolate at the same time. After a few steamy seconds, she succeeds in pulling away once more. "Oh Lawd, we really had better get home."

"Your ma's probably doing a hog roast for me."

"In chicken soup!" Laura laughs.

Charlie finds this so endearing that he pushes her into a single and rather pathetic bush that lurks right beside a column. She giggles as they both stumble, but he doesn't feel the time is right to go full horizontal.

Not yet.

THIRTEEN

Lexington, Kentucky. April 2004

Yet again the sign on the window reads '*C.D. MacNaughtan. Bestselling author of* The Forever Moment'. And stripped across it, in bright red lettering, so that nobody can be in the slightest doubt: '*TONIGHT!!*'.

At least they didn't spell it 'tonite', thinks Laura Griffin, as she stands outside the busy BlueGrass Bookshop in downtown Lexington. She has seen this lazy misspelling sufficient times on posters at her school where, as an English teacher, she has felt duty-bound to call it out. On one occasion she had told the student responsible that okay, she knew she was being a pedant, and could immediately sense, without anything being said, that the boy was wondering why his English teacher would so publicly and without apparent shame admit to child abuse.

She is about to remark on this to her friend and fellow teacher Kyra, who stands or rather looms right next to her on the sidewalk, peering easily over the heads of her fellow attendees into the crowded bookstore window. She realises, however, that she has already recounted this story, probably more than once, and wonders if this is what happens when you don't have a partner and tend to live more inside your head than perhaps you once did. Or – if you're also a mom – talk only in commands, entreaties and outright bans.

"Looks like they're gettin' a full house here," says Kyra, nodding towards the line of people now entering the bookstore. Being at least 6'2" in heels, she has to duck to follow them inside.

Kyra is a few years older than Laura and clearly several inches taller. She teaches biology at the high school and it is rumoured that even the dead frogs put their legs together when they know she is coming. She tries her damnedest not to be scary, but her unusual height, the vivid slash of her make-up and her entirely monochrome wardrobe don't exactly coalesce to calm young minds. Even Laura finds Kyra a tad intimidating and more than a little overpowering, but she also adores her, loves the humour, occasionally venomous but more often affectionate, that is never far from her lips.

They met because their kids joined school in the same class and only then discovered that they were fellow teachers. Unlike Laura, Kyra does have a husband at home. But as home is his favourite place and he is probably agoraphobic or at best antisocial, Kyra seeks out interesting places to go without him and asks likeminded people to accompany her. Hence tonight.

"Hi, Mrs Griffin, Mrs Nordstrom."

They turn to find a beaming young Asian student from their school. She is standing behind a table piled and strewn with books by C.D. MacNaughtan, including, of course, the one that is the subject of this evening's reading.

"Hi, Celeste," greet the teachers in unison.

Kyra taps a copy of *The Forever Moment*. "Any good?" she asks.

"I started speed-reading it just now," says the young woman. "Before the doors were opened. The word is it's fine and it's even gonna be a movie. Doing zip for me so far."

"Too romantic, Celeste?" Kyra smiles, opening bright red lips to reveal a formidable set of gleaming teeth.

"Too few corpses, Celeste?" asks Laura, who knows the smiling young woman slightly better, because she is one of her students. "Well, I never heard of it. Or him/her. I'm just here for the wine."

Laura looks around and is rewarded to see a table laden not with books by some obscure author but with glasses filled with white or red. They are being grabbed with gusto and going down as fast and easily as pulp fiction.

The small store already feels crowded. It is buzzy with chatter and anticipation. The management have clearly decided not to provide chairs, as they reduce the capacity and impede the milling around which booksellers prefer, since they do also have rather a lot of other books on offer. And there must be somebody here who hasn't yet read *The Da Vinci Code*.

Laura is always pleased to be here, as she has known the shop since her childhood and it represents to her the very essence of what a good bookshop should be. Replete with shelves in old or at least old-looking wood, it effortlessly curates wonder and magic between agonisingly tempting covers. Beams and walls are plastered with quotes about literature and the benefits of reading. Scattered around are recommendations from staff who often seem far more discerning and better read than their customers.

Laura Sherman, as she then was and to all intents is again, used to make a beeline for the children's section at the rear of the store. Now, she thinks ruefully, this same – although possibly more family-sized – Laura Griffin is edging and elbowing her way towards the alcohol nearer the front.

As she and Kyra arrive at the wine, they hear the chatter suddenly swell and then subside, and realise that the evening's main event is about to commence.

Grabbing her glass, Laura, being only 5'3" and not desperately wedded to heels, has to shuffle and strain to find a viewing point.

"Want me to lift you up?" offers Kyra.

"Oh, would you, Kyra?"

Laura glimpses the guy who seems to her to have been running the bookstore forever but who in reality, despite his impressive mane of flowing white hair, must still be only in his early sixties. She guesses that it is a family business, as she vaguely remembers an older couple, who would probably have been this man's parents and have now most certainly ascended to that great Barnes & Noble in the sky.

This proprietor, who she always thinks of as Mr Bluegrass, is already nodding and smiling to people, regular customers such as herself, as he works his way towards a portable lectern that has been set up in anticipation. Laura can't as yet see the guest of honour and still has no idea whether it is a Mr or Ms C.D. It seems to her that especially since J.K. Rowling, this *'initial'* business has become the fashionably profitable way to confound readers and override gender prejudices.

The lights flash on and off a couple of times, suggesting to the shop's patrons either an imminent power cut or the commencement of this evening's proceedings.

"Welcome to BlueGrass, everyone," greets the avuncular owner, proudly. "And I am truly delighted to see so many of you here, familiar faces and new visitors, on such relatively short notice. Our esteemed guest this evening has come all the way from London, England, and this is his only visit to the Southland. He confided in me that our fine city has held a special place in his affections ever since his youth. Imagine that. So, may I present to you the author of the – to my mind – perfectly wonderful *The Forever Moment*, Mr C.D. MacNaughtan."

By standing on tiptoe, Laura Griffin just manages to catch a glimpse of a tall, smartly but casually dressed man with neatly trimmed dark hair and olive complexion. This, combined with the recent introduction – and, of course, the now-familiar initials – suddenly causes her to sway and almost lose the glass in her hand.

"*Oh, Jesus!*" she says, as some of the wine spills onto the floor and she feels that she could soon be joining it.

Kyra turns to stare at their friend, who has gone quite pale and appears to be in a state of shock. The ridiculously small hands are trembling. "Hey, babe, it's only wine," she says, gently misunderstanding. "See, the kids are pouring out some more right now."

Laura can't speak. She just shakes her head, as she tries to peer around an unnecessarily large man, wearing what seems like a billowing summer kaftan but could just be a massive jacket.

"You okay, hon?" Kyra is just beginning to look concerned.

Her distressed friend simply nods and shrugs, tapping her wine glass as if to explain that the sudden giddiness and the look on her rapidly blanching face, the look that says the world is out of joint and spinning wildly, are simply alcohol-related. Which actually doesn't ease Kyra's mind one bit.

Meantime, Charles is making his way to the lectern.

Laura doesn't spot immediately that the man is staring into the crowd of total strangers, eyes boring into every face, or at least every female one, as if searching forensically for someone. But when she does catch a swift glimpse from him and suddenly realises what he might possibly be doing, she changes her modus operandi and instead of answering his glance with a smart one of her own, attempts to make herself as undetectable as possible.

Kyra, who really can't overlook her smaller friend's bizarre stretching and shrinking antics, leans down to whisper to her, "What are you like on a whole glass?"

"Good evening, and thank you," says Charles, still scouring the room. He glances at Kevin, who stands in a corner of the store, some distance away. The publisher is also looking around, as if he might suddenly recognise someone he has never met in his life.

Realising that he has held his pause just a fraction too long, Charles picks up the pace.

"Many years ago – twenty-two, to be exact – I came here to Lexington on a high-school exchange from Glasgow, Scotland. Some of you may still recall the rampaging horde of wee kilted Celts laying waste to your fine city. And I have to confess that this novel, whilst set somewhere totally different, is more than a bit inspired by that visit. Hence my somewhat sentimental return. But I must stress – especially for the lawyers amongst you – please don't go looking inside for anyone you know. It is all pure fiction!"

That voice!

Laura Griffin freezes.

Charles is gratified to see that the audience is on his side and already smiling warmly. Of course the wine helps. And if they're wondering why their speaker's eyes are zipping all over them like a meerkat on speed, frantically searching for something or someone, then let them put it down to a peculiar Britishness. Or something.

There's no mistaking that voice!

Perhaps a touch more gentrified than in their youth and at that lower pitch only maturity or nicotine can bring, yet the familiar Scottish accent has suddenly flung her back those twenty-two years. But whilst she might be listening right now – how can she help herself? – she sure isn't looking.

Like an incontinent penguin, Laura has sidled over to the table where Celeste remains on-duty, and grabbed herself a copy of the book. The Saturday salesgirl can only stare in confusion, as her respected and hitherto respectable English teacher begins flicking madly and in some frenzy through the pages, as if she has taken a super-advanced speed-reading course or simply doesn't want to splash out on a novel she might not wholly enjoy.

The author himself has begun to read.

> *"He hadn't intended that his fiftieth birthday should be a day for reckoning. For recollection. But wasn't this the very watershed between a youth sadly departed and that unwelcome senescence yet to come?"*

Charles uses this brief natural pause to scan the crowd once more. Kevin notices with some sympathy the look of disappointment just starting to cloud the Scotsman's face and can only hope that the audience will read it as a passion engendered by the written words themselves.

> *"Yet gazing once again at that crumpled photograph tucked away behind several others on his desk, Oliver realises that there are some things you have no option but to remember – because, whether you wish it or not, your heart won't ever let you forget."*

Despite her manic devouring of the printed word, these recently spoken ones, delivered with such sincerity, or at least a convincing semblance of such, appear to resonate far more with Laura. She realises with a jolt that she can't keep hiding, especially not in a room this small and with people she knows in the community, who she hopes have some respect for her. It occurs to her that perhaps she has always known this day would come. But she hasn't an idea in her head as to how it will go.

As Charles looks up from his own writing, she finally and decisively steps out from behind the larger members of the audience, which is most of them, and directly into his line of sight.

His still-familiar brown eyes land on her, linger for just a fraction of a second and then move on to search elsewhere.

Laura finds herself totally confused and in the unfamiliar position of not quite knowing how to react. Should she be offended, saddened, shocked, relieved? She really has no idea. Meantime, the oblivious and possibly shortsighted man reads on.

"'The sumptuous picnic his new American family provided was nothing like the poor excuse that he was accustomed to... white-bread Mother's Pride sandwiches with processed cheese by the side of a motorway... here were roast chicken legs, huge slices of watermelon...'"

"Have I really changed that friggin' much?" mutters Laura.

"Excuse me?" says Kyra, whose friend's peculiar and most probably alcohol-induced antics are rather distracting her from listening to that delicious Scottish accent and what sounds like a pretty good book. Something perhaps in the Nicholas Sparks vein, whom she adores.

""You go for many picnics back home?" asked his host.""

"Picnic," murmurs Laura, which makes Kyra believe that her novel-reading friend has definitely lost the plot.

Laura Griffin isn't listening to the words anymore. Or at least not to their context. Yet if a good book truly can transport you, this one is surely doing its job.

FOURTEEN

Mammoth Cave, Kentucky. May 1982.

"You go for many picnics in Glas-Gow?" asks Dr
Sherman.

It takes a few moments for Charlie to catch on that
he is being addressed, although it would be tricky to
find another person in the Sherman station wagon this
inevitably sunny morning capable of answering such a
question with any authority.

The addressee is ostensibly gazing out of his window
at the rear of the car, savouring the surprisingly green
and lush Kentucky countryside, watching out for as-
yet-unseen examples of the famed blue grass on hills
like verdant breasts, as those marvellous American
automobiles roar by. There's even a bulky camera held
one-handedly to his face to prove it.

Yet the vast proportion of Charlie Dickens' attention,
sensual if not visual, is focussed on some furtive but
dexterous hand-clasping going on with the person sitting

next to him. A person in the cutest bright red shorts and tiniest white tennis shoes, with a rather less cute and deeply suspicious twin parked bulkily right next to her. Suspicious, that is, when he isn't immersed in playing his noisy Mattel handheld football game, to which he is totally addicted and which Charlie for one finds really annoying. And a bit rude, actually.

Both handholding parties are aware of the sternly vigilant glances reflected in the driver's mirror and those of the equally wary woman sitting beside him. A lady who has an illuminated cosmetic mirror attached to her sunshield but is not averse to turning around in her seat at unnecessary speed, whenever she wants to speak to any of her three young charges. (And occasionally even when she doesn't.)

Charlie and Laura find themselves coupling and uncoupling their hands at such a rate that they might as well be clapping. But beggars can't be choosers and they need to seize every opportunity going for that essential, yearned-for physical contact. (Charlie would give anything just to touch, let alone stroke, those strong, tanned legs, or at least the one that is gently but regularly nudging his own. Too regularly, he is convinced, to be caused simply by the movement of the car.)

Such opportunities have sadly been rather fleeting of late, Brian and his family having taken over much of their guest's after-school and weekend entertainment. If there was a jump-seat in the car, the young couple's sexual frustration would be sitting opposite them like an extra passenger, taunting them to distraction.

"Er, not too often, Dr Sherman," says Charlie,

eventually. "I used to go more – y'know, when I was a kid."

"What are you now?" asks Dr Sherman, rather pointedly in Charlie's opinion.

"*Dad!*" protests Laura. "Charlie's going to college in the fall. Like Brian and me."

"Your father's just joshing, Laura," says Mrs Sherman, swivelling round like that girl in *The Exorcist*. As the couple's hands swiftly de-clench again, they can both sense that the older lady has noticed. Neither of them has chosen to question why they shouldn't, in fact, hold hands. It is as if they know instinctively that it has to contravene some rule about inappropriate intimacy within the host family, even though nobody has laid down any such rule.

"Well, Charlie, only a few days now till you're back home," says Mrs Sherman.

"Don't sound so fuckin' relieved," is what Charlie doesn't say. He simply nods, knowing that this will be reflected somewhere.

"I hope this visit has been all you were expecting," says Dr Sherman, very nearly smiling at him in his mirror. Possibly because the end is nigh and pretty soon he won't have to smile at anyone first thing in the morning.

"Aye. It has, Dr Sherman. Even better. Thanks very much."

Charlie and Laura watch the parents exchange a concerned look. Which merits another good squeeze on the fingers.

Very little more is said, especially as Brian has proved himself over the weeks to be a particularly poor conversationalist. (It had been the original intention that the American host teenagers would have their hospitality repaid in kind by a subsequent visit to Scotland, but for reasons Charlie has never understood, that bit of the 'exchange' – thankfully – has fallen through this particular year, although there is talk of resurrecting it in 1983.)

Fifteen minutes later they turn off the freeway and drive slowly into a crowded car and coach park.

Charlie hadn't really been paying much attention to where they were headed, knowing only that the entire Scottish contingent was having some sort of picnic with their Lexington families – which meant more time with Laura but still annoyingly not on their own. He sees a large sign and for some reason reads it out loud: "*Mammoth Cave National Park*," then adds a meaningless, "Uh huh."

Mums and dads with small kids are busily unloading baskets, rucksacks, blankets and industrial quantities of Tupperware from their cars, alongside other families who can be clearly recognised as this season's hosts, as at least one of their disembarking passengers has no tan whatsoever, worse teeth and is probably wearing either tartan or Doc Martens and sometimes both.

"Looks like the gang's all here," observes Dr Sherman, as he parks the car next to a dusty camper-van. "You ever seen a mammoth cave, Charlie?"

"Sadly not," says Charlie. "Mammoths got too scared to visit Glasgow."

Whilst her family smile politely, Laura affords this gem a tinkly yet surprisingly hearty chuckle, which makes Charlie wonder how she ever sprang from the same source as Brian and more particularly how she managed nine months locked up in there with him. And most probably his sodding football game.

He spots Norman, with his family, looking the palest of them all. This proud son of Falkirk, still kilted, is scanning the car park but stops when he spies his pal waving. Charlie finds himself torn between joining his friend and staying with his hosts. Laura, with the sensitivity that she appears to manifest on a regular basis, without even trying, as if it's – he doesn't know, instinctive or something – appreciates his dilemma and sets about immediately to resolve it.

"Here, take this bag," she says, thrusting a small rucksack out to him. "Mom and Dad aren't joining us. They've seen the caves a thousand times." Charlie's eyes light up – this is news to him and the best he has heard today. Now if only Brian could fall down a bottomless chasm.

Brian does the next best thing and goes jogging off to see Robbie and some classmates, still playing his football game. So much for looking after your guest, thinks Charlie, even though this is the last thing he would ever wish or need Brian to do.

"You go and see your buddy," says Laura, sweetly. "I'll join you in a second."

Pausing only to stroke Laura's hand, as if to say normal furtiveness will be resumed as soon as possible, he trots off towards Norman.

"So how's it going, pal?" asks the kilted one, as he watches his own host desert him for a handheld video game.

"Great," says Charlie. "They've been very nice. Very kind. Bit stiff, you know, but once they were assured I wasn't going to sacrifice any newborn babies—"

"I meant wi' yon Laura. She's not stiff. Although I bet—"

"Yeah, okay," says Charlie, feeling strangely prudish, as if Norman is about to sully something almost sacred. "It's, y'know… fine. She's more fun than her brother."

"My nan's more fun than her brother. And she's been dead six years." He stares meaningfully at Charlie. "Better hurry up, 'Chuck'. You ken? We're only here one more week."

"We're going to carry on. Laura and me. Writing. To each other."

Norman just stares at him. "PEN PALS?!" Charlie tries to calm him down, but Norman is on a roll. "Who are you – fuckin' Jane Austen?"

"No. Soddin' Charles Dickens. But we often get confused." They laugh as they join the rest of the group and walk on towards the entrance to the caves.

"What are you guys laughing at?" asks Laura, trotting briskly towards them. "We Americans, I'll bet."

"Not this time, hen," assures Norman, who clearly bows to no one in his admiration for her shorts. "Charlie wis just sayin' he canna wait to get back home and take a firm hold of his wee ballpoint."

"I'm sure that's rude, but I'm ignoring it," says Laura.

Once again, Charlie is lost in wonder at the way this young woman, unlike so many of her fellows, simply 'gets' them, him and Norman, their humour, their what he is only now starting to realise is a peculiarly British vulgarity. He also can't stop looking at her figure in those shorts – he is particularly taken by the little white socks that he reckons would look just so wrong and childish on a Scottish girl – or, as a pleasing alternative, the pearl buttons on her fetching primrose blouse and where they might lead. Although 'bloody nowhere' is the simple answer.

Talking earnestly to his friend but with her eyes forever straying back to Charlie, the occupier of the blouse says, "I've read some of his work, Norman. And I'm pretty sure one day scads more people will. You heard it here first!"

"Oh. Okay," says Norman, ignoring it here first and moving forward towards the darkness. Although the cavernous attractions are still a serious walk away, with some splendid scenery en route that none of the teenagers could give a toss about, he cries, "*Here come the caves!* Take off your shades, guys. Ooh. Spooky!"

On this warning, he scoots forward and begins mildly to scare some other members of their party and more profoundly a few random smaller children, who would find the sudden appearance of a man in a loud skirt sufficiently frightening, even without the accompanying caterwaul in a gruff and alien tongue.

When they can be certain that they are at the straggly tail end of the party yet fully out of sight of any host parents – those weary adults waiting patiently or not so patiently in the sunlight for safe returns and some food – Laura and Charlie simultaneously grab for each other's hands once again.

This time the grip is tighter, less sneaky or hit 'n' miss – more like an intention to remain attached forever than a simple, frenzied grasping for some basic and minimal physical contact. Their fingers play with each other like they've never encountered fingers before and need to secure a full sensory reading of every cell, knuckle and nail, just in case they suddenly lose all ability to touch or the opportunity never presents itself again.

Charlie can feel the darkening chill as they begin to enter the massive network of caves, yet the thermostat inside his shivering but hugely overstimulated frame appears to be completely on the blink. He might as well be in the sun-drenched deserts of Arizona or wherever they have sun-drenched deserts around here.

Again, working as one, they deliberately slow their pace until they can barely see anyone else in front of them.

Charlie has no idea whether he is lowering his voice in the interests of privacy or because it feels almost respectful in this darkly sepulchral setting. Yet it seems only proper in light of the intimate nature of a conversation that he knows is about to take place. One that he has been planning in his head for some days, but of course without her unpredictable response.

"It feels like we're always with some group or another or in a classroom or on an outing wi' your folks," he begins. "We've been to 'natural' bridges and baseball games and those funny wee horse races with the carriages and shopping in… in Cincinnati, wherever the hell that was. All very nice, but I don't think your mum and dad or Brian like me that much. I saw that Wicker Man in the garden."

"That what?" He just shakes his head. Why am I making crap jokes, he wonders, when we're talking about something so serious? Or at least I am. Is it some sort of incurable condition?

"They *do* like you, Charlie," insists Laura, although perhaps a wee bit too insistently. "They like you a lot. Who couldn't? You're just... different, is all." She grabs his arm and stares at him in the semi-darkness. "*One week!* Less than! Oh, Charlie, do you really think we'll ever see each other again? I mean, be honest, really?"

Charlie grabs her shoulders with both his hands. They feel so small and fragile beneath the intoxicating flimsiness of her blouse. Yet the warmth in his fingers suggests so much more. "I'll make bloody sure of it," he vows. "Laura..."

She looks up at him, waiting.

He can tell she knows immediately that whatever he is about to say is incredibly important but far from easy, so she is not even going to interrupt him with a nod of her head. Yet her eyes alone, so generous and trusting, are simultaneously making him feel bold and oddly intimidated. How do women do this?

"I know this sounds stupid." He is aware that she is waiting. Of course she's bloody waiting. She wants to know if it's as stupid as it sounds. C'mon, Charlie, get a move on. It'll be light soon! "And I do get that we're pretty young. I do. And we only met a couple of weeks ago, didn't we, although it seems... But please, Laura, I *know* what I'm saying." He's talking into her face. Well, whispering, but he is sure that she is catching at least a breeze from him in the darkness and possibly even some spray. *Jesus!* "I'm in love with you. And furthermore, I always will be. Always." There. He's said it. With a 'furthermore' and another 'always' thrown in for good measure. Now for the rationalisation. "It... it can happen. Right? It can! Look at... look at Romeo and... aye, okay, that didn't end well. But... Laura..."

Laura Sherman knows that she must help him out now, the poor dear boy. "Oh. Oh, Charlie... Charlie..."

"*SHIT!*" he says, too loudly, then has to draw himself down. Calm. Control. His hands move away. They brush against a wall of the cave, which is clammy and dripping. But probably no more than he is. "Sorry. I shouldn't have... Laura... I didn't... och, I've spoilt it now, haven't I? Bugger! I am so... stupid! *FUCK!*"

So much for calm.

Before he can smash his head against an available crag – and there are enough around – she sets her hand lightly on his bare arm. He can almost feel his hairs spring up to receive her. "*Spoilt it?* Oh, my darling Charlie." With the other hand she strokes his cheek, feeling the smoothness of this morning's ruthless shave. "No. You've made it. You've... *made* it." She laughs, sweetly. "You're so... romantic."

This surprises Charlie but doesn't displease him. It's how he would like to be considered and possibly even how he likes to consider himself.

For a moment neither of them says anything. They just stroll in a comfortable silence deeper into the maw of the ancient caves. He glimpses the water trickling down the rough, pitch-black walls and wants to touch it, to taste it. All his senses appear to have been dialled up to max.

After a few minutes, Charlie notices a small gap in the cave wall, most probably the natural entrance to another path, another cave. There is a rope barrier across it, although he has no idea whether this is simply to avoid stragglers and the adventurous from wandering off and getting hopelessly lost or if there are other more intrinsic dangers that the public might fall foul of and sue.

Impulsively, he removes the rope barrier from its supporting hook and with one firm arm pulls her towards the now blatantly unbarred opening.

"*Charlie, what are you doing?* We shouldn't!" says Laura, with what Charlie doesn't read as overwhelming reluctance. Although he accepts that he could well be wrong about these things and about women in general.

"Do you want to go back?" he says, as casually as he can, considering the obvious implications.

"Fuck no!" says Laura, surprising him all over again.

FIFTEEN

Lexington, Kentucky. April 2004

C.D. MacNaughtan is feeling guilty.

He is rapidly losing that glorious rush of excitement he first experienced only a couple of weeks earlier, when signing copies of his latest novel for patently enthusiastic and genuinely friendly American readers. (A rush that had endured – perhaps almost childishly – even longer than anticipated.)

The guilt is all the greater because this night's particular purchasers, waiting amicably in line, credit cards in one hand, wine glasses in the other, are still as open and welcoming as those locals he recalls from his very first visit to this town so many years ago. A visit without which, he has to keep prompting himself, he might never have written this book at all. Actually, no 'might' about it. Surely a pretty good reason why this evening's particular event – and hearing these glorious accents once again, redolent of so many fine and indelible memories – should be especially exciting.

Only it isn't.

Because the person he has most wished to find in this audience clearly knows nothing of the event or not sufficient to make her want to give up her Saturday evening. If indeed she even still lives here, which he very much doubts. Didn't he himself decamp some four hundred miles from his homeland many years ago and everyone knows that Americans can and do travel a great deal further in their own country, without falling into the sea.

From the cash desk, which is where his own interests lie, Kevin Roberts watches his mercurial author with some concern.

He can almost feel the currently rather dour Scotsman's sadness, even though the man is clearly putting a brave face on it, as he signs his books with an increasingly illegible signature and whatever new recipient name is thrown at him. He even politely asks for some help with the spelling, should the situation demand it. (Charles has heard some names on his travels that he never knew existed, including quite a few that really shouldn't.)

Of course, Kevin can't help thinking that the author's insistence on not using his real name on his books, for obvious reasons, hasn't exactly aided his quest.

Beside him, the white-haired bookseller, contentedly taking the money and working the credit-card machine, is sensing that something may be amiss.

"Does he always stare at people like this?" he enquires of Kevin.

"It's a… British author thing," explains the younger man, a bit feebly. "They all do it. Helps them build up characters." Kevin would explain this further and dig himself a deeper hole, as he can tell that his listener doesn't believe a word, but his attention is suddenly diverted back to the signing line. Because this time it is a customer who is staring, almost unblinkingly, through large yellow spectacles, at Charles.

C.D. MacNaughtan hasn't yet noticed the small, colourfully dressed woman in the line, as his head is down and the significantly bulkier BlueGrass customer ahead of her is tapping the title page of his book with a pudgy finger, to indicate exactly where the important signature should be.

"And just write '*Happy Birthday and a thousand apologies*' right there underneath," demands the man.

Charles is longing to know the full history behind this hyperbolic contrition and whether a copy of his book, even signed and in hardcover, could ever truly make amends. But there still remains a healthy line behind the remorseful Kentuckian and Charles really needs to sign the book, lick his wounds, drown his sorrows and possibly make a thousand apologies of his own to the indulgent young guy he can sense staring at him from the cash desk.

Then a voice, soft yet in its own way strangely insistent, halts his wanderings.

"Hello, Charlie."

Charles's head shoots up to find the woman smiling gently but tentatively down at him. He knows who she is in an instant. Of course he does.

Yet, even as he is recognising her, he finds himself quietly wondering whether he would have been quite so swift to do so, had he not actually been back here in Laura Sherman's own hometown and were she not practically the only person in the state or even the country to be aware of his real name and so confident in its employment.

Laura Griffin (née Sherman) is aware that this distinguished visitor, focal point of the evening in his sturdy signing chair, is now carefully scrutinising her from behind a pile of his own books. She knows that the hair is different, the bespectacled face a bit more careworn and lived in, whilst the figure after twenty-two years of kids and usage could hardly be quite as he remembered. Yet surely there is sufficient Laura Sherman here in front of him, the eyes, the bone structure, the mouth, one reasonably careful owner despite the mileage, that she isn't going to pass as just another stranger with a brand-new book in her frigging hand. And you're hardly Peter Pan yourself, Mr Dickens. Jeez!

"Hello… Laura," says Charles, only a few seconds too late.

"I wasn't sure… that you'd recognised me."

Charles laughs at the very idea, although the customers in the line behind Laura are beginning to seem less amused.

"*What!*" he says, in mock astonishment. "Of course I recognised you. It's been a long time," he adds, almost belying what he has already said.

Laura is aware that the good-looking man she has noticed standing beside the cash desk has suddenly turned up right next to them. He appears to be observing their exchange with some interest.

"Quite a coincidence," she tells Charles. "You being here."

They catch a snort from the new arrival. As they both raise their eyes to stare at him, he sidles just a bit more jauntily back to his post.

"It's no coincidence, Laura," admits the author.

They continue to stare at each other, neither one knowing quite where to go from here. Laura spots a female hand with a book in it, as it suddenly lunges past her with some urgency, in the direction and almost into the chin of the seated man.

"Could you sign my book? Or my babysitter goes into overtime. It's Jeraldine – with a 'J'."

"Oh. Sorry. So sorry, Jeraldine." He notices as he signs that Laura is slipping politely away. "Laura, don't go! *Please.*"

She nods briefly, as she moves towards the cash desk, only to find Kyra standing there. Her friend has been observing this exchange and is totally bemused.

"You *know* this guy?" she says, shaking her head, as if this is barely conceivable.

"I did, briefly," explains Laura, shaking her own head, as if the idea is just as inconceivable to her. "It was another lifetime ago."

"I'm gonna buy me that book!" says Kyra.

As her quizzical, if not downright nosy friend joins the line, Laura Griffin looks back at the author still diligently signing copies of his work. The tall man with the dark hair and the olive skin, the man with the interestingly asymmetrical face and flashing eyes, the guy she once thought not quite handsome, at least not in the clean-cut, wholesome, outdoorsy American way she had always pictured handsome, yet so far from unattractive. The person who she knew was going to be a writer some day. Or thought she knew – how can anyone be certain of anything at seventeen? When you're little more than children.

But we didn't think of ourselves as children then, did we, Charlie?

Oh God! Charlie, hon, we mustn't. We shouldn't... Oh Lawd! Don't stop. Did you bring...?

She can hardly see anything in the tight and almost pitch-black cave, which she thinks is probably just as well, because if she could see him, with his slim half-naked body on top of hers in the chill of endless night, she would surely stop him. Stop him unbuttoning and unzipping, stop him stroking and caressing, stop his cool lips from their breathless wanderings and explorations.

And she doesn't want to stop him. Because she knows now that this is surely what she most desired from almost the first moment she saw him.

She can hear the fumbling in the darkness, even as his lips breath the words onto hers.

Aye. Don't worry, Laura, he reassures her, attempting a smile in the hope that she can feel it with her own. Just watch out for mammoths!

She manages a giggle, before the passion returns. Unstoppably.

I love you, ma darling Charlie, she whispers.

I love you too. Always will. Always.

Something small and dark suddenly flies over their heads. She feels him quiver.

What the fuck was that?

Just a bat. Don't stop, my love. Just a 'wee' little batty.

"Sign it to Kyra. I'm another friend of Laura's. So – when did you two kids last see each other?"

Charles looks at Laura, as they both wonder who should speak.

"1982," says Laura.

"At the airport," amplifies Charles, who knows how important it is to set a scene.

SIXTEEN

Louisville, Kentucky. May 1982.

Standiford Field Airport, Louisville, feels a lot buzzier this Sunday morning than when Charlie Dickens first arrived here, less than four weeks earlier, wired and jet-lagged, on the second flight of his day and his life.

Or perhaps it only appears this way, because the disparate collection of Scottish schoolchildren, most of whom had never met each other before, and their equally random hosts, linked only by the school their own teenagers attended, have over these few heady, fast-flowing weeks evolved into a group who now know each other, have bonded with each other and in some cases even love each other.

Several of the Kentuckians are wearing items of tartan, not all of which are gifts from their departing young guests.

The noise level this particular Sunday has taken the airport staff by surprise. Especially when the parents of the host children rally together, as if on cue, to scream at their erstwhile charges – and be screamed at back – what Charlie reckons, should they ever document this story, could become the title song.

"*Y'all come back now weans!*"

At least, the majority of the parents are going for it. A certain doctor and his wife aren't quite so enthusiastic. If there was a local cry of '*y'all stay where y'all frickin' came from*' they might have sung along.

Even amidst all these painful and indeed teary separations, with promises to indeed all come back one day (and fulsome offers of reciprocal Caledonian hospitality totally unsanctioned by their unaware parents back home), Charlie Dickens appears notably more unwilling to break free than his fellows.

Whilst he cannot bring himself to expose his utter desolation quite so publicly (feeling the way he does right now, he reckons that the old hara-kiri business might not be completely out of the question), his face and that of the equally ruined person staying behind on the ground tell the story to any observer.

When the customary farewells are politely and properly delivered, with genuine expressions of well-brought-up gratitude (but no offers of reciprocity in this case, especially not to Brian), it is left to the young woman to murmur the final, definitive words.

"Don't forget to write, ma darlin'," whispers Laura Sherman.

SEVENTEEN

Lexington, Kentucky. April 2004.

Standing on the sidewalk, in the freshness of a mid-spring Lexington evening, some feet away from the wedged-open door of the BlueGrass Bookshop, Laura Griffin – with her brand-new signed book in her hand – thinks of those autograph hounds she has seen in photos, lingering outside the stage doors of Broadway, awaiting the emergence of an icon.

She wishes she could tamp down the fluttering of anxiety in her stomach, like one of those lottery machines in which fate, in the form of numbered balls, keeps churning mercilessly round and round. Feeling the newly signed book begin to slip in her clammy, trembling hand, she grips it tighter.

More than anxiety then – she reckons she may be in a state of shock. And how could she not be? Laura Griffin was simply expecting an unremarkable night out with a friend, plus maybe a drink or three. (A friend who has now gone soberly home to her husband, book in hand, confused but oh-so-very intrigued.) And now this blast – or rather tsunami – from the past.

He's a guy she knew twenty-two years ago, for Pete's sake! When she was plain Laura Sherman. It's not like she's been carrying a torch all these years, is it – and looking at him, the way he reacted to her (or didn't), she can't imagine that he has either. She tries to give herself some self-talk in the moments before he comes out, which she has heard is all the thing these days, but what if the self-talk is a whole bundle of lies?

What if he knows something she didn't think he knew?

As the lights are finally turned off in the bookstore, Charles comes out with the younger guy who made that funny sound back then, right after she had talked of coincidence. What was that all about? And didn't Charlie himself say...?

Charles smiles almost gratefully as he sees her, seeming just a bit more relaxed than at their encounter some minutes earlier. Yet she still senses that he is playing one of those spot-the-difference games, like they used to have in the newspapers and perhaps still do, with the 1982 Laura and today's 2004 model set side by side. She imagines that he has probably notched up well over a hundred jarring dissimilarities – a possible personal best.

Yet she can hardly blame him. Hasn't she often had a pretty hard time herself, equating the Laura she is now, separated mom, respected teacher, devoted daughter and, she's pretty sure, fairly ordinary suburbanite, with the girl she used to be? Or even, sometimes, with the woman that girl had once dreamed she might become.

"Kevin – this is Laura Sherman. Laura is a *very* old friend."

"You sound like my daughter!" Laura laughs, uneasily. "She thinks I'm practically senile." But while she is smiling at the men, she is observing her old friend's face and can almost watch his brain processing this new information. Well, kiddo, here come some more great updates. "And it's Laura Griffin now. Hi."

"Good to meet you, Laura," says Kevin, adding an, "at last," which his author doesn't feel is absolutely necessary. Realising that his author is probably correct in this assessment, Kevin decides to move on. "See you at breakfast, Charles. Early start tomorrow. *Back on schedule.*"

He goes off at his usual swift pace, leaving Laura wondering what that last little nugget meant and Charlie looking ill at ease once more.

For a few moments neither of them says anything. Where do you pick up after over twenty years, they both wonder, when you only knew each other for a matter of a few weeks anyway, in circumstances which in so many fundamental ways were totally unreal? Especially when there remain questions you might not want to ask, answers you might not wish to give.

"So. Welcome back to LexVegas," says Laura, finally breaking the silence. Then adding, with that smile he does of course still recall – oh my God! the smile that goes right up to her eyebrows, "*C.D.*"

"Aye. Well. My real name was taken, apparently." The voice is predictably deeper and the accent most probably tempered by those years away from home, but it's a voice – not simply a fetchingly 'foreign' accent but a distinctive Charlie sound – that brings so many memories bubbling back up for her like hot springs from warm earth. Memories she had held down for so long. "Is there somewhere we can go, Laura? You know, a bar or… Oh, sorry, have you eaten?"

Laura shakes her head, although of course she has eaten. Who wouldn't eat before – well, before this time in the evening? Maybe not in the UK, but here in the heart of Kentucky? Yet she is more than happy to eat again, because otherwise she will simply drink and… well, what with the shock and all, she feels that she needs to maintain a clear head. Okay, half a clear head.

She looks to Charles to lead the way, then realises that he would have absolutely no idea where to lead. The last time he was in Kentucky, fine dining was not exactly on the menu. Wasn't Colonel Sanders his chef du choix?

Please God, don't let the guy ask to go there again.

*

"I'd forgotten – about the southern portions."

Charles is facing down a massive chicken salad. Not fried and in a bucket, thankfully, but still formidable and resembling a medium-sized rainforest onto which a large cooked bird has clumsily crash-landed.

"That's why we Americans are so svelte," says Laura, smiling at him across the table. Part of her can't quite believe that she is here with him, Charlie Dickens, in one of her city's smarter or at least, in her limited experience, cooler restaurants! She also notes that locals whom she has only just seen at the reading are gazing towards their small, candlelit corner, wondering how this unexpected pairing has occurred.

And now she notices that he is staring at her again, examining her face like a critic in a gallery, as if still trying to compare and contrast the artist's naïve early work with today's more mature undertaking.

Just get over yourself, Charlie. Tempus friggin' fugits!

"You've kept your… you're looking well, Laura," he says, knowing instantly how clumsy this sounds. Not to say, insulting. He tries to add a complimentary smile, which he does genuinely mean, whilst realising that there actually aren't such things, unless you add on a building-site whistle or a sharp intake of breath.

"Thank you. So are you." She shakes her head. "You've hardly changed, Charlie."

"You should see the picture in my attic!" He laughs, then wonders if this is a reference Americans get. He is relieved that at least this American does.

"Doing well, too – clearly," she continues. "You must be so proud. Congratulations on all your hard work. Although I have to say, I'm not totally surprised."

Charles lowers his voice and leans in across the table. Here comes the serious bit, thinks Laura, steeling herself. Sooner than she might have expected, but perhaps he is tired and in no mood for small talk. Recalling with an inner smile his occasional misses last time round, she notices how well he has shaved today. She is also pretty sure that Lexington, Ky, is not the most obvious stop on a book tour such as his.

He is about to speak when he finds himself diverted for a moment by her hands. How strange to recall hands. And the way they felt in his. They still reveal those same almost mystical components of softness and strength, this time with two decades of experience adding what he might describe, were he to be as generous as he would always hope to be, as 'texture' to the mix. Charles gazes down at his own hands, as if only now noticing they've also been here for almost forty years. He is still looking down as he quietly broaches what he has to say next.

"Remember your very last words to me, Laura? At the airport." She doesn't respond. Of course she remembers. Yet she can tell, from his face and the tone, that he was clearly expecting she might not. Evidently he doesn't demand a response, as he moves on with more challenge in his voice. "Well, I didn't forget, did I? But after a very short while – you stopped writing back."

For a moment she says nothing, almost willing his head to rise and for their eyes to connect again. "You said that this – I mean, tonight – wasn't a coincidence."

Charles appears surprised, almost stunned, by this obvious change in direction. Yet he feels too wrong-footed to find a steady way back just yet.

"Er... no. No. I was here – y'know, in the US – and something, well, someone, suddenly made me think of you. And I had to..." He suddenly stops. And shakes his head. When he resumes, his tone is quieter, more pensive. Almost confessional. "Actually, Laura, when you read my book, you'll see that perhaps I never quite stopped thinking of you."

Now it is Laura's turn to be thrown. She can feel her

face becoming flushed and warm, as if she is leaning in too far towards the candle. "You said it was pure fiction."

"The story. Aye. Totally. But not… not the inspiration." Sensing her embarrassment and even perhaps his own, he aims, albeit clumsily, for an air of matter-of-factness. "Yet people move on, don't they, Mrs Griffin?" Her silence – or at least the slight, small shrug she offers, perhaps involuntarily – impel him forward. "Where's Mr Griffin tonight?"

"At home with the kids. Or more likely at a fast-food joint. Feeding their faces. It's his weekend with them."

As Charles takes this in, he tries to look nothing other than sympathetic. Yet he wonders where this slight feeling of satisfaction is coming from. Except he doesn't have to wonder too hard. Sometimes – well, too often actually – he is not that impressed with himself.

"Ah. Right. What kids do you have?"

Laura Griffin pauses for the moment, although the question would hardly seem of a sort requiring advanced mathematics. "Two. Yes. Sorry. Jess is thirteen and working to the teenage playbook. Henry's just eleven, so not yet monosyllabic. Although early onset grunting has been observed. Is there a Mrs Dickens – or MacNaughtan?"

Now it's Charles's turn to pause. He appears almost sheepish. "There was. Were. Twice. Not the same – two different ladies. No kids," he adds, with what does appear to Laura to be genuine regret, before looking down to take another mouthful of undergrowth. "Just… didn't happen."

Charles glances up once again, at some speed, to examine her face with new and perhaps challenging intensity. He senses all too swiftly that his dinner companion is finding this dramatic, almost scientific scrutiny just a bit perturbing. (As did another woman only recently, he recalls, a quite similar but considerably younger person.) So he switches focus into the middle distance and towards the people at other tables, who are still snatching furtive glances his way.

"I didn't know whether you'd even still be here in town," he admits, trying to roll back and normalise his gaze. "How would I? But I knew you loved books. And readings."

"Uh huh. And guess what – I teach English. At the high school."

"*Away ye go!*" says Charles. "Really? Not the same school…?"

Laura nods. "Hometown gal, I guess. My mom's still here and doing okay. And Brian too, he's a doctor himself now. Yeah – go figure. My dad passed about four years ago."

"I'm sorry," says Charles, because it's what you say.

"Thank you. Sadly, we weren't close."

"I remember he could never quite get over my…"

"Semitic roots?" says Laura. "No. You weren't exactly the fiery, redheaded Scot he was expecting."

"You weren't what I was expecting," says Charles, softly.

"Then? Or now?" she challenges, and his hesitancy is too long for comfort. "Twenty-two years, Charlie."

"Doesn't it sometimes seem like yesterday?" says Charles, and realises that it's a cliché he almost means. How sad is this, he wonders. "Maybe it's because all of us, we're still seventeen in our heads." He smiles to lighten his words, as he checks her out. "Or is that just me?"

They find themselves examining their food, as if it is chock-full of unidentifiable material that may well turn out to be toxic.

"So. Where do you land tomorrow?" asks Laura, eventually.

"Do you know, I can't even remember. Kevin does all that. But we're nearing the end of the tour."

"Then it's back to... London?" Charles nods. "Well, give me just a 'wee' bit more notice next time, please." She fishes in her pocketbook and hands him a neatly embossed card. "And don't forget to write."

He smiles at this. So does she. But there's a melancholy here, one that even diners at the other tables are picking up, as they wonder to themselves, what's he got to be sad about, for pity's sake – didn't we just buy his damn book? *And* in hardcover.

Is that it? he thinks, staring down at her card.

Is that all?

Like kids on a see-saw, Charles and Laura snatch looks at each other. As one head bobs up, the other goes down, each attempting to ensure that their confused but questioning eyes never quite meet.

Each wondering what the other recalls of those few weeks so long ago. During an earlier and even hotter Kentucky spring.

Charles knows what he wants to ask, what has drawn him so forcefully back to this place, but now that he is here, sitting opposite her after so many years, the whole enterprise appears strangely ridiculous. Almost absurd.

The distance between them is too great, the time that has passed is past retrieving. And yet…

"Did you ever get that short story I sent you?" he says, suddenly.

"A story? Sorry, Charlie, I… I don't remember," says Laura, hesitantly, still not quite meeting his eye. "But I'm sure it was very good."

"It was," says C.D. MacNaughtan. "For its time."

EIGHTEEN

Glasgow, Scotland. September 1982

The small photo has been sitting on his desk for months, propped up against a pile of books.

The desk is an old one made of oak, probably Edwardian, with a couple of ill-fitting drawers at the front, each with a wobbly bronze handle. His father had found it for him some years earlier at The Barras, the historic street market in the East End of Glasgow, so called because traders would sell their wares from handcarts or barrows. Once polished up and with a wonky leg sort of fixed by its purchaser, who has no profound carpentry skills but means well, the desk has served Charlie steadfastly through his eight tough O-Grade exams and the five diverse Scottish 'Highers' whose accumulated wisdom has now been consigned firmly to the ether, now that they have won him his place at Glasgow University to study law.

The attractively grained and carelessly scratched surface has played host to countless cups of tea and coffee, gallons of Irn-Bru and endless plates of sandwiches, shortbread and McVitie's chocolate digestives provided by the lady of the house. And born witness to all the agonies and ecstasies that occur with some regularity in a teenage boy's bedroom.

Charlie has written school essays at this desk, the odd embarrassing poem, more than the occasional short story and even first glimmerings of a novel.

It is a well-thumbed photocopy of one of these stories that he is reading again now, sitting in the repurposed and rather stern dining-room chair that had arrived in his room at the same time as the desk, a cast-off from his maternal grandma.

Charlie can't recall exactly how many times he has read and re-read these same words over the past several weeks, since he first carefully slipped the original typed pages into a proper envelope, so unlike the flimsy but heartfelt airmail ones he had been regularly sending. This time there was no long, rambling, passionate letter attached to it, simply a small piece of card that pointedly read '*I didn't forget to write*'.

He isn't scanning the story in order to make corrections or amendments. Far too late for that. The letter is posted; the ship has sailed. He is reading it – or at least attempting to read it – as if encountering it for the very first time. As if he hadn't himself written it in the first place. He is trying to get into the mind of someone meeting it afresh and imagining the effect his words might have. Well, not just someone. There is only one person whose reaction he is picturing. And hoping it has been all that he was desiring it to be.

Of course, he knows that this is nonsense. How can any writer totally divorce himself from something he has written, unless, of course, he or she has dementia and can't recall ever having written it in the first place? Or he has a split personality and it is one of his non-writer days.

Yet Charlie keeps on reading it. Again and again. Over and over. In his head and out loud. Addressing himself in a wardrobe mirror or, more regularly, narrating the tale to the small but magical photograph that sits unmoving, unchanging on his desk.

He reads it because he feels that if his recent impassioned but not totally uncrafted letters had been unable to elicit a sodding response from the person who little more than three months ago – and in her almost daily airmails of those early weeks – had said that she loves him to distraction and will do so for eternity, then surely his unannounced fiction should have done the job.

The story was like none other that he had written, one loosely based on the experience of some younger friends of his parents, overheard rather than recounted, a brief but hopefully potent piece that he had hoped would make the person he loves damn well do something about loving him back. (Even if she has gone and stupidly found herself someone far less worthy but considerably closer to home.)

A story into which he had poured his heart and talent. A story which might surely summon at least the barest smattering of affection in return.

Why the fuck hasn't she got back to him yet? It wasn't *War and Peace*! Surely there was nothing in it to…?

He reads it just one more time.

MISSING

A few weeks after the third miscarriage, he brought home a dog.

It was a curious-looking animal, an unplanned meld of German Schnauzer and something the Schnauzer had happened to meet in the park. Or so he assumed. He found it odd that, unlike other species that come to mind, dogs seem happy to mate with anything. But then he looked at his wife and himself and realised that humans were probably not so different.

He had always thought, until now, that the attraction of opposites was what made them such a team. But now he was at a total loss. He wanted so deeply to say or do something that would diminish her pain, yet the stoicism, the silences, the just-getting-on-with-things were so agonising that he could hardly bear to be in her presence.

He thought it would be so much easier if she just broke down and went to pieces or punched him or screamed at the God she never believed in for a moment and was hardly likely to turn to now.

Whenever they went for a walk these days – and they had always enjoyed walking, because open spaces and greenery appeared to make the trickiest conversations far easier and any problem that much more solvable – they would encounter children. Swarms of them, legions, multitudes. In pushchairs or wellies, running, climbing, sloshing, screaming. It was as if some government agency had alerted the local public that their town was about to be bombed to oblivion, so anyone under the age of ten must be evacuated forthwith to the nearest nature reserve.

He knew that a dog, even one as cute and cuddly as this, with its shuffling gait and hairy face like a dour old Scottish schoolmaster, couldn't replace a baby. He wasn't that stupid. He also knew that, so far as he was aware, she wasn't really a dog person.

Yet he needed so desperately to do something for her, if only as a gesture, an acknowledgement, and this was all he could come up with.

Naturally, he couldn't parcel up the creature and watch her face as she undid the string and removed the festive wrapping. But he did observe her as she slowly opened their front door to his unexpected knock.

He was taken especially by her large grey eyes (Schnauzer-grey, now he thought about it) as they followed his own eyes downwards. These had always been his favourite of her features, along with her soft, full lips, now gently parting to say, "Get that fucking wee thing out of my house this minute."

He had been expecting a tricky conversation after this, but the ensuing silence threw him.

In his head he had pictured her initial and quite natural reluctance to entertain the new arrival transforming in time to at least some appreciation for the misguided kindness that had prompted the purchase. And a sort of tentative yet inevitable bonding thereafter. The finality of 'one week – either that thing is out of here or I am' had rather taken him by surprise. Although, in retrospect, it probably shouldn't have.

Perhaps he might also have considered that, whilst he went out to his office every day, she could do her job from home. But he promised faithfully that until a new and more appropriate family could be secured for Barklay (the dog's very Scottish given name, the refuge insisting that a re-christening would be one change too many), he would walk, feed and do all the socialising with their temporary guest.

He was as good as his word. For five days, morning and evening, he tramped the streets of the quiet Glasgow suburb in which they had lived since they first got together, talking to Barklay about life, love and everything in-between.

He could honestly say that these were the most convivial conversations he was having at this point – Barklay was an excellent listener (and clearly motivated by his name being old Scottish for birch tree). Talk at home, when it occurred, was mostly about bills, elderly parents and household chores. It certainly didn't touch on anything emotional. Or canine. Or old Scottish.

On the sixth day, Barklay went missing. Or had 'gone bloody walkies', as his new mistress chose unhelpfully to call it. This apparently had occurred just minutes before the husband came home that evening. A door, improperly closed, had blown open and man's best friend, quite ungratefully and with a speed rarely associated with his lineage, unless greyhound was somewhere in the mix, had scooted off.

The man was thankful that his wife had agreed to accompany him on the search, although he suspected that this could be attributed more readily to a small but nonetheless appreciated measure of guilt than a genuine concern for Barklay's welfare. He had a feeling, however, that the quest – whatever its outcome – might not be totally unproductive.

As it was dark by this time, he carried a large torch. They tried to ignore the looks they were receiving from passers-by as they called out the errant animal's name into the crisp night air. It made him think for a moment that these people, commuters and strollers, would possibly assume that the couple had lost a child, which of course came close to the truth, but the pair would have been more careful and wouldn't have named him Barklay.

It was well over an hour later that they hoarsely abandoned their search of possible haunts and hiding places and returned in some frustration to their small, empty, terraced house.

Sitting on the doorstep, looking genuinely hangdog, was the escapee.

The solitary tears and sobbing could probably have been heard from there to the local shopping centre and beyond. Anguish and pain, so long contained, seemed to bounce off the walls of the sleepy little houses like gunfire.

"Finally," came the gentle voice.

He turned to look at her in surprise, as the tears continued to stream down his anguished face.

It was some days before he asked her, half-jokingly, as all three of them walked together in the sunshine, whether it was she who had let the dog out.

Charlie has just finished his third reading of the day, when he hears the metallic flap of the letter box in the hall.

Taking one last look at the photo on his desk, he leaps out of his chair and is down the stairs before his mother can even emerge from their small kitchen.

Mrs Kirstie Dickens, née MacNaughtan, arrives in the narrow hallway, toast in hand, to find her only child still in his pyjamas, squatted lankily on the welcome mat. His hands are scrabbling feverishly on the carpet, as he hurls envelopes and flyers around in a state of some agitation.

Sharing neither colouring nor build with her son, let alone temperament or talent, this relatively small woman with the pale blue eyes, open, round face (a Scottish face, as she has been told, but never quite understood whether this was a compliment) and conker-brown hair in a formidable perm, sometimes wonders if seventeen years ago the Royal Victoria Hospital had swapped infants at birth. At times like these she can often be found wishing that they had.

"It's been months now, darling," she says, not unkindly. Truly her heart goes out to the boy, but she sorely wishes that her Charlie would just bloody move on or go to university early or something. It has been a long, hard summer since he came back from that trip, and a four-year brush with the law might do them all the world of good. "The lassie's forgotten all about you," she says, trying to make her tone less harsh than the words themselves, yet failing to keep the frustration entirely at bay. "And you'd be wise to do the same."

Leaving the unwanted mail strewn across the hallway, Charlie glares at this ignorant, unfeeling woman for a precarious moment then stomps angrily back up the stairs. "How do you know?" he grunts. "How do you *fucking* know?"

A man's voice booms out from the open kitchen doorway.

"*Language!*"

Back in his room, Charlie marches over to his small desk and grabs the photograph. He glares at it, as if it owes him an explanation and it had better be good.

That was the very last full day of the trip, he recalls, staring at the object in his hand. It was at The Raven Run Nature Sanctuary, a beauty spot just a coach ride from the city.

Charlie had never been much into nature and had encountered very little of it in his tenement-heavy, suburban Glasgow childhood. Driving and camping holidays in his own country, probably one of the most beautiful in the world, left him cold and not just figuratively. Yet this place on that day was glorious. A consequence of the climate obviously but also the sort of wild and unspoilt scenery that he has been diligently teaching himself to appreciate and, in his own more recent writing, to describe. (One tree, however, is much the same as the next, in his opinion, and who, when reading a decent story, honestly bloody cares what sort of leaves there are on the trees or how the branches sway in the breeze like – like other things that sway?)

They had both been carrying cameras around their necks but had been too busy talking and yearning and emoting and touching to point them anywhere, and too reluctant to let go of each other's hands, even for the fastest shutter speed. Yet whilst they didn't say it, because it was too damn big and hard a thing to say, they were only too aware that these were almost the last hours and this certainly the final visit that they would be enjoying together, possibly forever or at least for years, and the thought of it was killing them.

Charlie remembers that he even pointed out a small stream running blithely beside them, as they strolled hand in hand, and had said that he could turn it into the nearby Mississippi with his tears, which Laura had decided was quite lovely, even though the Mississippi didn't run anywhere near there, and just the sort of beautiful thought that made him so special.

It was that sort of day.

There had been no reprise of the Mammoth Cave adventure, although it was not for the want of trying. Perhaps her parents had read everything in their faces when they emerged from the darkness, hands unclamped but faces glowing. Whether or not Dr and Mrs Sherman actually perceived that their only daughter had entered the attraction as an unspoiled young girl and returned as a worldly woman, in distinctly dustier shorts, they had certainly attempted to keep the pair on a pretty tight leash since then.

The young couple each decided that a photo had to be taken. Two photos. Before it was too late.

Just as Laura was about to capture Charlie forever, she noticed a kilted figure quietly slipping into the scene, a finger to its lips, behind the oblivious subject. She had taken the photo anyway and regarded Norman Gemmell as an unexpected bonus, to be cherished at a later date in the privacy of her room.

Glaring at his own photo of Laura Sherman now, taunting him mercilessly from his desk, even as she smiles lovingly upwards into his lens, he might himself have wished for some light relief, an unexpected intruder in tartan, to lessen the heartache he now feels and from which he knows that he may never recover.

He makes a sudden lunge for the photo and crushes it in his hand. Without the least hesitation he throws it in the bin beneath his desk.

Done.

Finished.

Closure.

"*This isn't how stories are supposed to end!*" he admonishes it.

Charlie is certain that his parents will be delighted. And perhaps he is even just the tiniest bit relieved himself, as if the second shoe has dropped, even though he knows that he has been stabbed right through his heart and the wound might well be fatal.

The photocopied story goes back into his file. At least that one came out alright.

The rejected lover is halfway down the stairs – in fact, his mum and dad can hear his approach and are already exchanging looks of some concern over the breakfast table – when he suddenly swivels and shoots back up into his room at full pelt.

The photograph will never fully uncrumple, but it has escaped the ignominy of the waste bin.

For now.

NINETEEN

Lexington, Kentucky. April 2004

The Morgan House, in downtown Lexington, is one of those boutique old inns which pride themselves on being called bed and breakfasts, although they resemble no B&B that Charles has ever experienced on his own home turf.

The rooms in this lovingly preserved and maintained historic home are inordinately spacious, decorated in an elegant southern style, with exquisite antique furnishings, original artwork by local artists, living and dead, and beds that take luxury to hitherto undiscovered heights. This is literally so as regards the bed in which Charles is currently fast asleep; hooked onto the rim of this massive, elevated item of furniture is a tiny but necessary set of mahogany steps, diligently placed to assist fortunate sleepers in their weary ascent and subsequently refreshed disembarkation.

When the room suddenly fragments, with a piercing sound, before the sun has even bothered to make wakening raids through gaps in the plush curtains, the bed's sole occupant almost quits his resting place in a far swifter and less dignified fashion than on first landing.

"*What the fuck?*" says Charles, but not directly into the room phone, which he finally realises is the culprit, as this is the object he is still struggling blindly to locate.

But first he has to find the steps, which have slid over during the night. He would see the whole business as farcical were he not still in shock. A shock only compounded by the many unsettling feelings that still linger after last night's less-than-fulfilling encounter.

What was I thinking? he berates himself once more, as he pads over to the infernal device, which by now is probably waking up his neighbours and most of the building. And what the hell was he expecting from the poor, stunned woman? Contrition, self-abasement, a PowerPoint explanation? Or maybe just the same seventeen-year-old girl he left behind so long ago, which even he realises, aside from being physically impossible, is more than a bit creepy. He is not averse to attractive younger women these days, Lord knows, but teenagers?

Charles is aware, as he finally answers the phone, that his voice must sound blearily unintelligible and extremely, gutturally Scottish, but what else should any moron who calls him at this godforsaken hour expect? Even Kevin, who he doesn't believe sleeps at all, wouldn't bother a fellow at six in the morning.

When the guy on the night desk manages to plough through the grunting and can explain all, the wind is taken right out of his sleepy guest's sails – wind which is probably a mixture of all the wine he had at the bookstore and beyond, plus the fine Kentucky bourbon he found in his room – to be replaced with an uneasy puzzlement. Charles informs the messenger that he will be down in a few minutes. Just as soon as he... well, no need to list the ablutions – as soon as he can.

Laura Griffin, waiting uneasily beside an American Empire chair, in the compact jewel that is The Morgan House's chintzy, parlour-like lobby, looks as weary as Charles feels when he finally makes his appearance. And from the jumpy way she is shuffling and clasping her hands, possibly a good deal more anxious.

Yet Charles himself is not exactly lackadaisical as he steps warily down the elegant but narrow staircase to greet her. He can't hide his surprise at seeing Laura again, nor his trepidation, and there is no reason why he should. Yet, despite this, he finds her unexpected arrival, after all the dissatisfactions of the night gone by, curiously intriguing.

The night receptionist, for this is still the darkish hour before day staff dawn, appears almost as interested in the event as his newly awoken guest.

"*Laura?*" says Charles, already lowering his voice as he approaches her. "What's wrong? Is something...? It's barely six o'clock."

If Charles thinks Laura Griffin née Sherman had seemed uncomfortable throughout the whole of last night, this was nothing compared to how she appears right now, this early Sunday morning, despite the casual neatness of her clothing and the half-smile of greeting that she offers him.

He can see that her eyes look even more sapped than he imagines his own must appear and, unlike last night, she seems to have done little in the way of make-up. Not that she needs much, he tells himself, trying to be generous, but not entirely meaning it, as he really doesn't think, harried and tense as she clearly seems, that she looks that great right now.

Charles wonders, even as she begins to speak, whether he is nothing more than an uncharitable, sexist pig – an educated, rather successful, sexist pig – and wonders almost simultaneously why his mind can't simply devote itself to the situation at hand, a situation puzzling enough without him having to describe her appearance in his head, as if she were a character in one of his books. And then he wonders why he should be berating himself for what are – come on – only thoughts. It's not like he's going to tell her.

Yet he suddenly feels an overwhelming sadness come upon him.

He has no idea whether this sadness is entirely homegrown or if he is picking it up from the uncomfortable woman standing just inches away. A woman who – he ruefully has to admit – he only ever knew back in the day for a few short weeks, albeit magical, pivotal, incandescent weeks. Weeks he has never been able to forget, hence this slightly aberrant detour, but spent with a person who is now almost a total stranger.

In fact, there's no 'almost' about it. This woman, pleasant enough, surely not unattractive, might be anyone just strolled in off the street, with a life and history very much her own. A life, from what he may also be picking up, that could in certain important ways have been more fulfilling. But honestly, what does he know?

Yet she does look, to his surprise, as if she might have been crying.

Of course, Charles admits to himself, he may be getting this all wrong, filtering it through his own perspectives and preconceptions. It wouldn't be the first time. Perhaps she has just brought him a hefty, self-penned manuscript to read.

He briskly interrogates himself yet again on his motives; forcing Kevin to divert them here on a fool's errand, deluding himself into suspecting that something miraculous, perhaps even mind-blowing, had happened? Prompted by what – a chance encounter in a strange university town?

When surely the simple and obvious truth of this morning's visit is that this woman whom he once knew intensely but so very briefly has decided to bite the bullet and explain, perhaps a bit shamefacedly (maybe she is not *totally* heartless), about her Mr Griffin and how he had won her heart so completely. And probably not so very long after that plane had blithely set off for New York on the first stage to chilly Prestwick airport. Hence the sudden drought of reciprocal *billet-doux*.

Hardly surprising that she couldn't quite open up about it last night, what with the sudden shock of their meeting. Perhaps young Griffin had been there in the background all along, but obliged to take second place, way back in '82, to an exotic Scotsman, if only for a few short weeks. He might even have been someone Charles had met during his brief sojourn here. Wasn't there a wee skinny redheaded guy at that writer's group?

All this is cannonading through his mind at a speed that impresses even him, considering his rude awakening only minutes before.

"Yes. I know. I'm sorry," she says, and he realises just a moment too late that she is simply talking about the infelicity of the hour, not her historic appalling behaviour. "Can we… go for a walk?"

Charles nods and finds himself yet again searching this Griffin woman's concerned face and uneasy demeanour for the Laura Sherman he still recalls so vividly, like one of those special cameras that can delicately scan a long passed-over work, in the hope of finding an artist's earlier and possibly more glorious masterpiece concealed beneath.

Unsurprisingly, the streets of Lexington are deserted as they walk out of the genteel, downtown inn. Who else would be daft enough to go for a stroll at this time on a Sunday? And would he want to bump into anyone who did?

Charles takes a moment to look around and realises that he has absolutely no memory of this place. Any recollections or images that he still retains are wrapped up in the person standing here beside him, or at least the person she used to be. It is these that he still recalls almost smile for smile, touch for touch, word for word.

As to the rest, he might as well be in any attractive city in any one of the southern states. What interest did he have at seventeen for architecture or history, what need for a briefing on the social conditions and ethnic mixes or conflicts of another distant country? Unless, of course, they related directly to a movie he had seen or possibly a book he had read. Wasn't it an authentic Kentucky Fried Chicken joint that he had demanded to see on arrival, not the site of the state's notorious slave auctions?

He does vaguely recall that the black students at the local high school tended to stick together, but this hardly impinged on his consciousness. The Asian lads at his own school and the Jewish ones too probably did the same. It's hardly unnatural that they would. He finds himself even today wishing that he had a crowd or a community into which he could meld, with whom he might seamlessly bond for comfort and companionship. Being half of something could often feel like being no part of anything. He has often thought that perhaps this is why he became a writer – because he was always on the outside looking in.

His mind must have wandered yet again during their silent meanderings along the inevitable Main Street. To be fair, Laura isn't opening up as yet and Charles definitely senses that he should be allowing her to begin any conversation. Yet, when she finally does, he is thrown to be confronted not with heartfelt explanations but with his own most recent book, extracted by his companion from her inordinately large, red-leather shoulder bag.

"I read your novel," says Laura.

"What – *all of it?*"

She shrugs. "It's easy. If you don't sleep."

Charles wonders whether this is a chronic problem or one provoked by his totally unexpected reappearance. He realises guiltily that he has been so preoccupied with himself and his own expectations, he has barely considered the effect on her. This poor woman pops along with a pal to her friendly local bookshop for a nice Saturday event with wine and is suddenly hurtled into a patently discomforting and possibly mortifying confrontation with her past.

"So – what did you think?" he asks. "Were you okay with the flipping backwards and forwards?" *Why am I asking about style now?* "Was it confusing?"

She shakes her head. "Revealing."

"Good. Well, that's… good. Oh, and sorry about the insomnia."

Laura smiles, for the first time this early morning. "I think I was right all those years ago. About how fine a writer you are."

For a moment Charles says nothing. The selfless generosity takes him by surprise. "Do you know, Laura, you were the first person to encourage me?" he says eventually, as they walk on, although he has no idea of their destination. "First one to believe in me."

It is Laura's turn to be surprised. "What about your parents?"

"Not a job for a half-Jewish boy."

"Bet they've changed their tune now."

"I think Dad did before he died," says Charles, wistfully. "I hope so. My ma just wanted to have grandkids."

Charles looks at Laura but says nothing more. Nor does she, for a moment.

"There's… still time," she says gently, after this curious hesitation. She turns to face him and taps the book firmly with a fingernail. He finds himself staring at her small but strong hand, recalling once more the glorious softness of it. "Charles, is this really how you feel? That what happened way back when we were just seventeen screwed up all your future relationships?"

Despite the chill that still lingers in the yet-to-warm-up city, Charles feels a heat rising in him. He doesn't know quite how to react, so he opts for both the head shake and the dismissive laugh, neither of which he suspects are particularly convincing.

"*It's a novel, Laura!* You're an English teacher, you understand. I was looking at what *might* have happened. Y'know, if a guy felt so rejected. Betrayed. Ask any author – we thrive on the 'what-if?'s." To his relief she nods at this. Now he can offer a normal smile, one of gratitude. "I really appreciate your wanting to drive over and tell me in person. Y'know, about the book. Means a lot. Even if you did stop writing. To me, I mean. I've no idea if you're still writing yourself. I hope so. You were very good."

As he talks, Charles realises that Laura Griffin is growing surprisingly impatient. And he suddenly knows, even before he has finished speaking, that there is something more. Much more.

"Charlie – that's not why I'm here," says Laura, finally. "Can we all sit down? Please."

TWENTY

They walk in an increasingly uneasy silence, looking for a bench or even a small wall. Personally, Charles would prefer a quiet coffee shop, as the morning's unexpected activities, coupled with last night's alcohol, are making him both anxious and thirsty.

They arrive at an imposing, two-storey red brick building, which Charles reckons, from his more recent delvings into architecture, must date from at least the early nineteenth century, if not before. Which he knows counts as old round here. Laura stops right outside and, as there are no available benches, sits herself on one of the railed steps leading up to the door. Charles follows her down, although a coffee shop would be infinitely more comfortable.

Before he can read the printed sign, Laura enlightens him on the building's importance to Lexington and to the world.

"This is where Mary Todd Lincoln grew up. Y'know, Abe's wife."

"'Aside from that, Mrs Lincoln…'"

"Exactly."

When she fails to move on, Charles continues to gaze across West Main Street. Waiting.

"This isn't easy, Charlie. And you may not ever want to speak to me again." She stops, looking at her hands, as if she has no control over how they are entwining, with some vigour and several strenuous variations, on her lap. "Can you say something, please?"

"I was listening, Laura. And no, I won't stop speaking to you. Not that we've been exactly chatty up till—"

"Did you ever wonder why?" she asks, turning to him. He just looks confused. "Why I stopped writing to you."

Charles does the laughing and head-shaking again, but this time in disbelief.

"*Are you kidding me?*" he says. "Of course I bloody did. I've never quite ceased wondering. I wrote you a few times. Well, a whole lot of times. Even after you'd clearly stopped. For weeks. Months, I kept on writing. Without any…" He can't quite understand why she should appear so surprised by what he is saying but neither can he allow himself to be interrupted right now. "Then, after a while, I just sort of assumed you'd met someone. Y'know, someone closer to home. Someone more 'suitable'. Or that you'd simply come to realise it was just a holiday romance. Built up out of all—"

"Is that what it was for you?"

"For *me*? God no! No, Laura. Read the bloody book. Oh, right – you did."

"You said yourself – pure fiction."

Charles feels himself floundering and is starting to feel angry as well as confused. "Yeah. Okay. So now I'm wondering. Now I'm asking."

Suddenly she is standing up and all he is looking at is her back, in a lightweight, pale blue blouson. She's broader than she was, he thinks, and wishes that he wouldn't.

"I was pregnant," she half-whispers into the Lexington air.

Charles has not the slightest idea how to react to this information.

He realises that it is totally devastating and has undoubtedly been equally as hard to deliver as it clearly would be to receive. Yet, confusingly, he is torn as to whether to treat the cataclysmic news as confirmation of something he has already been at least half-led by the strangest of circumstances to contemplate or as a sudden and earth-shattering shock to his system from which he might never recover.

As Laura turns to meet his gaze, he realises that he needs to go for the shock option, and fast. Which, to be honest, is near exactly how he feels anyway.

"*What?*" he mumbles. "But we only…"

"Once is enough," says Laura, resignedly. "As I tell my students."

"In English classes?" More head-shaking. "I thought I was being so careful. *Bloody Norman!*"

Laura, unsurprisingly, can't see where Norman, the sweet guy in the kilt whom she still remembers, comes into the dynamics. And she truly doesn't want to go there.

"Doesn't matter," continues Charles, thankfully.

He rises from the step, so that their eyes can at least be on some sort of level. Charles feels that he ought to be taking her hand, holding it, yet curiously senses, even in these life-changing circumstances, perhaps more life-changing than even she realises, that he doesn't as yet have permission. "Oh, Laura, I am so... Why didn't you *tell* me? Why did—"

"And ruin your life? Your dreams. You were three thousand miles away."

"3,743," corrects Charles. "To be exact."

"O-kay. Right. Another world."

"Laura—"

"And I'm pretty sure now that my folks didn't show me *all* those letters," decides Laura. "There really were so many?"

"Tree-loads. Some of my best work. At least you didn't get the story."

She turns away, as if not wishing to meet his gaze. He notices that the occasional car is beginning to drive down the street and wonders where they are going this early.

"Actually, that one I did get," she says. "Envelope must've snuck through, being so different. And it was beautiful. I cried, Charlie. Rather a lot." She laughs to herself. "How could I even begin to tell you about... after that?"

"Aye. Well, you would. Cry, I mean. In the circumstances. *Jeez!* I am so so sorry." She shakes her head. He wants to do the same, but more out of mystification at himself. "And that I could send it to you, with all that emotion wrapped inside, yet not put two and two together. Me – the writer. *The storyteller!* What a child I was! What a… child. So did you… er… you know…?"

Laura looks horrified. "NO! My dad wanted me to. It was against his principles, of course. Except when it came to his daughter. But I told him no way."

"You wanted to keep her?"

Laura freezes. He watches puzzlement rise like a wash over her face. "How did you know it was a her?"

Shit!

Charles looks flummoxed. And stunned. He shakes his head, hoping that she'll just move on and leave him to his ever-deepening concern. Which, mercifully, she does. Like a boulder tumbling inexorably down a snow-clad mountain, she simply has no choice but to build up and keep on moving. Building and rolling. She needs to get this story finished, preferably before he can say anything more.

"Well, it was. *She* was. And no, I couldn't do… that. But I wasn't ready for her, Charlie. A *baby*? I was seventeen, for Pete's sake. I'd only just turned eighteen when she… when she was born." Before he can ask, she fills in the blanks. "And taken away. Not that I was given a choice in the matter. Oh, Charlie, I am so, so sorry."

Charles feels like his heart is breaking. Breaking all over again, but this time a new fracture – from a very different source. The pain on this woman's face, the face of someone who is almost a stranger now, a faraway person from another world, is almost too much to bear. He knows that it isn't love he is feeling – how can it be, in a very real sense they've only just met – but he is certain there is compassion here. Empathy too –

hopefully. And an overwhelming sadness, a mourning for immeasurable losses.

Yet somewhere, he is certain, there is also hope. More than hope. Something – who knows – that may just miraculously be in his gift.

"Sorry? No! Och, Laura… please, will you sit back down?" He beckons to her. "C'mon. Please."

She sits down once more on the gently warming step.

Not knowing quite what to do, but knowing that he needs to do something, a gesture, he very tentatively takes her hand. Laura stares at it and after a moment moves her own hand away. She is starting to tremble. Charles feels so helpless, which he knows can often impel him to talk, to try to make things right. Yet, on this occasion, he senses that he has to let her tell the rest of the sorry tale unimpeded.

"My mom had – has – family in Ohio. Out in the country, beyond Dayton, on a farm. Good people. They sent me there. Told everyone I'd taken a year out before college. Gone to France, of all places, to work for a military colleague of my dad's." She hazards a brief smile. "Not certain how many believed them, but I sure did have time to learn French!"

"And when the baby… the wee girl…?"

Charles can see too well that every word, after this early desperate spurt, is understandably becoming more and more painful for her.

"Straight to adoption. Yup. My dad arranged it all. I barely saw her, Charlie. I didn't even get to…" She starts to cry, the type of quiet, breathless weeping that sounds almost like hiccups gone wrong. Now, almost immediately, with barely a pause in the sobs, she begins to berate herself. "I told myself – I *told* myself – I wouldn't friggin' do this."

Charles watches her face appear to crumble. He wants quite desperately to comfort her but sees immediately that this isn't appropriate. Not now. Not yet.

"How could you not… do this?" he says instead, scrabbling unaccustomedly for words. Words that aren't just words. "Laura, it must have been so… devastating. Traumatic. So unimaginably… agonising." He thinks he is starting to sound like a thesaurus. "And still has to be, even after… Bloody hell, of course it has to be. Even with all this time gone."

Laura looks at him, almost in gratitude. "Thank you. Thank you, Charlie. I had a whole heap of therapy, you know. Fortunately, there were some very kind people. Sensitive people. Even way back then. Not just the *'c'mon, gal, pull yourself together!'* gang. Although they were around too."

"*'Shit happens!' 'Get over it!'*"

Laura stares at him, like she doesn't need the commentary right now. "Mm. And, of course, in time, having my own kids helped. More than helped. But guess what Charlie, there's barely a single day… you know the rest."

"I can only imagine."

"She'll have just turned twenty-one now. The drinking age. I wonder if *she's* a writer."

Charles says nothing for a moment, which he hopes reads as if he is simply lost for words. "Or a drinker," he says, finally, which probably weren't the words to find.

"Who knows? But I bet she's beautiful, Laura. Like you were."

Laura doesn't react to this but simply nods. Charles is just starting to think that last bit might not have been quite the compliment he intended when they hear the sound of running on the still-empty sidewalk.

Kevin is fast approaching, on his early morning jog. Charles can't help noticing, yet again, how good-looking this guy is, albeit unnecessarily fit. And thinking once more how much he respects and indeed likes him.

"I see the Lexington Book Group is getting in an early meet-up," says the young publishing executive. Almost immediately he senses the mood and that three might not be company right now. Not that, as a devout jogger, he has any intention of winding down to a complete halt, even if invited.

"I'm interrupting… my morning run," he says, barely breathless. He can't fail but notice the sweet but solemn woman's liquid eyes. "See you at breakfast, Charles."

Charles just nods but the clearly bemused man is already half a block away. To his credit he glances back at the troubled pair no more than once.

As he watches Kevin go, Charles speaks into the distance, almost to himself. "To think you had to go through all that on your own, Laura. While I just – I dunno – simmered? Aye. And stewed. In Glasgow. Like a bloody kid!" He laughs without amusement. "Me – of all people. I should at least have *wondered*! How did I never stop to think…?"

"Maybe somewhere you did know. But you didn't know you knew. And that is garbage. Sorry. I should walk you back," says Laura, as if she herself can't take much more of this conversation or of this distressed man berating himself. For things he might just have guessed at but most surely did not know.

The streets of Lexington are gradually busying, as Laura and Charles make their slow and thoughtful return to his lodgings.

He notices again how so many of the shop and establishment signs, the names in neon, seem to be vertical in this country whilst almost uniformly horizontal at home. And he finds himself wondering just as irrelevantly what the early Sunday risers who are passing these signs right now would make of the momentous events occurring just feet from their oblivious and possibly carefree selves. Then he considers that each of these passers-by or drivers will have their own story to tell. Stories which, who knows, could be even more extraordinary than his own is turning out to be.

Pretty bloody unlikely, though.

"My family were okay, Charlie," continues Laura, without having been prompted. "Disappointed, naturally. And angry, well, that's for sure. But not totally unsympathetic."

"I imagine casting me as the villain of the piece helped a lot."

"Despoilin' the 'prahd' of southern womanhood."

"With my depraved Judeo-Celtic ways."

In the same relative lightness of tone and with a deliberate casualness, Charles poses his next and most important question. "Do you happen to know, Laura – where she went? Your... our daughter?"

Laura stops and turns to him in surprise. "I'm sure you know that's not permitted, Charlie. Neither here nor, I'm pretty certain, in the UK. When they're an adult, of course, they can make contact. Twenty-one again, I think, in most states. Through the adoption people, I suppose. But, y'know what, mostly they don't. And I guess – well, I guess she just doesn't want to. At least not right now. I try hard – *really* hard – not to overthink about it. About her."

She shakes her head sadly and starts to walk on. "It's not like I've gone anywhere far." To Charles's surprise she turns back to him, as if addressing something he hasn't yet said. "I would *never* ever try to force myself on her. If I even knew how. Who knows what that would do to her – or her poor family? And my kids don't even know."

"*They don't?*" says Charles, then wonders why he should be so surprised. It has to be tricky being any sort of moral benchmark to your brood with that sort of dubious history on your shoulder. 'Do as I say not as I do' has never, so far as he is aware, made the more reputable parenting manuals.

He feels that this is probably not an avenue that merits deeper exploration right now. "At least maybe this means she's content. Doesn't it?"

Laura nods a tad wistfully, as they arrive at The Morgan House once more.

Charles knows that he has to have the conversation – the one about what really sparked his sudden rerouting to this town, a town that has played so pivotal a part in his history and now made even more historic than he could ever have guessed. (Would I have come here anyway? he suddenly wonders, then swiftly brushes it off as another unnecessary diversion.)

"Laura, would you like to see her?" he says, quietly.

Laura Griffin spins round to him at a velocity that causes him to recoil. "*My daughter?* What do you fuckin' think!"

Calming down at almost the same speed, with a shrug which could be apologetic or simply born of resignation, Laura offers a despondent sigh. "I'm not a dreamer, Charlie," she says, staring straight up at him. "Not anymore. Now you had better go. Get your breakfast. You've got a good book to sell."

"You make it sound like the Bible! My tour is practically over. This was… a side-step."

"Uh huh. Not exactly what you expected, eh?" He doesn't answer. "Poor Charlie. So now what? Back to London?"

Charles seems unduly thoughtful, which surprises her. "Probably," he says, adding, "with mebbe just one more unscheduled stop on the way. Okay. So. Well… goodbye, Laura."

For a moment, on the still fairly deserted sidewalk, outside an old-fashioned and very closed department store, they look at each other a bit helplessly.

Charles wishes that he could gaze into her misty, almond-shaped eyes and feel the years instantly slipping away, that he could fall back into those golden weeks, that brief adolescent oasis, as he so often has and does. Yet, after such a dramatic conversation, with this now-mature, professional woman, homemaker and mother of two, he remains with at least one foot rooted in the immediate, early morning, middle-aged present. Whilst perhaps the other is still dangling free, seeking some firmer hold on a past that has just been momentously coloured and rewritten.

Clumsily, they give each other a slight peck on the cheek. Almost a courtesy, little more. As if they have already gone back into themselves and have nothing left to share.

Charles knows that there *is* still a connection here. Of sorts. How can there not be? Maybe born of biology now rather than chemistry, composed far more of cruel reality than fanciful first love. Yet without doubt something that has justified, at least for him, this unexpected, unscheduled but somehow predestined journey.

He watches her move away, this still devastated but hopefully a wee bit less burdened person. A new and very different person to the one he once thought he knew and truly believed he loved, leaving him entirely on his own, on the steps of a whole new day. Already planning the next and possibly most unpredictable part of the whole long story.

She doesn't once look back.

TWENTY-ONE

Abigail Chadwick is drying her hair in the apartment she shares with a fellow student when the cellphone on her desk rings. She knows that it can't be her folks, as they'll be in church this morning, so it's clearly not any sort of distress call.

When she gets there, still yawning, the number is not one she recognises. The voice, however, from the moment it responds to her, very clearly is.

"Oh. *Oh shit!* Sorry. Hello! Mr MacNaughtan – no, Dickens. Hey, I'm just going for C.D. like you said. Ha!" She knows that she is all over the place but has no idea how to calm down. And leaving her caller without any sort of gap or opening in which to respond with even one Scottish syllable is hardly the route to inner harmony. "I didn't expect… no, it's not too early, been up hours… you got the stuff? My writing. Yeah, course you did. Sorry for just dumping on you like that – but hey, you said I could."

"I liked it," says Charles, from his Lexington hotel room, leaping on a tiny moment of silence. He is packing up to go to yet another town, but one not as evocative as this – hopefully.

"YOU DID? ...Sorry, way too effusive. Dial down, Abi. Ha! Oh, well... wow. Thank you, Mr... er... Thank you so much. Well..."

"Can I maybe talk for a wee moment, Abi?" asks Charles.

"Good note, C.D. Sure. Talk away."

Charles says nothing for a few seconds, which he guesses must be confusing for the young woman, as it is he who has called her. Out of the blue. Yet he feels that he needs a moment, as he would say, to get his ducks in a row. And these are some bloody important ducks.

"This Wednesday," he says, finally. "I'm back in your neck of the woods. Would you... be free at all?"

"*SURE!*" she says, instantly. "Er... yeah, pretty sure I'm free. That day. Evening. Whatever. Are you giving another reading here?"

"No," admits Charles, "I'll be done with readings by then, thankfully. Where would you like to meet – same place as last week?"

"Same place is good. Perfect. But this time I'm buying."

"I was actually thinking of a nice dinner."

"Okay, you're buying." She stares across to her bedside and the book she bought only a few days ago. "But I'm reading your new novel, so the flattering's on me."

"Well, thank you, Abi. I shall be genuinely interested to know what you think. Will we say 7.30?"

"It's in the diary," she replies, then wonders why she has said this: A) this is not her vocabulary, B) it isn't in any sort of diary, and C) how likely is she to forget that an author whose books she admires is taking her out to dinner to discuss her work? "See you – Wednesday. 7.30pm."

"Great. Cheerio, Abi."

"Er, cheerio, C.D. And bye. Thank you. Okay."

When she is certain that he is gone – and probably with some relief, she thinks, after that debacle – she sets her cellphone back down.

"Who was that?" asks her flatmate, coming out of her own room. "You sounded excited."

"No, I didn't!" Abi tells the other young woman, excitedly. "It was just… my dad. Y'know, checkin' in on me."

*

The following morning Kyra Nordstrom catches her good friend Laura Griffin in the car park of the high school where they both teach and in which Laura Sherman once was taught.

Laura can sense that the other woman has been casually loitering in wait for her. When Kyra leaps away from her own car and grabs her firmly by the arm, Laura's suspicions are duly confirmed.

"*So?*" says Kyra, with an urgency her warm smile can't fully disguise. "You know me, Laura. I do not pry. I just expect true friends to be generous with the dirt."

With a sigh, Laura starts to move towards the entrance to the school, nodding over-demonstrably to kids she knows and to kids she doesn't know.

"There is no dirt, Kyra," insists Laura quietly but firmly. "It just turns out that Charlie – C.D. MacNaughtan – is someone I knew as a kid. When he came here briefly from his school in Scotland over twenty years ago." She decides not to elaborate on the billeting arrangements.

"And you had a sweaty teenage romance!" seizes Kyra. "That still burns in your aching hearts long after the zits have popped and the tits have dropped. Something neither of you have…" She suddenly stops, gasps dramatically and talks even louder than she has been doing, despite her friend's warningly *sotto* transmission. "*You're that girl in the book!*"

Unfortunately, the school bell doesn't sound quite soon enough to drown out the excited teacher's voice. Kids just stare at the tall, slightly scary woman, as they pour in to start yet another week.

"Oh, don't be silly," mutters Laura. "That's pure fiction, Kyra. You heard him yourself."

Kyra smiles. "So you read it already!" They are making their way to the staff room. This damn woman, thinks Laura, is like a dog with a bag of bones. "Laura Griffin, when was the last time a bestselling author – not to mention a cute Brit one – did a reading right here in Lexington, Ky?" A child pelts by, nearly knocking them over. "So, are the sparks still flying?"

Laura cannot believe how much her friend is enjoying herself. If she only knew, she thinks, as she sends a prayer that the woman never will. "We've both moved on, Kyra. Saturday night was what I suppose these days you'd call 'closure'. Not that there was much of an overture," she adds, hastily.

Henry Griffin walks past them, at the door of the staff room, on his way to class. He is laden with his schoolbag, books and a trumpet case.

"Morning, Mrs Nordstrom. Hi again, Mrs Mom."

"A lotta water. A heap of bridges," sighs Laura, giving her son's wiry hair a surreptitious ruffle.

TWENTY-TWO

New England. April 2004

The café-bar is the only element of the evening ahead of him that Charles has any confidence will remain much the same as on his previous visit. The music and the college-town clientele certainly seemed comfortingly identical, when he strolled in at 7.15 to secure his table. (He recalled that New Englanders do tend to eat early.)

Yet even now, as he sits alone and somewhat superstitiously at the same table they shared before, he wonders what the other patrons – locals, academics, students – will make of the pairing about to take place. There is no way that they can possibly guess at something that even to Charles is as yet little more than guesswork. Fortunately, the tables are sufficiently spaced out and the bland soundtrack just loud enough to ensure that what is destined to be the most sensitive and also possibly the most circumspect of conversations can at least remain private.

Observers might already have noted, should they be even the slightest bit interested, that the reasonably presentable man of around forty, who sits at a still pristine table with a barely sipped beer beside him, is finding it hard to stay still. If his legs aren't tapping, his fingers are drumming, and both these activities, which occasionally find themselves in less than rhythmic unison, are accompanied by some reasonably frantic head-swivelling.

Not for the first time Charles wonders whether Abigail Chadwick, who must be in her very early twenties, really does look – despite her own and her era's enhanced sophistication – the spitting image of a seventeen-year-old Laura Sherman of Lexington, Kentucky, circa 1982. And indeed, even if she does, why should a child of his and Laura's favour the distaff side so completely?

Yet hasn't he known people who are the shocking likeness of one or other of their parents, almost clone-like, in fact, albeit fresher, unlined clones? And surely the combination of Abi's so-familiar looks with the fact of her adoption at probably much the same time has to add some serious plausibility to the mix? As a storyteller, Charles knows only too well to avoid coincidences in his books, or at least get 'em in good and early. But wasn't it Einstein, at least he thinks it was him, who once said something to the effect that coincidences were simply God's way of staying anonymous? He finds this cheering, as he wonders exactly what God has up his celestial sleeve for tonight.

"*I am SO sorry, Mr... C.D!*"

Charles looks up to see a flushed but beaming Abi Chadwick shucking off her lightweight scarlet jacket as she manoeuvres to sit down opposite him at the small table. She slings a bulging bag over the seat-back, almost toppling it over, and ploughs on with her apology. "I had to deliver an assignment." Before he can enquire as to the nature of the assignment, the young woman is off and running. "It's my junior year and George Eliot is taking over my life."

Abi doesn't notice how closely Charles is examining her. Or at least he hopes that she doesn't, because he is finding himself unable to desist. She really *does* look so like…

"He can do that," says Charles, and is gratified to see the shock on her face. And the subsequent relief when he smiles. "I wish she'd taken over my life," he continues, "rather than the Crofters Holdings Act of 1886."

"Oh," says Abi in surprise. "Were you a lawyer?" He nods, but before he can explain how briefly and miserably that career path had turned out, she is practically yelping. "*That was you!* In your first book. The mom from Rio or wherever it was – the lady who wanted her stolen child back. I mean, you were the attorney, not the mom!"

"She's why I lost my faith in the law. Well, the case was." He realises that this is the relatively noble and selfless story he has been peddling all these years and has almost come to believe himself.

"At least you got a book out of it. And a whole new career. Way to go!" she enthuses. "Oh. Sorry. Was that callous of me?"

"Aye. But honest. Writerly honest."

She is surprised to glimpse a touch of confusion on his hitherto friendly – albeit a mite too unblinking – face.

This man, who she feels has every right to be supremely confident, suddenly seems quite lost. Abi guesses it must be memories of that extraordinary court case. If, of course, it was anything like the fictionalised version, which was pretty intense.

"Let's order food," announces Charles, shaking himself free. "Then you can tell me some more about yourself."

"And my writing," suggests Ali, picking up her menu, although she already knows what she is ordering. She has yearned for it many times.

"Aye. Yes, of course. And especially how the two – y'know, intertwine."

Were anyone to question him later, Charles realises that he would have virtually no recall of what he and the young woman discussed over their food and wine. His mind is too focussed on what is not yet being said. He would have a far more distinct recollection that it was Abi who did most of the talking. He is already thinking that if she writes the way she converses, her novel would make *Infinite Jest* look like a Cheever short story.

For most of the conversation, however, in which he hopes he doesn't make too big a fool of himself, Charles is just staring. He finds that he simply can't take his eyes off this young woman's appealing and so disturbingly familiar face. (He also realises that he has been doing a lot of staring of late and that he could be in danger of picking up an unedifying reputation.)

He has heard that certain mannerisms can pass down genetically, even when children have no contact with their birth parents, or identical twins with each other, so he finds himself searching for anything in Abi that he can trace back to himself or Laura. The way she holds a fork, perhaps, or turns her head, the furrowing of a brow, a flicking of the hair. Of course, this young woman bears far less a resemblance to the Laura he had only just encountered in a bookshop some way south of here. But, who knows, perhaps in twenty-two years she will.

"I guess I may have to do some journalism," says Abi between mouthfuls, "or even maybe teach. Hey, a girl's gotta eat."

"I can see that," says Charles, with a smile.

"Sorry. I was starving." She laughs. "And believe it or not, I don't get tenderloin every day!"

Before she moves on to address the looming issue, as he has always expected that she would, the expression on her face begins to change. She is brushing her long, ash-blonde hair away from her in a way that has become less instinctive and more as if she has grown increasingly uncomfortable with what even he would admit is now pretty blatant scrutiny. Laura would do that, he thinks, although surely most women with long hair don't just let it dangle all over their face and into their food like a sheepdog.

"Can I be honest with you – C.D.?"

Here it comes, thinks Charles, and with it the turn in the evening. "I would expect nothing less," he says.

Now it is Abigail Chadwick's time to direct her best stare directly onto him. A stare, he can't help thinking, not so very unlike his own.

"I think my writing's okay," she begins. "In fact, I reckon it's pretty good. But I'm not convinced it's quite so great it can make an A-list novelist, over here on a whirlwind tour, change his itinerary and flight plans just to come buy this wannabe young author dinner. Great dinner, by the way."

For a few seconds Charles says nothing. Despite his anticipation of the moment and even an admittedly one-sided rehearsal, he finds himself lost for words. Until a coherent sentence slowly forms itself.

"So, what do you think is going on? Come on, Abi – you're a writer."

"*Shoot!*" says Abi. She knows that this is a pathetic exclamation but still feels kind of uncomfortable cursing in front of older people and is only too aware that it smacks of lazy language anyway. "O-kay. When we met, C.D., you kept looking at me. Like, y'know, staring at me. I guess I'm not totally ugly, but this was like different." She pauses. Too many 'likes'. Guy's a writer, for fuck's sake! "It still is different but now it's kinda different in an even more different way and I really can't make it out. You said then that I reminded you of someone…" Charles doesn't say anything. "It's your turn now," she suggests.

"…Right," says Charles. "I do apologise – for the staring. But yes, Abi, you did remind me of… someone. And you still do. Very much, in fact. Or at least my memory of how that someone used to look."

To her surprise, he starts to take out his wallet. Abi wonders if she has totally blown it and that he is simply going to pay for the meal and go home. She also realises that, despite his patent oddness, she really doesn't want him to leave. Yet, instead of a credit card, he fishes in one of the leather sleeves and carefully removes what looks like a crumpled photograph.

Abi holds out her hand, knowing that the guy desperately wants to share his keepsake with her. She takes it very delicately, sensing both its fragility and its worth. Yet when she inspects it, sees the pretty young woman – no more than a teenage girl, really – smiling innocently out at her, she is not totally convinced that they are peas in any sort of pod.

"Hmm. Maybe a little," she concedes. "But I'm less crumpled!"

Expecting at least the hint of a smile, Abi is taken aback by the author's almost guilty wince. All too clearly she feels the imperative to move on, steer the conversation back on track, in a way that might hopefully appear organic. She can't help that she looks vaguely like someone else, can she? Surely, in this hugely overpopulated world, lots of people do?

"And hey, remember," she adds, "I'm reading your book. Only halfway through, thanks to old Georgie Eliot—"

"*That was a fiction!*" says Charles, a bit too insistently. "Okay, inspired by real events, granted. But then, y'know… embellished. Transmuted. Magnified. As we scriveners do." He leans in closer, across the almost-empty plates, just avoiding the tiny candle in its smoked-glass cocoon. Now or never. "And I think I did tell you, when we first met, Abi, that there had to be something in your own life you could write a book about. Remember what you said?"

"Sure." Abi smiles. "That I was born in upstate

Surinam. Oh – and I was adopted as a baby by fundamentalist Christian missionaries."

Charles is finding this almost too difficult but knows that he needs to press on. "*Exactly!* Exactly. Now, I don't really know how to say this. Or even that I should. Jesus! Forgive me. Er, Abigail… Abi…"

To his surprise, the young woman lays her hand gently on top of his. "I am so sorry, C.D."

Charles stares down at the slim hand, which feels so warm and comforting against his own. And why wouldn't it, when it could be composed of the same flesh and blood? He is rather upset when she takes it away.

"Abi, there's no need to apologise. None at all."

"There really is," she insists, looking more uncomfortable than at any time during this more than slightly strained evening.

When Charles resumes talking, it is almost to himself. "No, no, I'm intruding. This is going too fast. Far too… and I'm stepping over so many lines. Big lines. Giant steps. Dangerous steps. It's too soon. Too important. *Christ!*"

"It's bullshit," says Abi.

"Excuse me?"

"What I said." She tries to smile. "It's bullshit."

"I know." He smiles, remembering. "You're from New Platz."

"Paltz. Though Platz is better. No – I mean the whole thing is bullshit." Charles shakes his head, uncertain of what exactly she is trying to say. "Y'know – about my parents."

"They're not fundamentalist Christians?"

"Oh, sure. Well, they make the right joyful noises." Charles smiles in relief. "But they're not missionaries."

"Okay," says Charles, segueing almost seamlessly into work mode. "Well, hold on to the missionaries. It's a good basis for—"

"And they *are* my parents."

Now he pauses, brows wrinkling, confused yet suddenly fearful. "Come again?" he says, quietly.

"I'm not adopted. Though, d'you know something – I often dearly wished I was. Maybe that's why I threw it into the pot. But hey, I suppose most kids go through that some time in their lives." Now it is her turn to stare.

"*Charles? Are you okay? ...C.D.?*"

TWENTY-THREE

The café hasn't changed. It has simply moved to another planet.

A planet not called Serendipity. A planet where life is more complex and nuanced and unpredictable, where things that you believe are true or wish they might be true don't simply become true because that's the way good stories work. A planet where God, anonymous or not, is nowhere in the picture.

Charles is not quite certain whether he speaks the language.

"You're… *not* adopted?" he stutters, his jaws now as wide open as his eyes have been for most of the conversation. "Then why…?"

"Why did I – what did you call it – 'embellish'?" Abi laughs. "Why d'ya think, C.D.? To make myself and my life more interesting. Like yours is."

The guy is still staring.

She has to admit that she finds him quite attractive and – okay, sue her – she is enjoying being seen with him. Being stared at by him. If she is being brutally truthful to herself, she is a little bit turned on by his all-consuming interest, his unremitting focus. Even if it has been a whole chunk more intense than she is accustomed to from guys, including those who are clearly into her. But perhaps that's a Scottish thing, she tells herself. Think *Braveheart* or *Rob Roy*.

He's still staring, so she feels impelled to embellish some more. "Hey, you can't plumb depths, if the river is shallow. And it's pretty damn shallow in New Paltz. It's called The Wallkill and…"

Now he's holding his breath. Well, that's different, if nothing else.

"Mr MacNaughtan? Dickens? *Charles…?*"

Charles Dickens starts to laugh. Really laugh.

Laughter that wells up from a source that has been arid for some time. Laughter that causes heads to turn at neighbouring tables, as they wish they knew what the hell is so funny. Abi wishes the same, but it's infectious and it lights up his interesting, lopsided face, so soon she is laughing too.

When she takes in his face once more, as the laughter tails down, she notices that it has undergone some sort of dramatic sea change. If, paradoxically, the very absence of drama can provoke such a transformation.

The man appears to have relaxed beyond expectation, as if all the muscles in his entire body, which must only seconds ago have been so tight, have decided to unclench, hang loose and just enjoy the evening. His whole countenance seems so different now, not simply altered from what it was just before the laughing jag but from how she has ever seen him in their brief acquaintance. It's a good look. Perhaps a younger look.

"Hey, I made you laugh!" she exults. "Okay, scrap the George Eliot vibe. Screwball comedy it is."

She raises her wine glass to her lips and gazes at him over the top of it, her long, pale blue eyes slowly closing with her smile, as the muscles harmonise, but still laughing in the candlelight. Charles knows this look. And also knows now, with increasing certainty, that the look is sadly all this smart young woman's own. Yet the shock and disappointment he felt almost as a pain, a kick, a punch in the gut, just a few minutes ago, are slowly receding or, at very least, are being parked, until he can process the new status quo (or, more accurately, the *only* status quo there has ever been) and move definitively, if regretfully, on.

He knows exactly how the evening should proceed, now that the wildest of geese has flown. A return to his hotel alone, for a nightcap, perhaps, and some deeper contemplation on how this eventful trip has spun his entire world around, altered everything he had believed for so long about the events of twenty-two years ago, believed wrongly but almost religiously, and left him flailing and helpless. Still, and now possibly forever, in the dark.

So he genuinely surprises himself that he might not be ready for such a brutal reality check just yet and that the night could very well not turn out this way at all. Not with this brightly interesting young woman still looking the way she does.

"How old are you, Abi?" he says, tentatively.

"Old enough," she says, still smiling as she sips. "I took a coupla years out after high school. To make some dough. My folks aren't wealthy and the Lord doesn't always provide. I'm twenty-four." Now she laughs. "So, truthfully, you could be my dad."

"No, Abi," says Charles. "Truthfully, I couldn't."

Abi can recognise all too well the way that he is looking at her now and she is certain that it is not her writing or her parentage that are enticing him, although she hopes that they have added their own small share to the lustre. Yet something still gnaws at her and it isn't his age – Jesus, he's probably not even forty yet. It's not like he's one of her professors or, heaven forbid, a family friend. She dismisses it and continues with the game.

"No," she agrees, with an elfin smile. "You couldn't."

"Does that bother you, Abi? My being a wee bit older."

"It's bothering me less and less. What about you?"

The guy is looking confused but soon the warm, lopsided smile – a smile she senses, or at least hopes, is closer to the real C.D. MacNaughtan – returns. He raises his glass. "As George Eliot said, 'of course men know best about everything'…"

She raises her glass and sips her wine. Eyes twinkling in the dimly melted light. "'…Except what women know better.'"

TWENTY-FOUR

The small New England college town is just waking up.

For one sleepy, semi-conscious moment Charles feels that yet again he could be anywhere on his travels, anywhere on the planet, and predictably he has yet again mislaid the name of this particular way station. He has, however, fallen in love with the country's surprisingly elegant, repurposed old houses and has booked himself into one this time round, rather than the soulless chain hotel of his previous visit. But even this discerning traveller feels that sometimes you can have too much of old wood and nautical prints. There is also, for reasons unexplained, a small crucifix on the wall, which he would prefer wasn't staring down at him right now.

Charles can sense that the person beside him has turned to glance back, as she slips one warm leg gently out of the substantial and pleasantly employed king-size bed. Some seconds later, he is made aware by the sudden absence of creaking in the ancient floorboards, that the young woman has abruptly paused on her way to the bathroom. Charles has no idea of the reason but recalls that there is a full-length mirror in that vicinity and, whilst he most certainly wouldn't take time to inspect himself this early in the day, perhaps a younger and less careworn person just might.

What he doesn't see, and for which the newly risen Abigail Chadwick is quietly thankful, is her deft removal of a certain crumpled photograph from the wallet that lies on the dressing table. Nor does he witness her checking out the rather lovely face smiling innocently out from it against her own newly risen version. Whichever way she turns and however she mobilises her ruffled head, offering a fetching variety of fresh-faced smiles, Abi still remains unconvinced. But the old photograph is of course quite crushed, for reasons she can only imagine, and such items even at their best rarely offer more than half the truth and often a good deal less.

Charles suspects that eyes are once again upon him and not just those mounted beseechingly on the opposite wall. He rises slowly to greet the day and his most recent night-time companion.

"Good morning," he says, trying for chirpiness.

"Hey."

Sensing a lack of reciprocal chirp in her voice, which could simply be down to the hour yet he doubts it, Charles eases himself further up in the bed. He feels uncomfortably aware of his nakedness.

"Are you okay… Abi?"

"Yeah. Sure. No… I really don't know."

Charles suddenly feels an impelling need to stretch over to the nearby bedside table and put on some glasses.

As he doesn't yet wear glasses, although he has known for some while that he is on the cusp, he sees this more as a symbolic reaching out for some sort of elusive clarity.

He shakes his head. "This wasn't what it – I'd really like to see you again."

"How's that gonna happen?" says Abi, a tad more sharply than he would have wished.

"Well, right now, I have no idea. But I'm a writer – *you* understand this – we can work from anywhere. And mercifully, unlike most writers, I'm currently not without funds."

She shakes her head, slowly and a touch regretfully. "That wasn't me, Charles."

"What wasn't you?" he asks.

"The girl you fucked last night."

"Oh Abi, please," he reassures her, slightly shocked. "I truly don't think you make a habit of sleeping with guys on the first date. And look at me, I'm hardly one to pass judgment."

"It's not what I meant. And know what, I have slept with guys on a first date. Not legions, but I don't have a real problem with that."

Charles is nonplussed. Perhaps, he muses, now that Abi Chadwick can see him so clearly, with the less forgiving morning light just squirming in, the age gap really is more of a chasm than was perceived in a candle's waning glow.

"Oh. Okay. Then what…?"

"It wasn't me you were with last night." She expects his confusion and in this at least she is not disappointed. "It was her."

"Her?" He is now being seriously dumb, in her humble opinion.

"*The girl in the scrunched-up photo!*" she almost yells, pointing at his wallet for added clarity. "The girl I so remind you of."

"Abi—"

She is determined to complete the thought. "Your damn book. I told you, Charles, it's making me cry. How something that happened to him as a – well, as a kid – y'know, the betrayal, the silence, could like colour, even jinx, all the guy's future relationships. *Please don't shake your head – let me finish!* Could make him lose all trust and kinda keep him trying to recreate what he... can't ever get again. His 'forever moment'. So he just can't move on. Shoot – I sound like the worst kind of cover blurb, don't I?"

"*Exactly!* Because Abi, that is—"

"Don't you dare use the f-word."

He has to smile. "...fiction."

Abi starts to pick up her clothing. Charles had observed in passing that this is a rather neat person; even in the throes of passion last night she did her best to ensure that the items wouldn't be too creased in the morning. He wonders if she clocked at any point that he could still make such clinical character observations at times of maximum excitement.

"You seem a nice guy," she concedes, with a gracious glance back to the bed. "And for sure an excellent writer. I had fun last night. Truly. But you don't need me, C.D. Or maybe you do, I dunno, but it's sure not what I need." With some of her clothing still in her hand, although he assumes that she is going to take a shower first and that this has all the elements of gesture about it (or maybe she's going to dress in there too, who knows?), she moves closer to the bed. "Writing that book clearly didn't help so much, did it? You need a damn good sofa and maybe a Sigmund Freud or two."

Charles wants to tell her about Lexington. He wants to explain that all the years, all these decades of anger and supposed betrayal, were indeed crippling but also misplaced. That the grown-up culprit, once she had explained everything, turned out not to be callous and flighty after all. Simply an amiable, middle-aged 'stranger', someone he once knew and truly loved, with her own heartbreaking tale to tell and a whole other life unrevealed to him.

Yet he knows that this would be beyond inappropriate and wouldn't erase the sadness verging on despair that he is starting to feel right now and has been wanting so badly to evade. Sadness at that recent uncomfortable and disconcerting reunion. Sadness at a situation unresolved and now more than likely unresolvable.

Sadness also, Charles has to admit, with this young woman. For her crime of not being who he was almost convinced she was and most certainly in plot terms bloody well ought to have been. And now look what has happened, in this less than splendidly constructed world. He'd just slept with someone he once believed could be his daughter. And he thinks he could be easily persuaded to do it again!

He tries to shake it off. Abi is definitely not who he might once fancifully have thought she was. Abi is a grown woman of twenty-four. A woman of some apparent experience. Despite her recent simplistic, Oprah 'analysis', a woman he still rather likes.

"I suppose a bagel is out of the question," he says, as lightly as he can.

"Not at all." She smiles. "Here in New England, breakfast before check-out is part of the deal."

With this she skips into the bathroom, leaving Charles even more alone.

TWENTY-FIVE

Pan-Am flight, New York to Prestwick. May 1982

"Are you going to be miserable all the way home?"

Charlie is barely touching his airline meal. This distinguishes him from at least a hundred fellow Scottish teenagers crossing the Atlantic and is even causing puzzled frowns amongst the airline staff, who have never actually seen a group of passengers wolf down their only moderately palatable fare so feverishly.

The young man turns to look at his kilted companion. Less than four short but eventful weeks ago the guy was a total stranger; today most assuredly he is a friend for life. The tears that were glistening in Charlie's eyes at the airport in Louisville now appear to be a permanent water feature on the landscape of his seriously woebegone face.

"It's a distinct possibility," he sighs.

"I should be the guy greetin'," grumbles Norman, in a doomed effort to cheer up his new best friend. "I didn't get laid even the once."

Charlie stares at his new friend in shock. "How did *you* know that we…?"

"I didn't." Norman smiles. "But I do now. Jeez, it's always the quiet ones. I hope you used—"

"Aye. I did. Thank you. And for askin'."

After a moment Norman stops eating, which he has been doing almost religiously throughout the conversation. When he talks, it is in a more serious, almost sheepish tone. "Are we going to keep in touch then?"

"Of course!" insists Charlie. "She promised."

"Not you and Laura! That's a given. You'll be sodding pen pals till you draw your old-age pension! I meant you and me, Charlie! You and me. Hey," he smiles, "you never forget the first time—"

"…someone gave you their twenty-eighth-from-last johnny. You're a friend for life, Norman Gemmell."

"Well, that's settled then," says the contented son of Falkirk. "You can get back to your sobbing. Will you be wanting that roll?"

Charlie shakes his head. He can't even think of food. Not right now. Yet somehow his spirits have lifted.

He knows now that he is not just flying back home. He is flying into the future.

A future that has to have Laura Sherman, of Lexington, Kentucky, in it.

It just has to.

THE LETTER

TWENTY-SIX

Charles doesn't recall his mother muttering to herself quite so much when he last visited, but she's having a good old mutter now, as she rummages around in the tiny tenement kitchen. This is the kitchen in which he grew up and it hasn't changed much since, despite his suggestions and many generous offers.

The permanent smell of baking is also much the same. He wonders sometimes if she has a spray, like he's heard they have in supermarkets to encourage shoppers towards the bakery. He wonders also if the muttering is a first sign of something about which he should be concerned or simply what happens when you've lived on your own for too long.

He recalls with a start that he does it too, this disjointed talking to himself, asking questions of the air and loudly sighing, especially when he's wandering around his small but well-appointed bachelor flat on

London's Embankment. Charles can comfort himself that it's surely what all writers do, when they're working out elusive plot lines or the most naturalistic dialogue, but this doesn't reassure as much as it ought. Especially as he realises that he mutters the most when he has misplaced something trivial and can't recall exactly where or when he last saw it, which is pretty much what his grey-haired ma is doing now, in the privacy of her own ergonomically retarded kitchen.

"Now I had it somewhere, Charlie," she says, in a voice slightly louder than a mutter but still not entirely addressed to him. "I know I did. Now where…?"

"What is it, Ma? What did you have?" He pronounces this last word 'hov' and can hear in his head that his native accent has already grown stronger, as if a dial is turned the moment the train from Euston crosses the border. Yet, curiously, it becomes less the accent with which he himself grew up, which was strong enough, and more the one he now hears all around him in the city and has observed on others. He reckons he'll be saying 'haud yer wheesht' soon and pining for his ain folk.

"*A letter, of course!*" says his mother, turning to look at her grown-up son, as if the answer should be blindingly obvious. Especially to a renowned man of letters such as himself.

For one ridiculous yet heart-stopping moment Charles wonders if it's an old airmail from Laura, lost in the post for decades, such as you read about occasionally in the tabloids. Who else would still write to him here, in Glasgow, when he had left the city so long ago, after his unfortunate but probably inevitable brush with the law?

"Who on earth would send me a letter?" he says, almost to himself. "Hope it's not an overdue library book."

To his delight, Mrs Dickens laughs at this. A smoker's laugh, he notices, composed of equal parts phlegm and appreciation. It coincides with her retrieving a small envelope from behind a very old Oxo tin on a shelf, so her joy is unconfined.

Charles loves it when she smiles. It lights up her small and now sadly ageing face, shelving the wrinkles and reminding him how full of life she once was. Even though she wasn't the biggest cheerleader for his own literary aspirations, this woman, alongside his late dad, were the ones who first gave him his love of books. Witness his bloody name!

Charles is well aware that he wouldn't be picking up the irrevocable signs of life's one-way journey quite so clearly, were he to see his mother more often. He knows also that he will be berated for this at least once again before the afternoon is out.

"It was, in an envelope sent to me, actually," she says. "See, here. To Charlie Dickens, 'care of' me. To 'please post on'. But since you were coming up on a visit anyway – and not before bloody time!" Here we go, thinks Charles. But the old lady hasn't finished. "You've been back from yon American holiday for months now, darlin'!"

Charles simply shrugs. There's no point in explaining once again that it really wasn't so much a holiday, more a relentless and often quite taxing business trip, which more disturbingly had turned out to be less of a business trip than a blindsiding voyage of discovery and re-evaluation. And a journey into sadness.

It is not, he thinks, that his mother wouldn't understand, were it to be explained carefully and with sensitivity. But it would most certainly upset her to know that she has an untraceable and now grown-up granddaughter somewhere on another vast continent. He would be spending the rest of his brief visit consoling a dear, sweet person, who has had enough loss and disappointment in her life.

He realises yet again, with a regret that seems rarely to diminish, that despite his having the requisite number of friends, there isn't actually anyone he *can* tell about this, his most personal, pivotal story. Or at least no one who could provide him with what he needs. Perhaps this is why he became a writer. So that people he has never met, and most probably never will, might listen. And maybe even, who knows, 'get' it.

He opens the letter.

"Someone who doesn't have your address," deduces Mrs Dickens, leaning into him, to give her new bifocals their best chance. "I wonder who…"

Charles manages to glide the still-unrevealed letter away from his mother's unashamedly inquisitive gaze. "Ma, can I please just – *talk of the devil!*"

"What? *Who?*" yelps his mother, looking more excited than he has seen her in years. "Nice handwriting," she adds, pointing to the single page.

"Do you mind the guy I went to Kentucky with? The one who was forever in his kilt. We sort of made friends on the plane."

"Nigel…"

"Norman. Norman Gemmell. He and I stayed in touch for a few years. You and Dad met him a couple times, didn't you? But when I moved down to London, we kind of – y'know – lost contact. Bit sad, really."

"Is he wanting money?" asks Mrs Dickens.

Her son looks up from his reading to stare at her. "Why would he be wanting money?"

"Well, you being a successful writer, Charlie. People do, you know. Mrs Gordon's son has shares in a distillery and he's always getting begging letters from cousins he barely knows."

"Aye, okay," says Charles, who just wants to finish reading the letter and not get into this. He knows from experience that Mrs Gordon is only the tip of the iceberg. "Well, it seems like Norman's read my book – this last one. He must've worked out somehow it was probably me and it made him want to… reconnect."

Mrs Dickens is almost prepared to give the guy the benefit of the doubt. "Well, that's nice, isn't it? And lovely that he bought the hardback. There's at least a tenner more for you." Charles doesn't feel that now is the time to explain, yet again, the meagre share of the purchase price an author actually brings home. Especially as he's doing okay. "Does he still stay in… where was it… Stirling?"

"Falkirk. Aye, still there. According to the address he's given me. I *have* to see him."

"You only just got here, Charlie."

"Just for a drink or something." He sees his mother's disappointed face. "I didn't mean right now! Not at all.

Tonight, you and I are going into town for a good dinner. You're still my true love, Ma."

"Och, you! If it was a lassie writing you, I wouldn't mind. What happened to that wee girl you brought round last time? She seemed nice." She knows from his shrug that he doesn't want to go there. They have had this conversation more than once and it gives the mother no more satisfaction than it does the son. "Now tell me all about America, while I put the kettle on. Did you meet anyone famous?"

"No. Not famous. Memorable, mebbe. But people did seem to like the book."

"Well, why wouldn't they? Can I be truthful with you, Charlie?" He nods. "Even though it did have a sort of happy ending, it made me a wee bit sad. It was about you, wasn't it?"

"Only a wee bit, Ma. Every writer puts a bit of himself into his work. But it wasn't really me. Not at all. You read the book – my guy, my hero, he isn't even Scottish. *Or* half-Jewish. And his own mother's a dragon."

"Aye, I didn't take to her much at all. That thing she did to him with the cauliflower. So is yon book then what they'd call 'bitter-sweet'?"

"I suppose that's exactly what they'd call it. In fact, most of the reviewers did just that. *What thing with the cauliflower?* Are you reading two books at once again?" The elderly woman shrugs, knowing denial is fruitless. "Okay, well forget all about the 'bitter'. Because I have brought you the 'sweet'. Some authentic New England maple syrup. For those wee scones over there I can smell baking."

TWENTY-SEVEN

"I reckoned you'd be a bourbon-on-the-rocks guy by now."

Charles can't be certain that he has recognised Norman Gemmell instantly, on looking up from his pint, or that it is simply the obvious deduction to make, because no one else would be likely to approach him so cheerily in the beer garden of a central Glasgow pub on this pleasantly balmy summer evening.

His old friend, who already has a glass of Tennants in his hand, is still very blond, although clearly overcompensating for whatever is receding at the front with a proudly mullet-like abundance at the rear. There is a moustache of sorts but so fair that it almost wasn't worth the bother. Yet the smile and the warmth are exactly as Charles recalls them, whilst the kilt has been replaced by a pair of well-tailored shorts, as if a displaying of the hardy Gemmell knees has been the main focus all along.

Charles reflects yet again that it is only by encountering people you haven't seen for years that you can gauge how much you yourself might have aged and how you truly appear to others. Kills the Peter Pan thing stone dead.

"Or absinthe. Like Joyce and Hemingway," says Charles, then wonders if such literary references, so early in the proceedings, just serve to make him appear a bit up himself. He rises clumsily from the bench attached to his small wooden table and gives the other man a hug, although he is not a big hugger in general. Naturally, beer is spilled and an uneasy dance ensues, but at least a convivial tone is set for this evening's long-overdue reunion.

After telling each other how bloody great this all is and how fit and well the other looks, which thankfully is fairly near the truth, as neither man is infirm or using walking aids, Charles feels that he has to acknowledge what has happily brought them back together after so long.

"Thank you so much for what you said, Norman. About my book."

"I meant it, pal," says Norman, with refreshing earnestness, as he sets himself and his beer down. The grinning man smiles knowingly. "After all, I ken the real story, don't I? But the wife didn't – and she was weeping. So was my daughter."

There is so much information entangled in so few words that Charles needs time to unravel it. And he suddenly realises how weary he has grown of this business of reassuring people that it is all just fiction. Before he can respond, he finds a familiar hardback book thrust across the table, along with a ballpoint.

"Here, sign this for her, will you, mister romantic. To 'Isla'. She's the daughter."

"With the greatest of pleasure. How old is she?"

"Sixteen – going on thirty-six. She's my eldest. Of four." Norman laughs at Charles's shocked face. "Aye. Been a while. How about yourself, Charlie? Your book jacket wisna exactly saying much. It was only when I was in our local bookshop and read the wee storyline bit on the back that I even guessed it was you – C.D.! Last time I saw you, you were scootin' off down to London to be an ad-man or something. So – wife, kids, household pets?"

Charles is amazed how naturally he and this friend he hasn't seen, or even spoken to, in well over fifteen years, a person with whom he shamefully severed ties when the heady, nerve-wracking buzz of a southwards move to a whole new life took over (a move propelled by his aceing a major ad agency copy test), can slip so seamlessly into the same easy connection and speech patterns they once enjoyed. Even whilst the topics of conversation these grown-up days are so markedly different.

He wonders now, as he listens to the other man's liltingly mellow voice, remembering his simple decency and understanding, whether it was the very fact of their special linkage and what happened back then that gradually impelled him to loosen the connection. As if his friend had to pay the price for being an innocent yet painful reminder. How stupid was that?

"No. No wife… or kids."

Charles has no idea whether it is Norman Gemmell's gracious silence at this point – his not responding with some platitude such as 'och well, plenty of time' or even with a look of super-parental sympathy – but something compels Charles to reveal what he is convinced he had absolutely no intention of sharing.

"Well, actually..." he begins, then hesitates. Which may, he has to admit, have been deliberate.

"You either have or you haven't." Norman smiles. "It's fairly binary."

Charles leans closer towards his old friend, although the nearest table is some distance away and already the worse for drink.

"Norman, I haven't told a soul this..."

*

Night has fallen, a lot more lukewarm Tennent's Lager has been consumed and Charles is just wondering whether Norman's knees are beginning to feel the chill. But the man must have known that these were going to be staying out late, along with the rest of him.

Now that Charles has fully unburdened himself and told the man his labyrinthine tale (one that he is just beginning to think he had intended to tell him all along, since the moment he read his letter), there are probably fewer trains back to Falkirk. Yet his companion shows no signs of wanting to bring their evening to a close.

"Are you going to cry again?" asks Norman.

"Oh, you remember that."

"The whole plane does. I'm really sorry, Charlie – about the wee girl. And, of course, the condom."

Charles waves this off. Water under the bridge. Or something. He can see how genuinely moved his old friend is by the story and finds that he has absolutely no regrets about telling him. Yet, by the look on Norman's face, the man appears to have become surprisingly thoughtful.

"And there's absolutely nothing you can do at your end – to find her? *Nothing at all?*" Charles just shrugs, shakes his head and even sighs. "That is such a pity, Charlie. But hey, you never know – there may be something you've yet to think of. You're an ideas man, after all. And I mind you were a lawyer for all of five minutes." Charles is looking at him a lot more thoughtfully now, although Norman can't believe he has said anything the man doesn't already know. "So tell me a bit more about the lady. Y'know, Laura."

"Well, Laura – Laura Griffin – she's a teacher now, English, at the very school you and I went to. I *know*! Separated, sadly. Couple of kids. Still bright in her own way, sparky. But Norman – and this may be just me – it is so bloody hard to equate her, this woman, with the lassie I knew back then. The bonnie wee girl I was so in love with. It's almost as if they're two totally different people, although of course they're not at all. It's like – I dunno, like meeting Jodie Foster when she was in *Freaky Friday*, then catching up with her again at *Silence of the Lambs*. Okay, mebbe not the best analogy, but you know what I mean."

For a moment Norman says nothing. Charles realises that what he has just admitted, whilst easy to understand and almost stating the bloody obvious, even without the movie references, is perhaps more revealing than he had intended.

"We're all of us getting older, Charlie," says Norman, finally. He taps the book that still sits on the table beside their glasses and a couple of ripped-open crisp packets. "Some of us can mebbe handle it better than..." He stops as he watches his old friend wince at this and wonders if he has strayed just a bit over the line here. It's hardly like they're back to being bosom buddies all of a sudden, even if they do seem to be settling in surprisingly well. "Aye, okay. So, wanna ask me about the jaw-dropping glamour of running a neighbourhood pharmacy in Falkirk?"

Charles almost drops his head in shame and wishes he could retrace at least some of his steps this mellow evening. "Been a bit me, me, me, haven't I? Sorry, pal." For a moment he just stares down at his almost-empty glass, turning it round at an angle on the table like a skater pirouetting on ice. "What would you do, Norman – in my position?"

"Buy my prophylactics from a reputable pharmacist," says Norman Gemmell.

*

Lexington, Kentucky. May 1982.

There are some lights still on in the Sherman house.

They belong to two small adjoining bedrooms. A couple of parents sleeping nearby are thankful that these particular rooms aren't linked by a communicating door.

Wondering whether he will be presented with at least one more opportunity this trip, Charlie Dickens – who is far too inflamed to sleep after this momentous, cavernous day – lies in his comfortable American bed and counts his remaining condoms. He does this while staring at the internal wall in the hope that Laura Sherman, his Laura, is staring back at him, thinking very much the same, although perhaps not about the counting. He has no way of knowing for sure, yet still he senses that she is.

Perhaps she is dreaming on this prospect, even as she is writing in her diary, which he knows that she does every evening, as many teenage girls apparently do, and which he dearly hopes her parents never read.

He tries to guess exactly how she is describing, for her eyes only, what they did just this afternoon, deep within the off-limits darkness of Mammoth Cave. He hopes – his heart still racing – that he is given a decent review.

The first, he trusts, of many.

TWENTY-EIGHT

Pimlico, London. November 2004

The fireworks had begun almost immediately after the streetlights came on, as if a municipal heads-up had been given to all the pyromaniacs of the area.

By the time darkness had properly fallen, although pure darkness is unknown to most of the people who inhabit this part of London, so close to the embankment and the river, the recurrent explosions and accompanying flashes of many colours had started to get right up at least one local author's nose.

Charles realises, as he sits in his living room-cum-study, at the small trusty relic from the Barras that still serves as his writing desk, that he can't entirely blame his peculiar state of mind on Guy Fawkes and his abortive 1605 Gunpowder Plot. Had that daring gambit actually paid off or never occurred at all and there was nothing much either way to celebrate, no effigies to beg alongside or toss onto a bonfire each year at this time, the author is still pretty sure that he would be sitting here this evening, staring despondently at his laptop, wondering what in God's name he was doing and whether he would ever write another bloody book.

He glances around the dimly lit room and realises that, save for a respectable number of randomly shelved and precariously stacked volumes and a few framed posters of impenetrable European movies, the place is quite spartan. Charles would like to think of these four walls as the very hub and nerve centre of a highly fruitful writing practice but is too aware that, as this scribe does most of his creating in cafés, restaurants and bars around town, it rarely serves as such. So it is quite pathetic as a living room.

Curiously, although not the most outwardly social of men, Charles feels that he requires or at least prefers people around him while he's working. Those who know this about him are convinced that it is because, as a writer, he enjoys subjecting unsuspecting members of the public to his imaginative gaze and eavesdropping on their most intimate conversations. The truth is more mundane and far less romantic; he writes best when he doesn't feel too isolated and where there's decent coffee and a bun. A few years spent copywriting in major London advertising agencies thankfully gave him the ability to mull and write anywhere, regardless of the surrounding hubbub or revelry.

Except, patently, the sound of fucking fireworks.

He checks his watch. 21.55 GMT. And he isn't the least 'pleased to remember' the fifth of November.

Beside him, on the currently underemployed desk, he notices the manila envelope containing Abigail

Chadwick's writings and wonders for a moment why it is still there. He would simply pop it in the waste bin but this would be an unkindly response to a decent young person, someone who has done him no harm and is genuinely talented. He promises himself once again that he will get back to her, with notes and realistic encouragement, as soon as the dust has settled. But right now there seems to be an inordinate amount of dust and precious little settlement.

Charles has no idea whether it is simply mounting frustration with his own inertia or the taunting nudge that this envelope has just given him (bolstered, perhaps, by the most recent fond email from Norman, checking yet again with some concern as to how and where things are going), but he senses that if he doesn't do something soon to wrench himself out of his stultifying lethargy and ascend from the depths of his gloom, his brain will explode like one of those noisy and criminally overpriced Roman candles just outside his window.

His hand moves, almost of its own volition, over to the desktop phone.

For reasons he would find hard to explain, the phone he still uses is covered in fur and sports plastic fangs around the buttons, as if these are set in a slavering maw. This grotesque object is a relic of an advertising shoot many years ago, in which for some reason the telephone was meant to represent the enemy. Damned if he can remember what it was the enemy of or the exact product/service he was attempting to promote. Perhaps it wasn't even his account and he just lifted the prop from someone's office when he quit.

Whatever!

He finds himself pressing a finger to the fur and onto one of the pre-set memory buttons, hoping that some vaguely sensible words emerge from his mouth when the other person answers. If the person is even there at all.

"*What the Dickens?*" comes the surprised but friendly voice at the other end. A greeting Charles has heard more than once, even from this same person, but is nonetheless welcome this noisy evening.

Before Charles can speak, Kevin Roberts is on the case. Or at least the case he assumes he should be on. "Don't worry, C.D. The book is still doing gangbusters. In the mid-west particularly. Go figure. And I hear tell you had a meet over there about the movie."

"Aye," says Charles, "they're paying me very nicely to write the first draft." He ends what should be an upbeat response on a sigh imbued with so much sorrow that for a moment Kevin wonders if his author is about to tell him he has a terminal disease. (The young American realises almost simultaneously that he reads too much fiction.) "Between you and me, Kevin…" Here it comes. "I haven't written anything new in months. More than months. Not since… But that's not why I called. Although I suppose it very much is."

"I'm a push-over for the oblique," says the New Yorker. "Especially with sound effects. What is going on over there – is London under siege?"

"Oh, that. It's Guy Fawkes Night. Like July 4th but with baked potatoes." There is a pause but Kevin doesn't think this is in order that he can admire his author's limey wit. "Kevin, I think I need a lawyer."

"*Shit!* You in trouble?"

"No, of course not," protests Charles. "Well, yes, but only in my head. A family lawyer, Kevin. Someone who knows the US adoption system."

He can almost feel Kevin smiling down the phone, three thousand miles away, which sort of surprises him.

"Feeling a new book comin' on. Like it already. Told your agent or is yours truly being given a sneak preview?"

"It's not a book. Well... not yet anyway. Er... Kevin, do you have a few minutes?"

"For a guy who drags me all the way to the boondocks of Kentucky to recapture his misspent youth? Brother, I got all the time in the world."

The loudest explosion yet resounds down the phone line.

"Sounds like they're getting closer!" says Kevin Roberts in Manhattan.

*

The fireworks have been in abeyance for some hours, but this fails to afford one still sleepless resident of Pimlico much cheer. Not when he feels like a damp squib himself right now.

Charles checks his bedside clock. 4.15am. It is quite unusual for him to be awake at this time of night, as he generally sleeps fairly soundly, even when half-formed ideas and notions that wouldn't survive the light of day are swarming through his drowsy head like rats escaped from a laboratory. He sometimes thinks it is the very force and volume of these random thoughts, their swirling, unstoppable madness, that practically knock him out.

It is even more unusual for him to find himself dripping with a particularly pungent and noxious sweat, especially in late London autumn, when the nights are far from warm. Even the new beard, which is not exactly lush and the only thing he has produced in months, is full of moisture. He knows immediately that he isn't the least feverish, at least not diagnosably so, and that this discomfort is entirely stress-related. The accumulation of years, if not decades, of what he would have to call – melodramatic as it may sound – *torment*, finally seeping through his pores.

Charles has always regarded himself as a pro-active person. He knows that his sanity depends on rallying all his energies to the cause of making things happen rather than simply sitting around and hoping that they will. Wasn't this how he became a writer all those years ago? Yet these past few months…

He realises that last night's somewhat bizarre transatlantic phone call, where words came cascading out of his mouth, as if from a part of his brain he hadn't previously visited and barely knew was there, was the start of this season's current pro-activity. Spurred on perhaps by something with which Norman Gemmell had challenged him that very special late summer evening.

He also realises, as he slithers damply out of the pretzeled sheets, that last night's effort wasn't nearly enough. Not while he is feeling as he does right now. Not while he can't work. Or sleep. Or, well, manage.

No way.

Which is why his body, almost of its own volition, is leading him straight back to his desk. And to the computer that never sleeps.

TWENTY-NINE

New York City. November 2004

The view over Park Avenue South from his office on the thirty-fourth floor used to inspire Kevin Roberts far more than it does right now.

Perhaps it is because these days all he can see way down there is angry traffic and just as angry people, and all he knows is that soon he will have to push and shove himself through them all once again just to make the train back home to wife, sanity and his first young child. Even from way up here he knows that everyone looks angry. They walk angry, they drive angry, they cross roads angry. They even eat angry. And if he were down there amongst them, he would most certainly hear them talk angry. He can almost sense himself becoming just like them, in order to best prep for the journey. Which makes him feel – well – angry.

Kevin finds that he is yearning somewhat guiltily for another book tour, where at least, amidst all the organisation and the travel and the nights away from home, he can enjoy the warmth and leisured pace of small town (or indeed any town that isn't this one – even Chicago works for him) hospitality.

The phone on his desk rings at exactly the moment that there is a knock on his door. He decides to ignore the former and acknowledge the latter.

"Come in!"

As he turns from the window, he knows immediately what the call was about and who hasn't waited to be announced by reception.

"*Jesus Christ!*" he says.

"It's the beard," says Charles, entering the book-festooned office. Festooned on several shelves with multiple copies of the same unsullied books. He manages to glimpse his own amongst them, reassuringly, as he approaches the desk. "I was just passing. Did you find that lawyer?"

"*Say – what?*" Kevin Roberts is not a head-shaker. Never has been. But surely someone rocking up like this, someone to whom you spoke what seems like only hours before, when they were at least three thousand miles and an ocean away, can justify a good, solid and hard to contain cranium-swivel. "Jeez – again! Sit down, will you? And excuse me just a moment while I hyperventilate. Drink while you're waiting?"

"No. Thank you."

"Did the bombing in London stop? Say, wait – you're not my evacuee, are you?"

Charles just sighs. Kevin can see quite clearly that his author, most probably jet-lagged and patently insane, is not in the mood for small talk.

"Yeah. Okay. Sorry, Charles, let me just sit down and allow the shock to settle. No, not happening." The young publishing executive sighs, as he feels the slightly bleary-eyed stare into his soul from this writer he quite likes – in fact, really likes – yet still can't fathom. Although this could describe a good many of the writers on his books. "Okay, again. My wife's uncle. Works out of Brooklyn. Bright guy. He knows some people. We got to talking last night. And again this morning."

Charles sits down opposite the younger man and leans over the small stack of books on his desk, as if this will make the words come quicker. He wonders for a moment if all the books really need to be here and swiftly reasons that, in such an office, they would be conspicuous by their absence. He, for one, would be royally pissed off.

"*And?*" he says.

"And – we coulda done this over the phone, Charles." More head-shaking – this is almost becoming a tic. "You took a fuckin' peak-time flight – just for this? I hate to think what it's costing you."

"Nothing much," sighs Charles. "Just a big chunk of my script fee for the movie. Oh, and my sanity. So what did he say – this uncle of your wife?"

Like most people, or so at least he assumes, Kevin hates to be the bearer of bad news. Rejecting authors is, of course, part of his day job and rarely executed face to face. But this particular story, the extraordinary saga Charles finally told him on their recent call: a cruel adolescent rejection that actually wasn't; a newly discovered teenage pregnancy; a child taken away for adoption, now an anonymous adult; even a toothsome young woman with an extraordinary likeness, who sent his author on a different, more dubious journey – these are the stuff of a more primal, heart-wrenching dimension. The stuff of novels, he can't help thinking, even as he berates himself, knowing that life is a whole deal messier.

"Pretty much what you and I figured when you called," says Kevin, arms spread out in regret. "You don't have enough information. And it's up to the kid anyway – y'know, the 'adoptee' – to make a move. For obvious reasons. Usually at around twenty-one. Which – despite the cheesy stories you hear – they rarely do. So not the best news I could give you, Charles. *Unless…*" He pauses, almost as if he is waiting for Charles to react, but in reality trying to recall exactly what the lawyer told him. It was pretty late or pretty early and Kevin was still in some sort of shock from what he had been asked to find out.

"Yeah?" says Charles, leaping on it the way Kevin had just seen some of the angry walkers down below attack hot-dogs bought from the stand.

"Well, unless you go the private investigator route, which my guy wouldn't recommend. It can cost a fortune and cross into some shady territory. Plus – and I hate to upset you, friend – you're probably not even on the birth certificate."

"'Father unknown,'" agrees Charles.

"Indeed. And from what you told me, her dad – the late doctor – could've done all kinds of stuff under the radar. Maybe even changed the names, I dunno."

"A nice couple wanting a child. Suddenly there's one up for grabs. Few questions asked."

"Uh huh," agrees Kevin. He watches disappointment

cover his author's face like a shroud. The hope that must have transported him peak fare all the way across the Atlantic, along with the determination to find a daughter who, until a few months ago, he never even knew existed, is visibly draining away, alongside his energy.

Charles sinks into his chair, while his publisher continues to compound the obvious anguish with every well-chosen word. "I imagine if any person's thinking to do some kinda search or investigation, it'd have to be Mom. Yeah? And probably on her own. But even then it could be way beyond impossible. Not to mention prohibitive." Kevin pauses, as a new thought strikes him. "Charles, there's something I gotta ask you."

"No, Kevin, there's not another book in it."

"Shit, man. Do I look that crass?"

"I wouldn't blame you. But right now I'm wondering if I'll ever write again. Or if I even care. Sorry pal, what was your question?"

"Wow! I mean wow about the writing bit. Bummer. Er... have you told whatshername... Estella?"

"Since 'Estella' is the girl in my novel, no. You mean Laura."

"Yeah. Sorry. Laura from Lexington. Did you tell her about your quest?"

"You make me sound like bloody King Arthur. No. I haven't. It's far too early."

"Crissakes, Charles – *she's the mom!* And don't you want to see her again? Your first love."

Charles doesn't respond.

To his surprise this is a question he hasn't even thought to ask himself, at least not consciously, because the more pressing and revelatory part of the story obviously took over and has recently – in fact, since that long-overdue reunion with Norman – been dominating his every thought, waking, sleeping and all states in-between. This despite his attempting, in those fallow months after his American tour, to keep it in the box writers such as himself hold in their minds, that treasure chest reserved for myriad stories in progress, where resolutions have thus far failed to present themselves.

He wants to remind Kevin that he *has* seen her now, this Laura, first love, erstwhile childhood sweetheart, that they've both moved on with their separate and distant lives, and that this particular albeit pivotal aspect of his history is over. Done with. Closure. Charles is pretty sure that this is *exactly* how he is feeling and that the 'quest' for his adopted child is of a different order, a more pressing and far nobler journey. Hey, has he checked out that crumpled old photograph even *once* since he got back home? The one still in his wallet. He has not! Which has to say something, hasn't it?

"Laura's got her own life," he tells the young publisher. "Kids. Work. I can't just—"

"Sure, Charles, I get it. Anyway, she's twenty years too old for you now."

Kevin knows, even as the words shoot out of his mouth, that his foot has gone flying right into the gap. He can almost feel himself trying to claw them back in again, re-spool the tape, as he watches the face of C.D. MacNaughtan, the face of a very private man, one that never appears on book covers, dissolve in shock and hurt.

"*Fuck you, Kevin!*" says the author, pithily. "Fuck you very much."

Launching one final glare across the messy desk, Charles turns and stomps out.

"Oops," says Kevin Roberts feebly, knowing in his head that there is nothing left to say.

Through the glass of his office he watches his author walk away.

But then, curiously, the man appears to pause for a moment and to just stare back, unseeingly, at him. It is almost, thinks Kevin, as if the irate and wounded Scotsman has been caught short by a sudden paralysing notion or perhaps some new and even more unbalancing thought.

The workings of an author's mind, writ large.

*

Lexington, Kentucky. May 1982

Mrs Audrey Sherman waves her three young charges off to school.

She is trying not to pay too much attention to how perfectly the most recent – and thankfully most transient – of these charges is matching his stride to that of her only daughter, leaving barely a sliver of virginal Kentucky morning between their youthful bodies. A daughter who, she could hardly fail to remark, has been noticeably glowing over the past twenty-four hours, in a fashion that would normally bring a doting mother cheer but right now is flashing like a warning light.

As if acting as co-conspirator in the plot to cause his mother what her own mom would have called 'conniptions', Brian Sherman almost immediately quickens his pace away from the couple – for this is what they have clearly become, despite the almost excessive 'innocence' around the house – in order to catch up with some other school friends who are equally tree-like and live nearby. Mrs Sherman realises that her son hasn't exactly been the perfect host to his Scottish visitor but reckons that this is no excuse for her daughter stepping into the breach and taking that famed southern hospitality to possibly a whole new level.

She wishes that she could eavesdrop on the youngsters' conversation, if only to torture herself some more.

Which there is no possible doubting that it would.

"Are you okay, Laura?" asks Charlie, quietly, now that they are finally alone, for the first time since they returned from the caves. They both know that with the high school just a few minutes' stroll away, on this, his final day there, such time will be both precious and brief. "About yesterday, I mean," he adds, unnecessarily.

Laura nods but then shakes her head. Whatever glow she had – the one shining like a harbour light to the rest of her suspicious family – seems to have been replaced by a look of such desolation that Charlie feels as if his heart is about to break. This is a description so over-used he already knows that he would never reach for it in his writing, yet finds himself surprised at how cogently it sums up what is going on for him in real life.

"No! And *yes!*" exclaims Laura, confusedly. "It...

these weeks… they've been so… wondrous, Charlie. Oh, Charlie – just a few more days and you'll be…" Struggling for words, her fine hands, with those delicate fingers he finds so expressive, appear to take flight. "…and then in a coupla months you'll be off again. To college. You'll forget all about me. Us."

"No! *Never!*" protests Charlie, knowing already that this could not possibly be true. "Laura, you're a writer. I'm a writer. We'll stay lovers, y'know, through our letters."

"Like they did in the war."

"Exactly," says Charlie, although he's not certain as to exactly which war she's referring – they've had another big one here quite recently. "And I'll drip some blood on mine. For authenticity."

"And I'll drop tears – so you won't be able to read some of the ickier bits!"

Charlie's voice lowers, as the sadness returns. "What a shame we didn't meet in our twenties, Laura."

Her sudden peals of laughter, when he is being so deadly serious, take him by surprise. He turns to look at her.

"We still can, Charlie!"

"Oh yeah," says Charlie, breaking into a smile. "Yeah! *We still can!* We will! I'll come back here. To Lexington. Or… wherever you are. When I've made some cash. I promise."

Laura Sherman just nods and strokes the face of this sweet, unique, hardly handsome yet oddly beautiful boy. Brian turns round at this moment and the lovers spring away like clasps on a beer bottle.

They both go into their own thoughts, as the high school looms ever closer. Minds drifting into a world where everything is possible yet nothing too probable.

The only constant thing in this heartless universe – their unsullied, undying love.

*

Lexington, Kentucky. November 2004

"Welcome back, Mr MacNaughtan!" effuses the receptionist, at the historic Morgan House.

THIRTY

The small lobby appears much the same as when Charles last stayed here, except that the splendid floral arrangement on the central table has obviously been adapted to the change in seasons. He is not exactly sure what these adaptations are – he has to Google a lot when describing flora in his books – but he appreciates the effect and subtle warmth of their welcome.

The receptionist's greeting as he arrives at her modest but elegant desk is equally warm. Charles is flattered that the young woman recognises him. If not immediately on entrance, at least when he has provided his name.

"You remembered me?" He smiles.

"Oh, sure," says the young woman. "Well, the computer did. There's this program—"

"Yes, okay," says Charles, suddenly less than fascinated. He provides the requisite details and walks wearily, with his small suitcase and laptop bag, up the familiar staircase to the same room from which he had departed, a sadder but wiser man, some six months ago.

He had forgotten about the three-storey bed. "It's like the Princess and the fucking Pea," he mutters, as he ascends to the mattress as one would a scaffold.

For some minutes he simply lies there, enjoying an aerial view of the room. The card that Laura Griffin had given him, the one with all her contact details, is now resting in his hand. He wonders for a moment why he hasn't transferred the information onto his phone. There must be a reason, he thinks, but is too fatigued by travel and emotion to pursue it. Not when he's also quite preoccupied with going slowly insane.

Finally, he picks up the phone.

To his surprise, although it shouldn't be as he is calling a family home, a young boy answers.

"Hello?"

"Oh… hi. Can I speak to Laura Sherm… Griffin, please? You must be Hen—"

The boy has already moved off and is shouting to someone. He is therefore sadly unappreciative of the unknown caller's excellent memory for names.

"*Mom, it's a guy with a weird voice!*"

The guy with the weird voice can hear muffled conversation, a clinking of cutlery, the scraping of a chair and finally footsteps approaching. A domestic soundscape that should in some bucolic way comfort him but in reality does nothing to still the troublesome pounding in his chest.

"Hello – who is this, please?" He thinks once again that her voice may be slightly deeper than the one he still recalls from so long ago, more mature obviously and possibly less brimming with disarmingly innocent wonder in every note, but he finds that the years have done little to dampen its softly southern musicality.

"Hello, is that Laura? Laura, it's me – Charles. Charlie. Charlie Dickens."

Laura Griffin is grateful that this is a sound-only call, as she knows that she must look more stunned than even her unexpected caller might imagine. For reasons that are hers alone. She moves the phone away from its little table in her hallway and slips into the downstairs room that she has neatly converted into a compact study.

Ensuring that the door is firmly closed, she sits at her desk, trying to compose herself, before she engages in any sort of conversation.

"Charlie?" she says eventually and with obvious concern. "It must be past midnight where you are. Is everything—"

"Laura, I'm not in London."

"Oh. Okay. You back in the States again?"

"I'm back in The Morgan House. Again."

Whilst there is now only silence at the Griffin end of the line, Charles is certain that he can sense alarm. Perhaps, he thinks, it is simply him projecting his own stuff or maybe the phone is indeed amplifying and transmitting a detectably raised level of breath intake. Or, of course, it's the simple fact that a perfectly sanguine person would be saying something in response and not remaining utterly speechless.

"The…? *Why?*" says Laura, eventually. "Not another book already?"

"I wish! No, actually I'm writing the screenplay for

the last one. Well, trying to. Well, about to. I came here…
y'know, for inspiration."

As he says it, he realises just how flabby this sounds.
In fact, just how flabby it is. But how can he tell Laura
exactly why he has come here, when he is having a hard
job answering the very same question? And speaking to
Laura isn't making it any easier.

He suddenly remembers the wisdom his late father
passed on to him, when he was trying to decide what
'Highers' to take in his final year at school. "*What does
your gut tell you, Charlie?*" Is this what he's doing at this
moment – listening to his gut? Sensing that this new and
very different Laura should somehow, God knows how,
be the key. There's certainly a lot going on down there at
gut-level right now.

"I read your book, Charlie. Remember? It's not set
anywhere near Lexington."

She's got him there. "Then maybe… you're my
inspiration."

Where did *that* come from? More like his butt than
his gut.

Even Charles knows that what he has just said is a bit
cheesy, more than a bit if he is being totally honest, yet
somewhere he knows that it has also to be a little bit true.
Without what happened to them back in the eighties,
those short but sublime few weeks, there never would
have been a 'forever moment', would there? And he's not
just talking about the novel.

He hears a noise on the line that he can't make out,
until he realises that it is footsteps. The floor must be
uncarpeted and the person at the other end of the line

is pacing. Her breath is coming faster, and when she talks again, he can sense the anger and frustration in her words. And more than this – yet again, a certain panic. This is clearly not the reaction he was hoping for, but he realises that he has absolutely no idea what he was hoping for. Perhaps he was hoping that Laura could tell him.

"I'm sorry, Charlie," she says, brusquely but quietly, "you can't just waltz back into my life after twenty-two years. To do what – help you with a friggin' movie! You don't even know what my life is. I've got kids. Kids who know nothing about you. Or… *And* I might have a… a partner."

"Do you, Laura – have a partner?"

"None of your business. But it's not outside the realms of possibility."

"Like having a grown-up daughter."

The silence is even more ear-splitting this time round.

"I have to go, Charlie. Goodbye."

Charles can only imagine the effects of his final words on this person now fully disconnected from him yet connected in ways he has yet completely to process and absorb.

He can't begin to imagine the office in which she is now sitting, locked in her chair, unable to move. Nor could he possibly picture the formal-looking envelope resting in a metal rack right there beside her laptop. The one that is already opened and its contents read many times.

She reads it again now, with an even greater intensity. So much so that she doesn't hear the door from the hallway sliding open behind her.

227

"What's that?" asks Jess, sensing something of interest. Receiving absolutely no response, she moves on. "Oh. Okay. Can you help me with my English but like not tell Mr Leet?"

"No," says Laura Griffin. "But nice try."

"Who was the guy on the phone? Henry said he had a weird voice."

"No one. It was no one. Now go do your English."

As her daughter slumps out, her mind once more on something else, Laura takes the letter and swiftly locks it into an empty drawer of her desk. She almost wishes that she could join it.

THIRTY-ONE

Lexington, Kentucky. May 1982

Brian and Dr Sherman are in the den, watching the Louisville Cardinals go down fighting, while Mrs Sherman happily potters in the lush and spacious rear garden that is her pride and joy. All of which give Charlie ample time to relish staring at Laura's compact but entrancing body, as she sunbathes a respectable distance away from him on a lounger. Her short skirt has rolled, not entirely of its own accord, even further up her thighs; her flimsy, and to his mind impeccably filled, flowery top is discreetly, or perhaps not so discreetly, unbuttoned.

Charlie is ostensibly writing, but even the wary gardener has noticed that his pen barely moves, whilst his middle distance is having a field day. When she finally addresses him, he is surprised to discover that the older woman is now standing far closer to his chair. More alarmingly, she is holding a pair of large and very well-honed garden shears.

"So, Charlie, do your parents expect you to marry a girl of the Jewish persuasion?"

Whilst he has become familiar with the differing speech patterns and even topics of conversation in this far-off land, this overture still takes him by surprise. It appears to have come out of nowhere, although he is quite aware of its source.

"Not really, Mrs Sherman," he asserts, truthfully. "My dad didn't."

"And how did his parents feel?" she asks casually, as if she really couldn't care one way or the other.

"Just pretty glad to get out of Nazi-occupied territory."

"Yes," says Mrs Sherman, as she moves away, "that must have been nice. Laura Sherman, you will burn to a crisp in this sun!"

Laura Sherman manages to cover her modesty in a manner so overtly provocative that her mom might as well have instructed her to strip off and frolic butt-naked in front of her father's most traumatised patients on the newly mown hospital lawn.

Charlie Dickens knows that he will love this young woman forever. This is the memory he will take away with him in just a few days. And that she will never ever change.

*

Lexington, Kentucky. November 2004

He is so right-brained that he is practically off the map.

So it has never come as much of a surprise to Charles

that he has virtually no sense of direction. Having passed his driving test on the sixth attempt, at enormous cost to his parents, both emotional and instructional, he had promptly become so hopelessly lost during his first solo drive to a friend just minutes away that he had to find a phone box and call his father to come find him and lead him back home.

He has no illusions that what has drawn him to this particular part of the city of Lexington on this still clement early November afternoon, just a couple of days after his conversation with Laura, is anything other than the purest chance. In fact, he had simply been enjoying an aimless wander through the streets, attempting to get his head around a structure for his movie that didn't simply ape the book and failing miserably, concerns of a more personal nature stubbornly refusing to find a shady parking space.

He has almost sauntered past the gates of the hospital before he realises where he has found himself. Turning back, he decides that a stroll through the grounds might call up some of the happier memories, which are what he needs right now, amidst this chaos of his own devising.

The Sherman house, as it was then, is still there, looking smaller than he remembers. As he stares at it, having glanced up at the window of what he is sure was once his room, he notices in a far corner of the front yard an elderly lady pulling out some weeds. Sensing his presence, she turns and he realises almost instantly that this is Mrs Sherman. Not a vision from his past but today's Mrs Sherman, older, greyer, more stooped but clearly and somewhat surprisingly still the owner of the house.

She nods to him and offers a pleasant smile. "Another fine day," she says amiably, with not the slightest hint of recognition.

Charles decides that a friendly nod is quite sufficient, given that whilst his accent might not necessarily lead to total recall, it could at least act as an unwelcome reminder of the guy who ravished her teenage daughter and left the family with more than a bottle of The Famous Grouse to remember him by. And, anyway, he does enough mindless talking about the weather with strangers and passers-by back home, without exploring it in a town where they wouldn't know crap weather if they fell over it.

Yet gazing into this still well-tended garden, where he is pretty certain he has quite innocently meandered, does bring back other memories. More importantly, even in his directionless state, it gives him a nudge as to where he should sensibly – or perhaps not that sensibly – be heading.

THIRTY-TWO

The car park is relatively quiet now. Most of those students who own cars or get rides have departed for the day, ahead of the walkers, who Charles watches escaping homewards in larger, rowdier bunches.

Charles still finds it fascinating how many American kids roll up to high school each morning in their own transportation. Perhaps this is because he probably couldn't have found his way to school by lunchtime, had he even owned or had access to a car. He wonders idly how many teenagers back home have their own vehicles these days. Possibly still not so many, as he is aware of the schools he passes on his walks having only modest car parks. This one in Lexington seems vast.

He looks around. The school building doesn't appear to have changed much but he has far fewer recollections of the bricks and mortar than he has of the parade of high-school kids that he joined and enjoyed each morning back then, pupils of both sexes, unfettered by rigid uniforms, visceral football rivalries and the unassailable hierarchy of accents.

Charles soon realises that grown men standing outside school gates, without a child attached or expected, or even a small dog in tow, are just asking for trouble. So he is quite relieved to spot Laura Griffin as she walks briskly and purposefully towards an elderly station wagon not hugely dissimilar to the beast he vaguely recalls from so long ago.

He watches her wave goodbye to a colleague, as she opens the door of her car and slides smoothly in. Before she can drive out of the gates and away, however, he has moved towards her. Charles hadn't intended to shock her into a screeching halt, but this is the hardly unpredictable outcome of his approach.

"*I coulda been with my kids!*" she yells at him, out of the open window. For some reason he thinks that if this were early November in the UK, she would have had to wind the window down first, which would have been far less dramatic.

"I took a flyer that no self-respecting kid would want to be seen driving home with their teacher-mom."

"I suppose you'd better get in. Smart-ass," says Laura Griffin, without losing the glare. "I was hoping you'd have flown back home by now."

"No such luck," says Charles, as if it really isn't his fault.

He slips in beside her and they drive off in silence. He has no idea where they are going, geographically or emotionally, and for a while neither does Laura. But she does catch Kyra in her mirror, staring at her with undisguised fascination from inside her own still-parked car, which doesn't lighten her mood in the least.

Charles can see that they are driving away from the town. They're travelling through a suburb, which seems very green and pleasant, all the homes fully detached with their own sizeable plots of land. He marvels yet again, having been raised in a city famous, but hardly celebrated, for its cheek-by-jowl tenements, how much space these people have. Even those who would appear to be not so well off. It's like they've never heard of fences or party walls.

He assumes that Laura is not steering them towards her own home, where presumably her kids would by now be stuffing themselves and where he is pretty sure he is persona extremely non grata. Checking out her countenance, he and his first 'undying' love are far more likely to be en route to some deserted wasteland, where no one can see them, and she can bludgeon him into the dusty ground with a thick shovel.

"I always wondered what kind of women attract stalkers," she says, after a good few minutes of silence. "Well, now I know!"

"Ha ha. Laura—"

"I still don't understand why you're back here, Charlie. I told you every – I told you all you needed to know. Oh, and please don't tell me again that I'm your friggin' muse."

He notices a sign that says they're on Versailles Road and wonders what the hell this place ever had to do with Versailles. For some reason he tries to guess how they would pronounce it.

"I always promised you I'd come back," he tries. This meets with such a look of disbelief that he decides swiftly to move on. "Okay. To be honest, Laura, I don't fully understand it myself. I certainly didn't plan it. It just… where are we going?"

"I have no idea," she sighs.

"Oh. Well, the trees are lovely," says Charles, admiring the fall colours. "I bet people come leaf-peaking here, do they, like they do in New England?"

"It's 'peeping'. Not here so much, but in the Appalachias, they do. And Daniel Boone National Forest." What am I, she thinks, a goddam tour operator? She knows that a conversation must be had and she knows what it has to be about, but she's just not ready. Please. Not yet.

"Laura – I met this girl."

This wasn't that conversation.

She turns her head slightly, as if her profile couldn't do full justice to how royally pissed she is at this little nugget.

"Oh, and you just had to fly this three thousand and umpty hundred miles to tell me. Good – so now we're quits, are we?"

Charles wonders when she became so spiky. She wasn't like this when he first knew her. But he has to concede he might have changed a bit too. Just a tad, as he has heard them say in New England.

"I'm not explaining myself," he sort of apologises, bracing himself for what has to come. "I didn't tell you at the time, but I met this person – not a girl, a young woman – back here in the spring, at a reading. Well, not exactly back here. Another town. Keep forgetting its name. Miles away. States away. She was from upstate

236

New York. Quite lovely person, she was. Bright. Funny."

"This isn't getting any better, Charlie."

"Trust me. It will. Laura, she looked so like—"

"Like who?" she steams in, sharply.

"Just gimme a bloody chance to pause. For pity's sake! *You!* She looked like you. Well, like I remember you looking."

"Like *me*?" She shakes her head, wondering where this is going. She also wonders where she is going. And where they are both going. She realises there's a lot of wondering going on and is feeling increasingly uncomfortable. "Sometimes our memories play tricks. I can hardly picture my dad now, unless I go back to old photos."

"Me neither. *My* dad, I mean. Sad, isn't it? Anyway, when she told me she was adopted…"

Laura doesn't say anything.

She wants to stop the car right now but can see no place that's safe to do so. There's a turning up ahead, where a few cars are going. So she decides to join them, which enables her simply to sit in a barely moving line and stare fully at this man without causing an accident. This once briefly familiar face that had lost focus for her over the decades but which she is now seeing again, in a very different form but all too clearly.

Charles realises that he has just unforgivably provided this poor woman with false hope, which he really hadn't intended at all. In fact, this is the last thing he would have wished. Silently berating himself for his ineptitude, he shakes his head with some force, as if this will somehow make up for the overweening crassness.

"*Wait!*" he almost shouts, although she is clearly not going anywhere. "No! I'm so sorry, Laura. To… y'know, build up your expectations. I found out later, when I went back to see her for a second time – in April, right after you and I last met – that she had just made it up. Well, the adoption bit. The missionary bit too, although that's maybe secondary." He knows that he is rambling now but can't bear to confront her reaction head-on, which he is certain will happen the moment he stops talking. "Anyway—"

Laura does indeed look horrified. "Why would *a person*—"

"To make themselves and their 'history' more interesting, I suppose. People do this to authors. Maybe to others too, when they feel a bit – I dunno – wanting. Or maybe she was just a wee fibber. As you lot say, go figure. But at the time, when she first told me, well – it did make me wonder."

Laura smacks her steering wheel hard with both hands. Unfortunately, it sets off her horn, so she has to wave excuses to the bemused driver up ahead. All the cars in the line, both of them now notice, are larger, newer and very top of the range. There are Bentleys, Rolls-Royces, BMWs, Mercs. "*That's why!* Why you came here back in April. Wasn't it? It's why you set up that reading!"

Charles nods, relieved that he is finally able to be frank with her. Well, vaguely frank. No need to go overboard.

"It brought things up for me, Laura," he explains, gently. "Well, she did. Things that were, to be honest, never really that far from the surface, but I just didn't dare confront them head-on. Couldn't actually bring myself to find you, intrude on whatever sort of life you'd made for yourself. And have that awful rejection, as I saw it, from way back confirmed for all time. So I never did. Confront them. Confront *you*. Until this kind of, well, forced the issue. I mean, how could I know you'd even still be there – here – in this wee town? Actually, not so wee – it seems to go on much further than I remembered. But I thought I could – well, finally pick up the courage to find out why you just stopped writing like that. Just dumped me so casually, as I thought. I had to, didn't I? Find out, I mean. It's been—"

"It's been twenty-two years!" she practically yells, as this appears to be turning into a monologue. "That's what it's been. *Jesus!*"

Charles can almost see the cogs in her brain shifting. She must realise now, from what the crazy person next to her has just burbled, that an undisclosed teenage pregnancy had at least been suspected before she drove over and revealed all to him. So her painful revelation that early morning in April would, in truth, have edged more in the direction of hopeful confirmation than full-on, hold-the-presses astonishment. Well, the guy certainly put on quite a show.

"This girl – this young woman," says Laura, "she's not our daughter."

"Sadly not," confirms Charles.

"Because our daughter lives in Austin, Texas."

It takes a while for Laura Griffin's words, spoken so matter-of-factly, to make any sort of sense.

"Excuse me?" he says, finally.

"I got a letter. Wanna see some horses? Kentucky's famous for 'em," says Laura, because of course she realises exactly where she has aimlessly driven them and needs time to decide exactly what to say next.

THIRTY-THREE

The name Keeneland means absolutely nothing to Charles but patently a great deal to everyone else around him. Especially, as Laura informs him in her hyperactive state, to the very important people who have come here today, from all over the country and beyond, with their chequebooks and bankers to hand.

With its lush, meticulously landscaped grounds and fine stone buildings, this iconic landmark, according to a leaflet now helpfully thrust into his unwilling hands, lays claim to being the world's most beautiful racetrack. He is certain there are more than a few other racetracks around the globe that would take issue with this, but he has to admit, whilst not in the most receptive mood for beauty, that it could be regarded as breathtaking. From April to October it is apparently a testament to southern gentility, where ladies still sport white parasols and the men are all dolled up in seersucker. They've surely never been to Ascot, he thinks, a testament to overpaid people attempting to be posh and posh people being completely up themselves.

But on this November week, he discovers, to his total indifference, it is the Breeding Stock Sale, where some of the top broodmare and broodmare prospects are sold.

Laura is still pointing all this out to Charles, nervously and in unnecessary detail, as they walk through the hallowed grounds at some speed to nowhere in particular. It is unfortunately just too late in the day, and indeed in the season, to catch the magnificent thoroughbred beasts on their morning workout, sweat on their priceless flanks, hot breath rising in the crisp fall air, but at least visitors can see and marvel at the proud animals close up and, if so inclined and endowed, take one as a going-home present.

Having only just now been furnished with quite possibly the most momentous news in his entire life, Charles Dickens doesn't give a flying fuck for the broodmares, weanlings and stallions that his overwrought companion is manically banging on about in all the unnecessary detail that she can muster. Yet he knows only too well what she is up to: attempting in some desperation to cling on to the reins of normality. To complete the metaphor, which he insists on doing, if only in his forever-scribing head – she is straining to maintain a good seat, in case wild, untamed horses drag her sanity screaming down the track.

So, for the moment, he will allow her to continue extolling the pride of Kentucky horse-hood, in this the home of horse history and horse millionaires. Even if they both know it is all so much horse shit.

A young woman in a bright blue Keeneland shirt is leading around a splendid example of mane-tossing equinity, just part of the multi-million dollars' worth of matchless flesh on show this afternoon, brought here into this roped-off pen from one of the larger local horse farms for which the state is justly famous.

Ranged high above them, on a wooden platform, are the auctioneers. Charles checks out the starting price on the notice board, which is well into the zillions, and concludes that he is so in the wrong game. He smiles to a generously proportioned gentleman from the Middle East and nods with eyebrows raised towards the price indicator, but the gentleman, whilst acknowledging Charles politely, appears to be not quite so bowled over.

Suddenly a distant memory leaps into his head, like a thoroughbred leaving the starting gate. "*I remember something about the horses!* Yes! Your family took me one evening to the – they were in funny wee carts! What was it called?"

"Harness racing. That was over at the Red Mile. Dan Patch himself won his world record here in Lexington. Yes, the town is famous for it. That and slavery. And, of course, George Clooney."

"Yeah, the last two weren't on the tour. TELL ME ABOUT THE BLOODY LETTER!"

People nearby turn at this. People not so nearby also turn. Even the horse takes a supercilious look round.

Laura gently but firmly leads Charles away, to a less-populated area of Keeneland, right between the library and the gift shop. She can't for the life of her understand why they are here, now, in this place, but realises that a conversation such as this – one she was dearly hoping not to have, at least until she could choose her moment and possibly not even then – would hardly go any easier or feel less uncomfortable if they were to have it languishing by candlelight in warm baths full of asses' milk. It is what it is.

"Okay," she says, thoughtfully. "Well, it was very formal. Businesslike. This person – the 'adoptee' – has decided she would like to get in touch with us. Well, with me."

"Because I'm not even on the birth certificate," sighs Charles.

"No. Well, I suspect not. Knowing my dad. But rest assured, there's no doubting the paternity."

"That's a relief. Because they can do DNA—"

"Yes, okay, Charlie."

"Sorry. I joke when I'm nervous."

"Good to know. Anyway, they do it, the… thing, y'know, the searching – through intermediaries. Agencies, that kinda deal. I don't know for sure, of course, but I'm guessing it was something she'd promised herself. That when she reached twenty-one…"

"Which she must have done earlier this year. I expect you'd know the exact date. Aye, of course you would." He finds that he can't look at her and marvels at how some of our most important conversations in life are conducted whilst we examine our footwear. "So, what did you say?"

He waits for her to speak. For some seconds she says nothing. She appears transfixed by the purposeful flurry around them. C'mon, he thinks, wanting to shake her. It wasn't that tough a question.

"I didn't say anything, Charlie." She is not surprised at his surprise. It hardly begins to match how surprised she is with herself. "I've had the letter for a few weeks.

Maybe longer. Just sitting on my desk. Staring at me. I'm..."

"Apprehensive."

"That's a writer's word."

"Crapping yourself?"

"More in the ballpark," says Laura. She makes a sound like a laugh but the pain is mortifying. "Funny, isn't it? I've been waiting so long for this – more than half my life – and now..."

They can sense that the people hovering around them and even some casual passers-by are staring just a little bit longer than they might normally. As if they are picking up, from the couple's faces, that the conversation in progress, important as it clearly is, might not be about horses. Or, if it is, that the difference of opinion between them as to what to buy or how much to pay is of such magnitude as to cause them both to look as if they are about to dissolve into tears.

Charles knows in his head that he shouldn't shift focus right now. Not when the poor, tortured woman standing right in front of him, yet still keeping a schoolma'am distance, is going through the twin agonies of doubt and fear. And probably a few more. But bugger that for a game of soldiers, this is about his flesh and blood too.

"And were you going to tell me – this time?" he challenges.

Laura Griffin says nothing. She simply shrugs.

"O-kay," says Charles.

She wants to say that how could she tell him this time or any time, when she can't even quite tell herself. She wants to say that he has been out of her life for so many years, it hardly seems part of a natural or organic process, regardless of the biology, just to reel him so seamlessly back in. She wants to say that she feels helpless and scared and trepidatious and floundering.

She wants to say a lot of things, but she doesn't have the chance, because he comes straight back in with a suggestion so outrageous that she can hardly begin to process it.

"Well, could I maybe meet the children who aren't mine?" he asks quietly.

THIRTY-FOUR

Charles and Laura say very little in the car coming back into Lexington, but even Charles, with his flawed or non-existent sense of direction, can just about tell that they aren't making straight for The Morgan House.

On suburban front yards children are shooting hoops. Just like you see in the movies, thinks Charles once again, whilst reminding himself that this – real life – is where the movies got it from. He looks in vain for white picket fences but might as well be seeking old grey-haired ladies carrying hot apple pie. He does, however, see the occasional woman of colour and finds himself wondering if they are returning home after a day's gruelling domestic work, before telling himself that they are far more likely to be local residents out for a stroll. This isn't 1982 anymore, nor is it a land paying serious obeisance to a Scotsman's flawed preconceptions and prejudices. But it is still Kentucky, with all its history, and it is the gateway to the south, so he could be totally wrong.

"*Hey, you guys, this is a person I knew for three weeks some twenty-two years ago!*" comes the voice from beside him. He wonders for a moment who she's talking to. And why.

"I'm sorry, Charlie," she continues, turning to him so deliberately that he fears for his safety on this by-now-rush-hour road. "You weren't my 'forever moment'. I truly thought so at the time, but some people move on."

He wonders why exactly she is being so vehement about this. So far as he knows, he hasn't come onto her in any way, on either of his visits, and has absolutely no intention of doing so now or in the foreseeable future. Then he works it out, although surely what she has just said should have provided him with a more immediate clue.

"Ah. That was fiction, Laura. I told you. I've moved on. Moved on a lot, actually. As indeed does the guy in my book, if you recall. And seeing you again right now only reminds me just how much I've moved on."

"Well, that's good, isn't it?" she agrees. "Except now you're back."

"Er, yes. Now I'm back. But not…"

"Not for me."

"No. Not for you. I suppose I came back for closure. After what you told me in April."

"When you came back for closure."

"Er. Aye. Right enough. But of a different ilk."

"'Ilk'?"

He hears himself talking as if each word has to be clearly separated from the one before and etched into some sort of permanence. "I came back now – this time,

Laura – to see if we couldn't somehow write this final important chapter, y'know – together. You and me – pooling our resources, as it were. Utilising our different skills and connections. Although to be honest, before I heard about this letter of yours, I couldn't for the life of me see how."

"*And you thought I could?*" She seems suddenly incandescent. "Like I hadn't frickin' thought about it – about finding her, seeing her – a trillion times all these goddam years. Only every single goddam day! Like a great big piece of me was missing."

"Laura…"

"Well, now something *has* happened, obviously. But it's *my* letter, Charlie, my *chapter*, as you say, and right now I feel like I've found myself smack in the middle of what you'd probably call a 'cliffhanger'. One I haven't yet worked out how to navigate my way into, through and out of in safety. That's if I even take any next steps. *Big* 'if'. Because I'm… well, never you mind how I am. I didn't need you here, mister, not with all this going on. I don't *want* you here!" She shakes her head in pure frustration, trying desperately not to raise her voice or ascend to that pitch she has heard can simply stop men listening. "I'm not a writer like you, Charlie, but I am a reader. And I know that sometimes it's necessary just to cut out the subplot, because it's no more than… than an unnecessary distraction."

Charles starts to laugh, but clearly not in amusement. "So the father of your oldest child, that poor wee girl in where is it, Austin, Texas, who you haven't seen in twenty-one years and could just possibly see again – if you get off that white picket fence currently up your bahookie – is a *subplot*!"

The car is turning into the driveway of a small but well-maintained home.

"Maybe we should talk about this later, Charlie. Or not at all. Ever. Is there anything you don't eat, by the way?"

"I don't eat shit or humble pie. Other than that, I'm fine."

"I have no idea what that means."

"To be honest, neither do I," admits Charles.

"Jesus, this is going to be a long evening."

*

"*Hey, you guys, this is a person I knew for three weeks some twenty-two years ago!*"

Charles didn't think that she was going to say it out loud, just as soon as they walked into the small, sun-speckled hallway, but he can tell that Laura Griffin is still pretty pissed and emotional.

He supposes that he should be grateful she has even brought him here, but he knows too well from those relatives and acquaintances of his, the ones who've achieved parenthood, or had it thrust upon them, that they'll leap on any opportunity to show off their kids, however uninspiring they might be.

He realises, as he checks out the pleasing décor, embellished with some strikingly vivid examples of what he guesses is Native American artwork, mostly woven but also in an array of bentwood boxes (and flaunting the happy absence of any military memorabilia or weaponry), that this reaction of Laura's is hardly surprising or excessive, given the present, unsettling circumstances. One of which clearly being his arrival unannounced in this city once again and, more specifically, in Laura Griffin's own schoolyard.

Yet, paradoxically, Charles also reckons that in his own way he might just be the best thing that has happened to her recently (well, perhaps second best), even if she doesn't quite realise it yet. He is, however, starting to wonder why the hell he asked to meet her blessed children. What is he trying to prove?

Or – more obviously – who is he trying to persuade?

Laura is clearly thinking the same, as she silently questions herself on why she went and agreed to this exposure. This home-front threat. He can see it in her face, the anger and the fear, just before it changes to accommodate descending thumps on the staircase and the noisy arrival of her kids. Yet she knows him well enough, surely, that he is not going to give anything away, blurt out the big secret. At least she trusts him not to be that mean.

She hopes.

Jess and Henry's total indifference to meeting their new visitor is parried with a genuine, adult smile from Charles, one that this slightly intimidated guest dearly trusts is chock full of transatlantic bonhomie, whilst hopefully masking his surprise that the Griffin kids are of what he would call mixed race, but might be termed here what – multiracial? He hopes to God that they're not called anything else and realises how little he still really knows about the country and the state he is in.

"Guys – Jess, Henry – this is Charlie. Charles. Charles Dickens. From the UK."

"Yeah, right," says Jess Griffin.

"No, I really am from the UK. In fact, Scotland, originally."

"I meant about the name." The 'dickhead' remains unspoken.

Charles and Laura both laugh. "He knows what you meant, Jess. But sadly it's true. Blame his folks. Now you and Henry go upstairs and finish your homework, while I make dinner."

"I've done—" begins Henry.

"Well, go do some more, scoot. I'll call you when it's ready."

The kids trudge upstairs, looking puzzled. When he hears their doors shut, Charles looks at Laura. "You are scared I'll tell them, aren't you?"

"I have no idea what you'll do."

"Then why bring me?"

"Honestly – I do not have a clue. I'm not making the best decisions these days. Just help me chop some vegetables. It might be a change for you to feel useful."

When dinner is finally served and the four of them sit uneasily around the small table in the kitchen-diner, Charles has to concede that Laura is a pretty good cook. Admittedly, what they are eating is a leftover from something she had prepared over the weekend and of which the kids have probably already had their fill, but to the first-time guest it is as delicious as only home cooking can be. Depending, of course, in whose home it is being cooked.

Conversation isn't going down quite so easily, as the younger pair aren't asking him anything and a clearly nervous Laura is just chattering over-enthusiastically about Keeneland, to which the kids have been more than once, which was more than sufficient and which they had until now assumed was also way off their mother's radar. Not everyone is horsey in Lexington, even if the town is famous for it.

"This is delicious, Laura. What is it called?"

"We call it burgoo. It's very traditional. Folks got together to make it and bring their own ingredients. Y'know, squirrel, opossum, raccoon." The kids look at the confused man in their kitchen, as Laura smiles. "Don't worry, it's just chicken. With some lima beans, corn, okra... chipmunk."

"Well, it beats KFC," says Charles. "That's all I wanted last time I came here."

"Why've you come back?" asks Jess.

"*Jess!*" chides her mom, although she has herself been repeatedly posing the same question. Laura suddenly wonders if her daughter thinks that a new suitor has just been wheeled in for approval. She feels the urgent need to disabuse her swiftly and in every way that she can.

"*What?*" asks Jess, innocently. "I was like just, y'know, showing interest."

"And I'm glad you did, Jess," says Charles. "I've actually come to write a movie."

"Jesus Christ!" says Henry, excitedly, bits of traditional stew flying out of his mouth.

"*Henry!*"

"What? We're not religious."

"And *you* say it all the time," says Jess, defending her brother for once. "You only have to look at the kitchen clock in the morn—"

"Do you have delinquents in Glasgow?" asks Laura.

"I think you'll find we invented them. And at one time they were our major export."

"You're making a movie here?" says Jess, who doesn't want the conversation to move on before she has exhausted this hot item.

"Whoa. Hang on a wee bit, Jess. I have to write it first."

"And it's about you and Mom!" announces Henry, which stops the conversation dead in its tracks. Charles and Laura exchange looks, before realising that this only serves to confirm for her children what until now has just been a fishing trip.

"*What?* Who told you that?" says Laura, just a fraction late.

"Josh."

"*Josh?*" says Laura.

"*Josh?*" repeats Charles. "Who's Josh?"

"I work with his mom," explains Laura, with a sigh of resignation. "You met Kyra. The one who invited me to your reading. She's put two and two together—"

"And made six."

"You didn't hear the worst," says Laura. "She coaches in math."

If Laura thinks this touch of whimsy will halt her kids, she has sorely misjudged them.

"But you guys did date back in the old days," says Jess.

"When the world was in black and white," says Charles, which gratifyingly makes them laugh. Well, not all of them.

"We didn't 'date', Jess," insists her mom. "Charlie was Uncle Brian's exchange student."

"No wonder you stuck with Mom."

"Jess Griffin!" says Laura. "Sorry, Charlie."

"Och, not at all. I'm having fun. And the food is delicious."

"Better than haggis?" says Laura swiftly, hoping for a deft but almost unnoticeable change of subject.

"What's haggis?" asks Henry. Yess!

Charles turns to Henry and talks to him in a tone of extreme Caledonian seriousness. "You dinna ken what a haggis is? Och, Henry, it's only our national dish and a great Scottish delicacy to boot. Haggis, my young Kentucky friend, is animal heart, liver and lungs minced up with the finest oatmeal and suet, all wrapped up in a sheep's stomach." He watches their repelled faces carefully. "And you know what the hardest part of it is?" Jess and Henry shake their heads. "Getting the bloody sheep to eat it in the first place."

For a moment the children just stare at him. Then they burst out laughing and Laura finds that she has no choice but to join them. More burgoo comes out of Henry's mouth and nose, but this is probably excusable in the circumstances.

The conversation doesn't return to 1982, even though, listening to these spirited, youthful Kentucky voices, as he sits once again at a dinner table with Laura – albeit a greatly changed and some ways unrecognisable

Laura – a part of Charlie Dickens can't help feeling that he has never completely left.

*

The station wagon is well out of earshot and way out of her neighbourhood before Laura Griffin feels able to talk.

"So, you successfully ingratiated yourself with the junior Griffins," she says.

"I wasn't *trying* to ingratiate, Laura. I liked them a lot. They do you proud. I'm suspecting the next part will be a wee bit harder."

"Like gettin' the bloody sheep to eat it."

Charles says nothing more, until he recognises the Mary Todd Lincoln house, from their last cataclysmic encounter. He tries to sound a whole lot more casual than he feels. "Any clearer... on what you want to do?"

"Since four o'clock this afternoon? Curiously not, Charlie."

Not unnaturally, Charles assumes that the comment she has just delivered, in tones that no one could term collaborative, marks the conclusion of this particular conversation. He certainly doesn't know how to lead it anywhere the other party might happily wish to follow.

So he is more than a little surprised when, having finally parked the car outside The Morgan House, nodded to him to open the door and presumably get out of Dodge, Laura Griffin talks thoughtfully into her steering wheel.

"I think I want to meet her."

Prudently, especially for him, Charles doesn't say anything. He is already halfway onto the sidewalk when Laura turns to face him.

"It's just so scary, Charlie. For me and, of course, for her. But I have to, don't I? Now… now that she's asked."

Contorting his frame right round to her, as if he is trying to screw his entire body firmly into the tarmac, he simply nods. And holds his breath. He fears that anything he might say now could send her straight back to first position.

"On her home turf," she continues, talking to herself once again. "Thanksgiving's coming up. The kids are with their dad's folks in Maryland this year. They don't need to know anything. Not yet. And maybe not…" She simply stops but clearly the thinking goes on.

"Uh huh," says Charles, because he feels he has to say something and 'Maryland's supposed to be nice' would seem a bit irrelevant.

Actually, what he has been wanting to say since the moment they left her house is '*you never told me your ex-husband is black*', but as there is no earthly reason why she should have done so, nor that it should matter in any way whatsoever, he is rather glad and even proud that he has kept this observation unvoiced.

"Maybe she and I can just, y'know, have a coffee or something," says Laura, still half-talking to herself. "Somewhere safe. What do they call it – 'baby steps'?" At this, she begins to tear up and starts wildly to shake her head, as if trying to suck the loaded words back in.

She suddenly finds Charles back in the seat beside her and his door gently closing once more. "Laura – now

257

that you've come to your own decision, about what you have to do, which by the way I think is the right one, has to be the way to go – can I make just a wee suggestion?"

"Is it what I think it is?"

"Why don't we drive together? To Austin. I'll rent a car."

"Nope, that came outta left field." She gives a sigh that sounds suspiciously like despair. "Charlie—"

"Just hear me out, Laura. Please. It'll take, what, a couple of days?" He actually has no idea and waits for her to give him the driving times from Lexington, Kentucky, to Austin, Texas, allowing for Thanksgiving traffic, but she is remarkably unforthcoming. "Let's say a couple of long days. And, well, by the time we get there, we should know whether you want to do it as a double act or a single. I'll follow your lead. No pressure. Totally up to you. And up to her too, of course."

Laura says nothing but her silence says everything. Although nothing good. Finally she turns to him, wishing so much that he had stayed on the sidewalk.

"Are you serious? *Seriously, are you serious?* I haven't even spoken to her yet! I said baby steps, Charlie. Not baby friggin' mammoths! And why all did I just say that?"

"We shall never know. What's her name, by the way?"

"I have no idea. Oh, right, of course, authors. You need a name before you can move on with the plot."

"Doesn't everyone? Listen, Laura, there'll be absolutely no arm-twisting. I promise. You'll decide whether you even want to broach that I'm in the picture. *Back* in the picture." Her face hasn't altered one scintilla from when he made the first tentative suggestion. It is almost as if she has been replaced by a life-size pop-up of herself. Of herself with her mouth wide open in astonishment. "Oh, c'mon, she's bound to ask, isn't she? I mayn't be on the birth certificate but you're not the Virgin bloody Mary of Kentucky. So I'll... I'll just follow your lead."

This time her head-shakes have a totally new and disturbing rhythm, as if she is trying frantically to ground herself in a world that is spinning right off its axis. "I don't believe this! *A road trip!* A goddam, freakin' road trip! You're imagining it like... like it's a story. Like it's, I dunno, something out of a movie."

Charles shrugs. It is how he thinks, but he's sure as hell not going to admit it. Not that he needs to.

"And ooh, hey, maybe – who knows?" continues Laura, staring straight ahead. "We might get *kidnapped* by an evil Colombian drug cartel just outside of Bowling Green! Lotsa drugs in this state. Or whoa, one of us will topple into raging white-water rapids on the way – I'm sure we can find some – and the other must dive in to save them on peril of their life because they can barely swim! Or – *or* we'll realise that the past twenty-two years were no more than a fucking blip and just nothing compared to the lifetime of a Galapagos tortoise. This is my *life*, Charlie! More than half my past and possibly my future. Maybe even hers too, seriously doubt it, but who knows? You can just go back to... Glasgow. London. Madagascar. Wherever. Write your books. Your movies of your books. I've got kids. I—"

"So that's a no, then," deduces Charles.

Laura Griffin, teacher, homemaker, mom, who many years ago, in another life, another world, was a young, impressionable teenage girl called Laura Sherman, turns and stares at this almost total stranger, who is becoming stranger by the minute, in bemused amazement.

Charles alights from the station wagon once again. "I'll be around," he promises, or threatens. "For a while. Y'know. In case you, or indeed she… Thanks for the supper."

Laura doesn't know which of her available options – sitting in her family car outside his hotel, stationary and stunned, or driving smartly but furiously off, gears grinding – will give this intrusive, maddening, jabbering Charlie Dickens the deepest understanding of how she genuinely feels right now. Somehow, without any planning, she manages to do both and contrives to look to Charles, who somewhat forlornly watches her lurch bumpily away from The Morgan House, like a zombie who's just been given the keys to a brilliant but baffling new machine.

He hopes the mother of his child gets home okay.

*

When Laura Griffin returns to her home, quite safe but deeply shaken, there are fewer lights on. Without even thinking, she makes straight for her tiny ground-floor office, where naturally the first thing her eyes go to is the drawer lodging that printed letter. It seems to be taunting her from the darkness. She is about to release it and read it just once more, seeking a clarity that may have eluded her the last forty times round, when she hears a voice from the doorway.

"Are you two dating?" asks Jess.

Laura spins round to see her daughter – her *younger* daughter, she now surprises herself by thinking. The girl, small for her age but with a taut, athlete's body, is looking serious. More than serious – concerned. Or at least, thinks Laura, looking intrigued.

"We knew each other for three weeks, when we were seventeen," protests her mom. "Jess, come on!"

"Stacey says you should go for it."

"Tell Stacey thanks, I'll get back to her. Now scoot. I'll be up in a minute to drag you screaming away from your homework."

Jess nods, offers her mom a slight smile then turns and goes.

Once she has firmly closed the door, Laura Griffin moves slowly but decisively towards the desk.

THIRTY-FIVE

The amiable, white-haired proprietor of the BlueGrass Bookstore appears pleasantly surprised when he spots the only Scottish author he has ever met strolling in.

Charles is equally gratified that the patrician-looking southern gentleman, with his dapper waistcoat and only slightly affected pince-nez, should have recognised him so immediately. Without even a computer to guide him.

"Why, it's Mr C.D. MacNaughtan, isn't it?" announces the man over-loudly, causing patrons in the store to turn and stare with puzzled interest. "Did you fly thousands of miles back to us, just to see how your delightful book is selling?" He posits this latter question at an even greater volume, calculating that it may incite a sudden flurry of book-buying and possibly another few impromptu signings.

"Not exactly," admits Charles. "But now that I'm here…?"

The elderly gentleman gives his visiting author a reassuring thumbs-up. "So indeed, why *are* you here, sir?" he asks, not unreasonably.

"Well," says Charles, who has the stock answer so firmly lodged in his mind that he almost believes it. "I'm here on a sort of research trip. For the movie. Of the book."

The affable bookseller beams at his new favourite author. "Why, how very exciting. A movie, no less! Need any good diversions, while you're thinking? Something to fuel the creative fire?" He spreads his arms around his emporium, to emphasise the riches within, just waiting to be devoured. "*The Five People You Meet in Heaven* is our bestseller right now."

"Sounds uplifting." Charles laughs, wishing he could remember the dear man's name but knowing that it probably isn't Mr Bluegrass. He scans the shop, as his mind makes its own tour of possibilities. He is very partial to a hardboiled American police procedural.

"Actually – do you have any really decent road maps?"

*

It is some days later when Kyra Nordstrom catches her friend and colleague on the way to her car. She can tell that the poor English teacher looks frazzled.

Laura has indeed had a particularly difficult session with her ninth-grade class. As she explains, they have all been reading *The Sun Also Rises* and decided almost as one that they should write their essays with the stark simplicity of Hemingway. As an exercise in parody this most probably worked fine but stylistically it swiftly became repetitive and irksome. 'I had my nuts blown off and it was sore' was probably the worst of the culprits and she hasn't been in much of a mood for finding things amusing these days. Too tense, she supposes, although this would be an overshare for Kyra. A life once almost boringly predictable suddenly being lived on the edge. As her ninth-grade would say, it is hard.

"Did you know your guy is still in town?" asks Kyra.

"My guy?" repeats Laura, sounding disingenuous even to herself. She knows exactly to whom Kyra is referring but most certainly didn't know that he was still around. Damn the man. The information clearly unsettles her.

"Don't be coy, girl. Why's he still here?"

"Playing hard to lose? Oh, I don't know, Kyra. He's researching the movie of his last book. Or writing it. Or something. I haven't seen him since—"

"Everyone knows you're that girl in the novel," persists Kyra. "The one he has such a hard time getting over. Estella, right? Funny name."

"It's from *Great Expectations*," says Laura, a memory suddenly rushing up. That first day, the airport, those crinolines. Dear Lord! Was that really her?

"Uh huh," says Kyra, taking her word for it. "They say sequels are big these days."

"Not with me they ain't."

Laura is about to change the subject, just as soon as she can manage to think of one that has nothing to do with the current, mortifying discussion, when her cellphone rings. Kyra watches her friend with some concern, as the younger woman, usually so grounded and in control, suddenly begins to tremble.

"It's him, isn't it?" says Kyra, hoping that the concern

plastering her face will convincingly mask the all-consuming glee inside.

Laura Griffin shakes her head and moves briskly, definitively away from her inquisitive friend and her car.

"Hello?" she says quietly, when she is certain that she can't be overheard. It's a number she doesn't have on her phone, so it could be anybody. Only she knows that it isn't. "Yes. Yes, this is Laura Griffin."

When she hears the voice at the other end, a voice that in normal circumstances ought to be as familiar as her own but of course isn't recognisable at all, Laura knows that she has to sit down somewhere – anywhere – before she collapses. She is pretty sure that all the colour has left her face. She wonders if her legs can manage to deliver her to the nearest and lowest wall.

"Excuse me. Please. Sorry. I just need to… I have to…"

Laura Griffin knows that Kyra is still staring and coming to all sorts of erroneous but infinitely novelettish conclusions. Laura doesn't care. All she cares about is that she is shaking so much that she is more than likely to drop the phone onto something brutally destructive and never hear from the caller again.

"Hi there," she murmurs, shakily. "I'm so glad you called."

*

Later on that night, in fact so late it might already be classed as morning, a troubled Scotsman in a very tall bed in a very smart place receives a call that wakes him up and gives him the shock of his life.

"Yeah?" he burbles.

"Her name is Erin."

THE ROAD TRIP

THIRTY-SIX

The long road to Austin. November 2004

The rental car is smaller than Laura had expected.

She berates herself for thinking that Charles is a man of infinite funds. He is certainly a fellow of infinite surprises, which is something entirely different.

To her own surprise, as she watches him pull up, she recalls one of his earliest letters. A flowing, gushing airmail received in that brief, carefree time before she made the racking discovery that not all of him had departed Kentucky one late spring day. And before so many of these equally lovingly penned letters, which she now knows had indeed been mailed and were apparently beginning to express deep puzzlement over the total lack of response, somehow ceased to reach her sad but still yearning eyes.

He had joked that she shouldn't bother shaking the envelopes to see if any money or gifts fall out, because, Laura Sherman, you made the awful error of falling madly and deeply for a guy who was both Scottish *and* Jewish. As she had not even the vaguest clue what he was talking about, she had asked her mother. On that same day she learnt a new word, 'parsimonious', which she has read several times since but doesn't believe she has used even once. Nor does she believe the sentiment.

Laura has just a few remaining seconds to ponder on why her normally super-logical and sharply focussed mind is firing off in all directions like a Catherine wheel. She decides that it is because she is way beyond frantic this morning, utterly wrecked and totally hyper-anxious. She has made the most terrible mistake in agreeing to this insanity. Sharing possibly the single most pivotal moment in her entire life, or at least some crucial preliminary elements of it, with an almost total stranger – *what had gotten into her?*

Too late.

She has no choice now but to acknowledge the arrival of Charlie Dickens, in his small and, in her opinion, way too sporty rental car. She does so with the most cursory of greetings, hurling her large and seriously overpacked suitcase into the paltry trunk (what's the generally accepted outfit for meeting an adult daughter you haven't seen since birth?) and dumping herself into the vehicle that is growling inanely beside her. All the while silently offering a prayer for these potentially interminable days to pass.

And the car isn't even a colour she likes.

"I told myself again last night," she tells him, without any introduction, "right after I called you." To his surprise she comes to a definitive stop after this.

"Told yourself what?" asks Charles, reasonably, as the car moves off.

"Huh?"

"What did you tell yourself?" She looks at him as if he is the confusing one. "You said you told yourself something last night."

"Oh. Yeah. Well I did." She is certainly not going to apologise (or indeed admit that she, unlike the stupid car this guy has rocked up in out of nowhere, might not be firing on all cylinders right now). "I told myself that I should be taking a plane today. To Austin. *On my own!* And why did you get this car? Did you specify 'backbreakingly uncomfortable' and 'especially loud' or do these come as standard?"

"It was all they had. Other than the Chelsea tractors, which I hate." He senses her puzzlement. "You know – SUVs, the rugged, rough-terrain machines that mothers use for school trips down the road. So why aren't you?"

"Why aren't I what?"

They both already know that this has to be the most uncomfortable and stilted of conversations, and indeed they also know why, but neither has a clue how on earth to fix it.

"Going by plane." He feels that he is simultaneously taking leave of Lexington and his senses.

"I have absolutely no idea," admits Laura, staring out of her window at the landscape with which she has grown up: horse farm country, large houses, warm southern hearts and occasionally, she knows, small southern minds, but somehow safe, secure and lush. A landscape which right now, even in the late November sunlight, seems suddenly all too remote and threatening. As if the time is out of joint and the world no longer as it was. Quite possibly it never will be again.

"Maybe you felt bad towards me," suggests Charles.

"*Bad?*" She swivels and he knows he's going to get it directly into his right ear, which is not the normal aperture of chastisement for a British driver. "*Bad!* For my not telling you something way back in '82, even though Lord knows I might dearly have wished to, because I felt it could maybe screw you up too and it wasn't something you could do a damn thing about anyway? *Bad* – for finally moving on, after a pretty rough few years, and making my own life? Bad? We were seventeen, Charlie! If people even still call you Charlie."

"Perhaps I'm just more in touch with my feminine side." He doesn't see her face but he can hear the groan. "And Charlie's fine."

"Good. At least there's one thing that hasn't changed out of all recognition."

"Aye." Charles chooses not to explore whatever she has meant by this. He remains quiet for a moment, so that only the car appears to be carrying on the conversation.

The man seems to Laura to be composing his thoughts, attempting to find just the right words, which doesn't surprise her in the least, although she does wish he would get a move on and spit out what he has to say, so that they can get a quieter, more peaceful show on the road. "See, I thought I *had* moved on, Laura. Truly. Moved on from what happened. From… what I believed had happened. It was when the book kept writing itself over and over in my head over the years that I realised I still had some way to go."

"And when you wrote it…?"

"I reckoned 'job done'. Then I saw Abi, and I suppose it all just came shooting back – the full monty. The hurt, the 'betrayal', the lack of trust. And, of course, the loss."

Laura seems puzzled for a moment, until it clicks. "Abi's the girl who looked just like I used to – right? Well, apparently so. In your storybook mind. Let's just hope she has better luck than me when the rot sets in and she hits thirty-nine." She pauses for a moment. "You can contradict that if you like. I've left space."

Charles has the grace to laugh at this, before thinking that, whilst he hasn't driven in the States before, he vaguely recalls hearing that you can turn right on a red light here.

"*Whoa!*" yelps Laura, as cars behind him hoot angrily and he nearly gets hit by a massive horse box. "Wait until Texas for that one."

"Sorry," says Charles, a bit sheepishly, thrusting an apologetic hand out of his open window, to the driver and the horse. He recalls what they were just talking about. "You look fine, Laura. Honest. Barely changed." He ignores the snort. "And you're right, yes, I am a storyteller, a pretty good one by all accounts. Yet until that evening, the time back in April when I first saw her, Abi – it's short for Abigail – it had never ever occurred to me. Can you believe that? About the pregnancy – the baby."

"So basically you trusted the condom in your wallet more than the girl in your heart." He tries to protest but her voice just grows louder. "You just thought I was so skittish, so fickle and…and flibberty-gibbetty, that after a brief exchange of passionate and soul-bearing letters, swearing eternal love, I ticked you off my list, put Charlie Dickens right out of my little southern mind and happily glided on to someone else."

"…What else could I think? And… well, you did glide, didn't you?"

"Jeez! *Eventually!* People do, Charles. Well, some people."

"I know," he says, sadly. "Funny, I never expected…"

"That he'd be black?"

Charles had promised himself that this wouldn't figure in any conversation between them, yet somehow he always knew that it would. "I bet your parents were thrilled."

"You have no idea. I sometimes wonder if I—"

"Don't go there. You loved the guy and you share two terrific kids. Sometimes… things just don't work out."

There is something in the way he says this, however casual he may think that it sounds, which makes her turn to look at him. She can tell that he is aware of her look and is equally determined to ignore it.

"Hey, now that we've all this time," he announces, as they hit the Bluegrass Parkway, "and a thousand miles of possibly the world's most unchallenging roads – druggy Colombian bandits and treacherous rapids aside – why don't you start?"

"Start what?"

"You know, filling in the blanks."

"The blanks," says Laura, blankly.

"Yeah. Your life. Since I last saw you. Start at, say, 1983."

"You *know* what friggin' happened in 1983."

"Oh yeah."

They carry on driving for what seems like forever, in total silence. Charles has no idea what Laura is thinking. Indeed, he has very little idea of what he himself is thinking, as it appears to be a whirling kaleidoscope of half-familiar place names, half-baked memories and half-formed ideas, combined with the overwhelming tension of wondering if the woman beside him is ever going to unfreeze and let him in.

Dear Lord, he's not asking for a relationship, only for some basic understanding. And yes, acknowledgement. Of his part in the proceedings, in an albeit supporting yet still pivotal role. It is only when they see signs to Mammoth Cave – Charles has no idea whether this is a spur or mere coincidence – that his travelling companion starts to speak.

"O-kay," sighs Laura Griffin, eventually, as if she has been beaten into submission. "But if you whip out your pencil, mister, I'm breaking the 'bloody' thing off."

THIRTY-SEVEN

"So I came back home from Ohio – not long after the birth. Erin's birth. Can't believe I actually know her name now. *Oh God!* ...Sorry. Good name too. Pretty. No reason to stay there any longer, was there? In Ohio. And I knew French by then! So we all kinda pretended absolutely nothing had happened. Which was weird. Except they had to put up with my frequent crying, wailing like a banshee more like, and, of course, little stuff like wanting to die."

"Did you ever think of actually—"

"Was I talking?" says Laura.

"Sorry. Please – carry on. You were wanting to die."

"I *know* where I'd got to – don't need a friggin' prompt." She ignores his sighs and the fact he is making a gesture to God knows who, maybe the Lord himself, that involves his taking both hands off the wheel and spreading them out in despair.

"I was wanting to die. *Okay?*" she continues. "But eventually, after some pretty good therapy and when it looked to people that I had no more tears left – ha, like that happened! – I resolved to, what do the kids say, 'man up' and go to school right here in my hometown. Life had to go on, didn't it? And it's a good school. UK. University of Kentucky. They have an excellent fallen women's program."

Charles knows better than to comment or to interrupt. He has always thought that Laura had a good sense of humour, but back in the day it was far more about her appreciating his wit than responding with her own, which he imagines goes the same for most young men and a serious proportion of the older ones. He wonders if he will ever be able to find humour in his own adversities and would have to admit he hasn't done such a great job of it so far. He also realises that his mind has wandered off again and begins to wonder about his own mental state.

"Of course my folks were keeping a careful watch on me," she continues, without any audible hint of bitterness. "Brian was too, God bless him, when he wasn't off sowing his own seeds. He wanted to kill you, by the way. Oh and re: the careful watch – we are talking nunnery here. As overseen by the Gestapo. Say hi to the Hester Prynne of Lexington. It wasn't exactly how I'd pictured my late teens."

It is several seconds before Charles concludes that Laura has ended this chapter of her story or at least taken a serious pause. He decides to leave her to her own thoughts, which have probably once again been uncomfortably stirred up by the narrative, as if they weren't already on the cusp of boiling over. He can only imagine what is going on in her head and knows that he is still hitting nowhere near the reality.

Time now to admire the rolling and far from unpleasant Kentucky countryside and to muse, as he often does, on how he might describe it, should this be necessary. He reckons that he would afford it much the same treatment as he did the varying locales of his latest book, which was sufficient to give his readers a decent sense of where they were, without burdening them with a feature worthy of *National Geographic*, one that simply steered them away from the momentum of his tale.

Yet there was no road trip for him to navigate and chronicle on that earlier tumultuous voyage of discovery. No thousand-mile drive for sixteen hours over major and predictably massive roads, some of which, when converging, will probably look as if they were knitted together by a gaggle of demented urban tricoteuses, if pictures he has seen of American junctions are anything to go by.

Through Kentucky and Tennessee, Arkansas and Texas, legendary states all, making for iconic cities that he has always wanted to visit – Nashville, home of country music (which he now recalls he can't actually abide and appears to be on every radio station he can currently pick up), Memphis, mecca of blues, soul, rock and, of course, the King – and totally bypassing them all. Without, he guesses, catching even a whiff of their flavour or what makes them so unarguably great.

From the maps he had noticed that the optimal route to Austin passes through wildlife refuges, parkland and national forests, but he is beginning to realise that whilst there may be some wonderful green stuff and far from lonesome pines way off on either side of him, there is plenty enough on which to concentrate closer to home, what with the unfamiliar driving (which even back in his own 'hood', living as he does near the heart of London, he very seldom attempts) and whatever conversation his clearly anxious passenger might wish to share with him.

Perhaps selfishly, as he himself would acknowledge, Charles wonders how much Laura is even thinking about what's going on for *him* right now. Has she the least sense of his own inner turmoil? He also wonders if she is regretting, with every driven mile, that their paths once again have crossed. Maybe she is still mystified that somebody whom in truth she barely knew when she knew him, and about whom she knows even less now that she doesn't know him, has somehow oiled and insinuated his way into joining her, at least for part of the way, on this inevitably life-changing and quite possibly earth-shattering journey.

Well, too bad, Erin is his bloody daughter too.

He wishes now that he could slip out of this cursed Interstate, just for a while, and into something more comfortable, like a familiarly narrow, badly marked British road, with passing places and dry-stone walls and tractors. So, when he spots a sign saying Glasgow, he practically leaps over the other lanes to get to it.

"*Hey!* Where do you think you're going?"

"There's a place here called Glasgow!"

"And?"

Fair point, thinks Charles. "I just thought... a change of scene. A smaller road."

"We're not on a goddam sightseeing trip! And even if we were, Glasgow would be a hell of a curious place to start."

"Maybe not for a—"

"*Even* for a Glaswegian." She looks at Charles and can tell that the man is disappointed. "Hey, I know these roads are boring as hell. I'd share the driving with you, but I don't think I'm in a safe place right now and I hate this shitty car. But tell you what – tonight, rather than getting stuck in some big city, which could take us hours to navigate our way round and even longer to escape out of, maybe we can just drive off to somewhere small and find a cheap motel or something. So at least you can get a break from the endless freeways. Deal?"

Charles nods and takes advantage of this unexpected but welcome diversion into a far more cordial zone. "So you studied what – English, at uni? Er... university."

"I *know* what frickin' 'uni' is!" So much for cordiality. "Yeah. English. And, of course, I loved it. I suppose after that I just wanted to pass the love on, so I got my teacher certification. Did my field practice at the same high school I went to as a kid. The very one you were skulking around outside of."

"I wasn't exactly skulk... *Pygmalion*!"

"Excuse me?"

"Don't you remember? You took me to see it at your school. Their English accents were terrible."

"Yeah, well, I doubt the high school of Glasgow doing a great Kentucky play would have given Professor Higgins a hard-on."

"Depends on the great Kentucky play. Which one?"

"…Not relevant."

"Do you not remember that night, Laura? After the play, when we first…?"

Laura seems suddenly uneasy. Or even more uneasy. When she next speaks, it sounds as if she is toppling over her words, like logs in a fast-flowing river, in a rush to get to the next sentence, the next year, the next rest of her life.

"It was at UK – 'uni' of Kentucky, not the United Kingdom – that I met Colin. You know, my husband. Ex-husband. The black one." It is Charles's turn to ignore this. "He came here, to the university, to do his PhD. He's a biochemist. We met in the library, of all places. UK has a great library. Famous. Anyway, naturally my folks thought I married him just to spite them. First a half-Jew knocks me up and then… But I really don't think I did. Hope I didn't. Glad I never told them about Osama Bin Laden's cute cousin."

She gives a tiny laugh, so Charles does too. Which he would have done anyway but right now he is finding it safer to take all his cues from her.

"Nothing really awful happened. In case you were wondering. The first years of marriage weren't bad at all. Not easy, how many young marriages are, but fine. Colin was a good father. *Is*. He still is. And a good man. We just grew apart, is all. The way folks do." She shakes her head, as if it's full of tiny whirling balls and little holes and she has to slot the one into the other, one ball at a time, in order to put things in order. "I guess there really isn't so much more to tell. A pretty uneventful life, I imagine, at least compared to yours. Save of course for… you know.

'Laura Sherman, the blunder years'. Even if the marriage was rocky at times, my kids, my job, my home, my friends have all brought me contentment. That sounds so mealy-mouthed, doesn't it? They've brought me joy. Truly. But maybe sometimes I'm scared to admit it, even to myself, because then it might all be taken away."

"So, you're happy, Laura."

She pauses for a moment, but Charles isn't certain whether she's contemplating the nuances of her answer or the impropriety of his question.

"Happy? ...Sure," she says, thoughtfully. "Well, least I was, until..."

"Until I came along and rippled the calm Kentucky waters. It wasn't me who sent you that letter, you know. About Erin. Which I'm betting you still have with you."

"Some people would call that coincidence. You coming back right now. Needing to find her, so soon after she decides she wants to find me. Maybe that's all it was. Coincidence. Happens far more than we think. But, you know, Charlie – okay, maybe this is all too new-agey for you – but I sometimes believe there are energies at work here. Energies we all send out and pick up. Right across the globe." She appears to be talking to herself now, convincing herself. "Energies swirling all about. Energies that no one can see or feel or even sense – certainly can't be measured like... well, like your electricity or your gas – yet they carry their own unique force with them, their own power, and it's only afterwards we start to wonder *what the hell...?* Could be I sent some extra-special energies out this year. It being twenty-one years on. It's possible, isn't it?"

"Could be I did too," adds Charles, a bit petulantly, wanting his own energetic efforts to be taken into consideration. "Laura, I can sometimes walk into a place, I dunno, maybe a wee café or a pub, even one of the museums, or… aye, somewhere outside, like a garden or a park, and I'll think, hey, I can write here. This has good – sounds corny – good 'vibes'. I can sit here and the words will come." He thinks for a moment and is suddenly saddened. "Well, at least I used to be able to. But it could well be, as you say, energies. I can buy that, just about. Even worked for me once at Highgate Cemetery. Until it got chilly. And dark. So, do you date a lot?"

"Wow! That was left field. None of your bloody business." Charles just shrugs and the silence appears to last a good portion of whatever state they are in. Until something, who knows what, causes her to answer the question he has almost forgotten that he asked or even why he asked it. "Sure, I've dated since Colin and I split. Good guys. Decent people. But nothing serious or lasting. Maybe I'm just happier with my own company. You get set in your ways after a while, don't you think?" Before he can answer, she carries on. "I don't mean calcified. More like… well, comfortable."

"I'm not sure I've ever felt comfortable," says Charles. Sensing her eyes on him, expecting some elaboration, he checks out the road signs with a new intensity. They all appear to be telling him to go straight ahead until forever. "You just carry on. With the story so far."

Even though Laura Griffin reckons that, in truth, she has precious little to inform her inquisitor about herself, or at least not much that she really wants to hear herself saying or have this guy knowing, she does still manage to puncture the silence with occasional sharp little memories, which her companion of the moment might find vaguely interesting. Or which, perhaps by their relative novelty, will evade her own jaded disinterest and help just a bit to quell the maelstrom building inside her with every mile, threatening her small and currently quite vulnerable frame.

"I'll say one thing for you, Charlie Dickens – you're a good listener."

From the driver's seat come a loud snoring.

"Oh, very friggin' witty," says Laura Griffin, digging into her voluminous bag. "I made some sandwiches, cold cuts, so we don't have to stop at fried roadside hell. Want one?"

THIRTY-EIGHT

It is just beyond Little Rock, Arkansas – a city that Charles is convinced features in an old but popular song he struggles vainly and perhaps unnecessarily to remember – that he decides he has done enough driving and passed enough oversized trucks and over-disciplined motorists for a day and perhaps a lifetime. (He has found himself almost longing for discourteous, tailgating, lane-leaping Brits.) They have to find somewhere off the beaten track to rest up, refuel and resume their reminiscing and squabbling and lack of any meaningful connection face to face.

"Seems like there's some small towns just off the 365," offers Laura helpfully, examining the map. A piece of paper falls out of it, which she recognises as a receipt from the BlueGrass Bookshop. "Jeez, how many maps did you buy! And *three* guides to Texas?" Charles just shrugs. "I thought *I* was anal."

"Just searching for somewhere to stay that didn't look too ropy."

"'Ropy'? Okay. But no funny business with the room arrangements."

"Why, scared you'll get pregnant? I'm bloody over you, Laura!" he responds with unnecessary vigour. "Now you just have to get over yourself."

Charles has absolutely no idea why he said this or indeed whether either of them needed so tart an exchange at all. He isn't even certain why he is still quite so angry with this woman. Obviously he is anxious and frustrated – who wouldn't be? He would prefer, however, to justify the ire still-simmering inside of him as a simple reaction to her own palpable anger. Anger at his reckless muddying of the waters, at his unwanted involvement in what should simply be a fraught yet hopefully heartwarming mother-and-child reunion. (A reunion, he would hasten to point out, that he has been more than instrumental in encouraging.)

Yet he does wonder somewhere – and this is a thought he would far rather park than entertain – whether a large part of his own disgruntlement might simply be because this person, this Laura Griffin, has the effrontery not to be the sweet and gentle seventeen-year-old Laura Sherman he left behind so long ago. At least left behind physically. The one still doggedly taking squatter's rights inside his head.

After all, he tells himself quite sternly, he should hardly still be feeling raw from that sudden and inexplicable dumping back in '82, because there now appears to be an almost textbook explanation. One he should patently have been onto. To his relief, as he drives, he feels able to start dialling down the resentment.

But hang on, he suddenly thinks, *what has been bloody stopping her from telling me the truth since then?*

In all the ensuing years, decades that he's been plenty old enough to take it, didn't he have the *right* to know that somewhere out there he has a child? A daughter. Who is now a grown-up herself. And who they both now know is Erin something or other. From someplace.

Charles feels himself getting royally pissed off all over again.

Perhaps it is exactly this silent and suppressed rage that is causing him to reject every motel they spot on the road until, after forty-two more miles of less than perfect driving into deepest Arkansas, which to Charles doesn't look much different from deepest anywhere else, although perhaps slightly less safe and a bit more depressing, Laura tells him that even if the next place is a condemned crack house with a communal, open-air john, they're taking it.

The Starshine Motel exceeds all these rigorous specifications. Or near enough. Charles is so relieved simply to park the car and unfold his aching body out of its triangle of pain that he only wishes for a matter of seconds that he were back in his comfy, three-storey bed in The Morgan House. Although this dream does return quite vividly, when they open the door to the converted garden shed that serves as motel reception and it wobbles precariously on its single hinge until it just hangs there like a threat.

"Welcome to The Starshine Motel, folks," says the sweet-faced, elderly lady behind the desk, in the deepest female voice Charles believes he has ever heard. "Where you can enjoy the fall from your private balcony."

"She means autumn," explains Laura to a momentarily confused Charles. The lady is seriously engrossed in a well-thumbed paperback and, before looking up, has to fold over one of the corners quite tightly – its many predecessors remaining equally ruckled – so that it looks almost like an exercise in origami.

The woman notices Laura trying to ease the door back into place. "Don't you worry about that door, hon. Been meanin' to get it fixed. I told the owner we should get us one of them automatic ones, but I won't say what he told me to do with myself. Room 15 is free. It's our most romantic, 'cos of the stream that runs right down below it."

"*We want separate rooms!*" insist the newcomers in unison.

The lady appears quite alarmed at this, as if she is being harangued by two vocal representatives of a new and threatening cult of celibacy. She takes off her reading glasses, so that she can examine them with long-sighted suspicion.

"We're brother and sister," says Laura swiftly, with a disarming smile, before Charles can make up some ridiculously arcane explanation or, worse still, tell the old dear to mind her own effing business. The motel clerk sighs with relief.

"Well, isn't that nice? I can see the resemblance now. Can I get you both to do some signing?" She thrusts an old-fashioned ledger towards them.

Charles, who looks less like Laura than anyone he

can think of, approaches the desk. "By the way, is there anywhere to eat around here? Somewhere that doesn't involve more driving."

The woman pauses in her scrabble for keys and stares at him oddly for a long moment before she speaks. "Well... well, I'll say there is. Look no further than the Corner Diner. It's... oh, you can't miss it. It's..."

"On the corner?" ventures Laura.

"How come you two speak so different?" the woman asks, warily. "Being kin and all."

"I was adopted at birth and taken far far away," explains Charles, instantly. "We've only just magically discovered each other."

He decides to ignore the groan beside him.

The excited clerk lays out two clunky metal keys. "I seen a programme on that very thing! You should tell the TV folks. They would love you. Pay you a fortune too."

"We might just do that," says Laura, snatching her key and walking towards the door of danger.

The last puzzling words the elderly motel clerk hears, as she returns to her kitty-cornered book, will confuse her all the way to bedtime.

"*I cannot believe you said that!*"

*

Half an hour later, tempers appear slightly less frayed.

Charles meets his long-lost sibling coming out of the room next to his own, in the rundown, two-storey building. She is waving her hand, not as a greeting but in some way to disperse or at least indicate the fumes she has encountered within.

"Aye," says Charles, with a nod, "curiously, mine wasn't strewn with rose petals either. Let's hope the Corner Diner saves the day."

"The name alone conjures up all the mystique and elegance of Belle Époque Paris." Charles just looks at her in astonishment. "I'm an English teacher, Charlie. I do read. *Seriously?*"

"Sorry. So, are you up for whatever delights Mr and Mrs Corner can provide?"

"Tempting, I'll admit. But only if you fill me in on your own history since we last 'stepped out'. You've been *way* less... forthcoming. And, by my reckoning, it's your turn."

After a few minutes and with a firm eye on the uneven tarmac beneath their feet, Charles talks quite quietly, without looking at her. "I may omit or fabricate the odd thing. And, y'know, embellish. To make me look better."

"You're a bestselling author, writing a major movie. How bad can it be?"

"I impregnated a wee seventeen-year-old American girl, then didn't speak to her for twenty-two years."

"Now you're just making that up."

THIRTY-NINE

The Corner Diner lives up to its name in almost every way.

Charles is disappointed that there aren't the traditional, red-checkered tablecloths and that there is no sign of a jukebox, but there is a fake-marble lunch counter with tall, uncomfortable stools, barnacled with discarded and now-solidified chewing gum, plenty of snug little plasticky booths, those traditional napkin and ketchup dispensers, and a smiley waitress called Darlene with a serious amount of piled-up white-blonde hair and a pencil behind her right ear. The fact that she is a dental student in her final year and just helping her parents, who own the place, is slightly chastening, but he can live with it.

They are well into their meal before he decides to talk – which happily coincides with Laura being even remotely capable of listening.

Charles had no idea how ravenous he was until he saw the menu (realising on receipt that he had read and written shorter books) and knew that he had immediately to find something on one of its many colourful pages that was both sizeable and speedy. Laura, who had been equally famished, assured him that he would have no trouble round here with the size part and indeed the juicy steak he is demolishing, whose photo should have come with a scale or a comparative object, such as the Statue of Liberty, turned out to be slightly larger than his head.

"I did become a lawyer, after uni, as predicted," he says, when his stomach eventually allows him to speak and the food remaining on his plate bears some resemblance to a normal, as-yet-untackled meal. "But I'm afraid I was total rubbish at it."

"At least you made your parents proud," says Laura, whose own meal is also a thing of substance, with fries.

"Aye. Well, until I got sacked for inappropriate behaviour. That sort of took the edge off it." Laura doesn't know how to respond to this, so she doesn't. "I had an affair with a client. When I was sorting out her divorce. Och, don't make that face, Laura! I was very young. And she was very... We do law as a first degree in the UK. Straight from school." He realises immediately how pathetic this sounds.

"Yes, okay. Sorry... about the face. I was picturing my own lawyer. Yucch."

Charles returns to his steak, determined that a huge slab of southern cow won't defeat him. "And then I applied for a creative traineeship in a major London ad agency – happily, they liked my copywriting and my profound superficiality – so I moved over the border. *Well* over. Bit daunting at first – well, more than a bit –

not the friendliest city on earth, but gradually I got into the swing of things. You know, selling people things they never knew they wanted or needed. You probably still remember my slogan for Finnish Airlines – '*Disappear into Finnair*'… Er, that was a joke…"

When he glances up again, Laura's face has taken on a look unlike any he might reasonably expect a cod slogan or a youthful peccadillo to provoke.

"Charles, I have to ask you something – something that has been on my mind for some while."

"Ask away, Laura. It's what this 'trip' is all about, isn't it?"

"Please tell me you didn't sleep with that young woman."

For a moment Charles is genuinely confused. Yet even when the confusion clears, he resolves that some semblance of it should remain.

"…What young woman?"

"I think you know which one, Charlie. The girl in New England. The girl you thought looked like me. Like I used to look. Possibly." Charles's involuntary hesitation is all the confirmation she needs. "*Oh my God!* Oh jeez!"

"Laura—"

"Talk about *arrested* development. Yours… yours isn't just arrested, it's found guilty as charged and sent down for frickin' life. *Who are you, Charlie?* How does someone who can write so maturely about love and relationships still remain such a… *Oh my God!*"

Charles is thrown by both the vehemence and the incision of her response. As are those suddenly fascinated customers around him. He finds himself unable to form any sort of suitable denial or, as it already appears far too late for that, at least some modicum of justification.

"Laura, it was a… I didn't… And she wasn't a 'girl'…"

"No? *She was young enough to be your daughter!*"

"She was a grown woman of twenty-four, actually. Our daughter, as you may recall, is barely twenty-one." Charles realises, as he says this, that he is only digging himself in deeper. "Anyway, to use a phrase I recently heard somewhere, what bloody business is it of… So, would you like to hear some more about the years in-between? Or at least the early ones. How I got out of advertising and into novel-writing? I know it's a bit late and we've come way further off the main roads than intended. But we've a whole other day's driving to get through."

His face becomes infinitely more sad as his voice lowers. He stares at her fearfully, willing her to look at him. And to understand. But his dining companion has her eyes fixed firmly on her half-cleared plate.

"And, well, there are a few wee things – important things, Laura – I'm thinking I do still need to tell you."

Laura doesn't respond. Perhaps she has stopped listening. Or perhaps she simply doesn't want to know.

They finish the meal in silence and don't even check out the seven full-colour pages of tempting Corner Diner desserts.

*

There are just two lights still on in the Starshine Motel this midnight and they are in adjoining but not interconnecting rooms.

In one basic and unprepossessing bedroom, with for some reason a poor reproduction of Edward Hopper's *Nighthawks* nailed to the wall, in tones that unimaginably render it even more bleak, Charles lies awake, laptop on his knees above the fraying blanket, feeling utterly alone and unusually perturbed. Especially after the silent stroll back to their lodgings last night.

He looks to the wall between his and Laura's room and wonders if she is equally restless and troubled. He also wonders if she is spending the night with a rendition of the same or another equally gloomy example of American realism, like perhaps that stern old couple with the pitchfork. The woman, as he recalls, had a face, or at least wore an expression, not unlike the one latterly adopted by Laura Griffin at the Corner Diner.

It takes only the slightest nudge of memory to remind him that they had been in similarly adjoining rooms once before, on those precious and all-too-short weeks he spent in the Sherman House. He can hardly believe how different are the emotions in play this time round.

Laura, awake in her own lumpy bed, is not thinking of the past at all. Only of the future. In her hand she holds the original printed letter, which she reads one more time, as if there is a code encrypted within it that will tell her more than the brief, sterile words in type could ever impart.

When she has read the final and not over-significant last line for the umpteenth time, she turns to stare at her side of the same bland wall that has momentarily captured her neighbour's gaze. Yet her curiosity leans less towards what the aberrant Scotsman might be thinking at this very moment and more in the direction of what the hell has he been thinking all these years?

FORTY

The one thing about Arkansas, decides Charles, although he is certain that The Natural State (as the large 'Welcome' signs proudly proclaim) has far more in store to excite the jaded visitor, is that the mornings are gorgeous. At least this morning is.

The fall colours, in the middle distance just beyond the road on which they arrived, are quite spectacular in the early daylight. Recognising the maple and having a guess at dogwood, he berates himself for having failed to notice the obvious variety and technicolour richness of the foliage on most of the way here. He now recalls that there was indeed some distraction from the endless green but his head was too deep in his own particular and often threatening clouds fully to appreciate it. He intends to make up for it now, on this final day of their drive. (Laura had already specified before leaving home that she would be returning from Austin by plane, in time to meet her Lexington kids.)

But, of course, he must make up with Laura first,

which he reckons could lay claim to his most conciliatory words and the best part of this splendid morning. Although what his past or even current behaviour has to do with Laura Griffin of Lexington, Ky, and why she should have been quite so outraged, is still, to him, rather questionable.

Before knocking on her door, as he had promised to do after their uneasy silence last night, Charles has to admit to himself that his chances of meeting his daughter any time soon – and indeed of Laura even telling Erin anything that would make his identification a possibility – have diminished from an already less-than-promising base. And because his paternity is probably unrecorded, without Laura he would most likely never find the young woman again, however rigorously he might investigate. He certainly has no more details than her first name. There are probably legions of Erins studying at the massive University of Texas in Austin, and the way Laura is right now, or at least was when he left her last night, she could spin any number of yarns about him to the one Erin that matters. 'Your father's the only immature bastard in this scenario' could well be the words to seal his fate.

It is as if she has been unable to find a suitable biological father for a child that has already been born.

He tries to render his first wake-up knock as full of contrition and good fellowship (and lack of anything even hinting at the predatory) as his simple Scottish knuckles can convey.

After a good few seconds, when his remorse code has provoked no response, Charles knocks again and addresses the peeling door with her name. He takes a few breaths then proceeds to do the same again, only louder and with maybe a slight urgency creeping into the mix.

He notices that other motel residents, either returning from the reception hut or re-packing their cars, are watching him with a mixture of fascination and compassion.

"Laura…? Good morning. Time to go, Laura. Maybe pick up some breakfast on the way. *Laura*…?"

Wondering if she has taken herself on an early morning stroll – and why wouldn't she, on this fresh, crisp start to such an important day? – he walks as casually as he can across the crunchy gravel towards reception.

Once he has navigated the potentially lethal doorway, he notices that the clerk behind the desk this morning is a long-bearded, grey-haired man about the same age as the lady of last night. For some reason he wonders if they might be a couple. Like the 'mom 'n' pop' Corner diner, perhaps the Starshine is a 'mom 'n' pop' motel and that talk of the absentee 'owner' was just that.

The old guy gives Charles a friendly nod.

"Hi. Morning," says Charles. "The lady in number 14. Have you seen her at all? Maybe going out for a wee stroll."

"Hey, you're the long-lost brother! My old lady talked about you."

Charles just nods, silently congratulating himself on his deduction. He is about to ask again, when the clearly intrigued clerk-of-the-daytime leans over the desk as if to scrutinise his unusual guest more rigorously.

"Your accent… I meet a lot of foreign folks… well, mostly outta state… but I just can't place it."

"What does that…? It's Scottish. I'm Scottish. Can you just…?"

"*Scottish?* Whoa! We sure don't get many Scottish people here. Although I do like a drop of the Scotch. Prefer it to bourbon to be frank with you, but don't tell anyone. Wouldya mind sayin' something else?"

"Excuse me?"

"In Scottish. Go on."

Charles leans over until he can smell the older man's breath, which is not the freshest smell this fall morning. The accent he adopts is one from his Glasgow youth, or almost a parody of it, which he and his schoolmates would take on, when they were being wee hard-men in the playground.

"Do ye want yer fuckin' teeth to play wi', pal?"

The elderly clerk takes two steps backwards. "She left about an hour ago. I called her a cab."

"*A cab!*" says Charles, in more modulated, genteel tones, yet the astonishment is almost as formidable. "Where to – the airport?"

"What airport? We got a small rail station not too far away. Don't get many trains though. They're thinking of closing—"

"Austin. She's going to Austin."

"Austin, Texas? I hear that's a nice town. Pretty expensive, by all counts. Well, good luck with that. She didn't tell you – that she was going?" Charles shakes his head. "Kinda says to me she didn't want you to know. By the way, you speak English real good." Charles nods in gratitude, without thinking. "Watch out for that door when you leave. We keep tellin' old Mr Starshine to fix it."

FORTY-ONE

"So I wrote my first book when I was still in advertising. A number of copywriters have done the same. Maybe it's the long lunch hours. Or just wanting to pen something a client doesn't bloody fart around with. Look at Scott Fitzgerald or Salman Rushdie. Mind you, we're not all of us *that* brilliant…"

The car is moving at some speed, as Charles retraces his steps back to the Interstate. He pays even less attention to the November foliage this time round, even though the trees have been favourably late this year in strutting their variegated stuff. This resumption of his life story is intended to be ironic, as the only thing sitting next to him on the sporty car's bucket-like seat is his collection of maps and guidebooks, courtesy of a delighted BlueGrass Bookstore. There is, of course, no one other than Charles to appreciate the irony, but for a writer this is sometimes sufficient.

"Of course, you don't want to know any of this," he adds, "or you wouldn't have buggered off at lark's vomit this morning, without even a note." He is on a roll now, as he overtakes another gargantuan truck and breaks another speed limit. Not that he has any idea what the speed limit is, but he can tell by his fellow motorists' shaking heads that it is considerably less than what he is achieving. "But you don't escape that easily, Laura, on your 'griffin-like' wings. And what's it to you who I bloody sleep with? You're not my girlfriend. You're not even my friend."

A thought suddenly gallops into his mind, one which upsets him so profoundly, even as it shoots nauseating darts of fear up from his stomach into his throat. He feels himself sweating and his hands go clammy on the wheel.

"*Just please don't tell Erin!*"

He tries to calm himself down. "If you even bloody mention me to Erin at all, that is. It means 'Ireland', by the way. Wonder if her parents are Irish. Her adoptive parents. They'd be gratified to know that their gift of a girl really does have a respectable chunk of Celt in her DNA."

Charles decides that he has done enough of his perturbingly familiar 'talking to no one' and has heard that they don't do irony in America anyway, so he switches on the car radio. Only to discover that almost every station is still relentlessly playing Country 'n' Western music.

He makes a unanimous decision to revert to irony.

*

The Amtrak train is moving at an unimpressive speed, a victim of its own nineteenth-century pioneering spirit. A spirit that laid out tracks across the land with righteous zeal, enabling bustling cities to grow up around it but spawning a network sorrowfully unsuited to a twenty-first-century demand for travel that is straighter, faster and a good deal more comfortable.

Laura Griffin sits on the train, almost grateful for its slowness and its rattle, wanting to cry but having either no tears left or not even the strength to shed them.

Her eyes wander down to her bag, which the kids are forever joshing her about, because of its resemblance to the one used by Mary Poppins. More than once Jess has asked her, when they've been together on a vacation, if she could borrow the coat stand for a while. Laura digs deep inside it now and fishes out her copy of Charles's latest book.

She wonders why, at the last minute, she has grabbed *The Forever Moment* from her bedside and dropped it in. She also wonders why it has remained by her bed for so many months, but puts it down to a single mom's 'my room, my rules' rather than anything more symbolic.

The book might possibly serve, she had thought when she packed it, to show Erin who her father was. And still is. Should the appropriate moment present itself. But right now she is having second, third and fourth thoughts about providing her newly found daughter with any such definitive clue. Being impregnated at seventeen, however, by a total stranger, whose name and provenance she has somehow completely forgotten, doesn't speak wonders for her character or her judgment.

Perhaps there is a middle ground: I only ever knew his first name – he specifically wanted nothing to do with

303

his child, he died at sea. (She also knows that her having never even attempted to *tell* the father, over two decades, that he had a child somewhere might not exactly help to seal that precarious bond with her rediscovered daughter, the belated connection for which she is so desperately praying.)

It's a quandary, as is having the infernal man so unexpectedly back in her life, stirring things up, meeting her children, stalking her goddam schoolyard. A man who is disturbingly still bewitched not by the woman she is but by the naïve teenage girl she was. (If indeed she ever *was* that girl.) A man whom she tells herself she has managed, with some admitted early difficulty, to relegate to the past, only to have him rudely interrupting her future. And reminding her so heartlessly of all that she has lost, of who she isn't but might have been yet patently can't be any more.

Inside the back cover of the book she sees the two pieces of paper that she must have slipped in there. She finds that she can't even recall doing so, having clearly been in such an anxious state. Removing the top one, that first and by now quite crinkled official letter, she sets it on the small table in front of her to pore over yet again.

Her mind goes back once more, as she almost knew that it would and perhaps right now even wishes it, to the time of Erin's birth. A time when she hadn't even considered names, because really, what was the point? A time when she was knowingly growing and nurturing someone else's child.

Her own mom is sitting beside her in that tiny hospital room, looking in at least as much anguish as the young mother-to-be. Perhaps, thinks Laura as she revisits it, the older woman was in even worse torment, due to the added element of shame. A shame Laura couldn't honestly find it in herself to feel, despite every encouragement.

The midwife is there, of course, kindly yet ever so discreetly disapproving. To Laura's mortification her father is also in attendance, although he is not her obstetrician. (Nor, indeed, any sort of obstetrician.) He hovers sternly around, waiting like an impatient courier for the package to be placed in his hands for seamless onward delivery.

Whatever the agony of the birth, and she recalls there was plenty, it is soon to be outdone in intensity as the newly born child, a perfect but still anonymous baby girl, is abruptly seized and transported away.

Laura returns the innocuous yet life-changing letter to the safety of the novel's back cover. A glossy flap of shiny paper which gives inordinately little away about the creator. Which could be the ideal template for what she intends to do tomorrow.

She slings the book back into her voluminous bag.

FORTY-TWO

Austin, Texas. November 2004

Whenever Charles has heard it spoken of, although this is far from frequent, Austin is described in terms that distinguish it from the state in which it happens to find itself, rather than as the capital and proud embodiment of the same.

"Oh, Austin's not like Texas," people have said to him, when the city came up in conversation, perhaps with reference to the South by Southwest music and movie festival, the world-renowned Austin City Limits or the flagship University of Texas with its famous tower, but more generally in terms of its character and outlook. "And people even walk here," they add, to elevate it above Houston or Dallas. Despite being the state capital, it appears to Charles to exist in a state all of its own and in that sense rather alluring. In other circumstances he would quite look forward to seeing it.

The Austin train station, however, is far from being

one of America's landmark termini, those lavishly endowed temples, with endless staircases and Beaux-Arts design, iconic clocks and ceilings just scraping infinity. For which, on this balmy evening, Charles finds himself inordinately grateful. The unrevered brick depot from the forties has an excellent café, which he finds a haven after all the manic, un-American driving, and is happily not a venue in which a person can lose track and become easily disconcerted.

So, romantic as it might have been in a grander forum (although he seriously doubts even this), Charles Dickens' reunion with Laura Griffin is not composed of his barging a frantic way through grey and teeming crowds, all rushing rat-like in the opposite direction towards the barrier. This is not a man terrified that in a bewilderingly overpopulated arena, even with both his hands waving madly, he might just miss the one small but vivid person he most wants to see and whom now he might never find again. If a person were going to film that scene in Austin Station, they would have to be one hell of a director.

When the train pulls in, Charles has absolutely no problem making out the sad-looking figure with the heavy bag and overstuffed suitcase, as she tentatively alights from her carriage into this new and portentous world.

Equally, Laura would have had no problem at all in noticing the man, even if he weren't rather nervously holding up a large white legal envelope, the only suitable thing he could find at a nearby store, on which is hastily scribbled 'MISS HAVISHAM' in blue sharpie. (They had run out of black but he hopes it reads okay.)

Laura simply sighs and shakes her head.

Charles is not convinced that she is secretly delighted, owing to her looking far less secretly livid. Nor is he sure that she even registers the badly scrawled allusion. He does feel, however, that a look of surprise at finding him here, just waiting for her, could have been writ a tad larger on her face, or that she could at least be exhibiting some modicum of admiration for his doggedness and wrong-side-of-the-road driving skills.

"I thought you might have gotten the damn hint," is all she says.

"I'm no good at subtext," he says, attempting to take her suitcase, which she resists quite firmly.

"Kind of a problem for a writer."

Charles suddenly feels oddly embarrassed – although there is no one around who knows him or is ever likely to – by the image of this poor woman being obliged to carry her own heavy case in his company. He then immediately feels equally unsettled that other people he doesn't know from Adam might have been watching him in disapproval, thinking he was attempting through brute strength to disempower a proud and capable female. He wonders why all this should bother him, when he can so shamelessly brandish a self-made sign bearing the name of a famous and totally fictional character from a classic Victorian novel.

He turns to face her, obliging her to stop and face back, as she has no idea where she is going, having been in this new place an even shorter time.

"I'm so sorry, Laura. About… well, you know. Not my finest hour, I'll grant you that. I'd love to explain, but it probably wouldn't help much."

"No. It probably wouldn't. It's your life. *And this is mine!* What are you doing here, Charlie?"

Charles pauses before he speaks, knowing that he must get this bit right yet having no idea what a right bit might sound like. "Y'know, I'm not sure. I suppose… well, I didn't want to leave you on your own with this. Not for a second time." This sounded okay to him, probably because he meant every word of it.

"I'm a grown-up now, Charlie. I had to grow up a long time ago."

Charles nods, realising that his words, whilst heartfelt, hadn't really done much by way of thawing. "It's your call. Of course it is. But my car's down the road. Er… block. If you think we should start looking for a place to stay tonight."

"We?"

"See, you do speak French well!"

"Jesus!" says Laura. "That is terrible. You should be ashamed of yourself."

He starts to walk towards the exit. Hoping that she will follow. Knowing now that she will follow. Probably.

"I've been racing Amtrak all fucking day," he mutters into the mild fall air, as they walk out onto North Lamar Boulevard. "Gimme a break, why don't you?" He realises that he has never actually used 'why don't you?' like this before, but when in Austin…

They don't walk far up Lamar (or down Lamar, as they have no sense of the city's geography) when they come to BookPeople, an attractive and clearly well-established bookstore. Charles, who has never passed a bookstore in his life without at least looking in the window, stops. A discreet notice reads that this shop, established as long ago as 1970, has been voted best bookstore in Austin several times.

"You're looking for your book, aren't you?" says Laura.

"*No!*" insists Charles rather too adamantly. "I'm just thinking that if a district has a fine-looking shop like this in it, it must be an okay place to stay."

"Uh huh," says Laura. "Didn't you once tell me that the best theatre in Glasgow was in the most rundown and dangerous part of the city?"

"Aye. The Cits. The Citizens. It was in the Gorbals. Still is. *You remembered!*"

"I didn't forget you, Charlie. I'm not senile. I just didn't want you coming back and trying to take over my life. And know what? I still don't."

"Looks like there's a nice hotel over there," says Charles, pointing across the road. It might be or it might not be, it could be a hellhole, but he doesn't know what else to say.

FORTY-THREE

The hotel is modern and extremely clean.

Whilst lacking in the character that appears to abound in the city itself, or indeed any character at all, at least the doors stay on. What's more, Laura can have a room as far away from Charles as possible, and has already demanded such, to the consternation of a smiley staff member. So there won't be any wondering what the person in the next room is thinking or doing or thinking of doing.

Happily, Charles's reluctant companion has at least consented to having a swift dinner with him, as it is evening and they both need to eat. He intends to make it as cordial as possible. He supposes, as he loiters in slightly smarter clothing in the large but soulless lobby, that simply by refraining from any further mention of persons with whom he has inappropriately slept, in a work or mentoring context, he would already be ahead of the game.

As he waits for her, Charles finds his mind wandering back again to Lexington, as it does more often than he might wish. Yet the journey this particular evening is perhaps more excusable. He has heard that memories of traumatic events are literally etched more deeply into a person's cells than those everyday or more pleasant recollections. He has wondered recently whether happenings which, on their occurrence, are quite sublime but are later transformed utterly in character and resonance by subsequent occurrences or discoveries, will inevitably undergo this same deep-etching process.

Charles also wonders if he spends far too much time on his own.

*

Lexington, Kentucky. May 1982

The Lexington High School Writers' Group is meeting again in the same small, dusty room.

Charlie recognises most of the faces now, as he has seen them around for the past couple of weeks and has even chatted to some of them. The redheaded boy still looks as if he would like to kill the young Scotsman but Charlie decides not to allow this to put him off. He did say '*whasgwanonwiyoupal?*' as they walked in together, but so speedily that he doubts the local could have picked up a word.

This time it is Laura Sherman who opens the proceedings, with a poem that she has only just composed. Charlie almost wishes that she hadn't, because the piece, whilst not overstaying its welcome by a pentameter, feels mortifyingly endless. This is due to it being addressed quite unselfconsciously by its creator to him alone. He knows immediately that he and his fellow writers are witnessing less a reading than a declaration. What had been mere suspicions up to this point have donned for the assembled group the delicious mantle of incontrovertible fact.

> *"How long does love take?*
> *A moment to fall into.*
> *A lifetime to test its power.*
> *But in that moment's fall, will we ever know if an*
>   *eternity awaits us there?*
> *Can we truly sense that it is a forever moment,*
> *Until forever is no more?"*

Even when she has concluded her reading, Laura's eyes stay focussed on Charlie's unmoving but not unmoved face. They only shift when her fellow writers round off this first offering with polite applause and an almost choreographed sequence of raised eyebrows. Charlie can sense their attention shifting as one onto him, to check out his reaction. So he applauds too, looking everywhere but at Laura, until the eyes have moved on.

Before the next reader is invited, he swiftly jots something down in his trusty pad.

One of the other girls, a friend of Laura's, now turns to him. "Your turn, Charlie."

"And not William MacGodawful, please!" Laura laughs.

Charlie finishes his scribbling and stands. He has no idea what he is going to say and the only items in his pad are rough ideas for stories yet to be written or rambling first impressions of America. There is one slight piece he has just bashed out this morning but he knows that it is most probably shit. And he is already aware that he doesn't want to be associated with anything less than great. He doubts his audience will know the difference. Excepting, of course, that Laura will.

"O-kay. Thanks. Howsabout my homage to George Bernard Shaw? Y'know, 'Separated by a common language.'" He begins to read somewhat tentatively from his notepad.

"*I used to pound the pavements, do I now dollar the sidewalks…?*'"

Which thankfully, on completion, garners the odd clap and a few polite smiles.

*

Austin, Texas. November 2004

"Charlie?"

Charles turns with a start, as if awoken sharply from a dream. He seems almost alarmed to see Laura standing beside him. She looks quite elegant in a plain cream blouse and well-tailored pale grey slacks, a woollen shawl of navy blue over her arm. As his ma would say, albeit at times backhandedly, she 'scrubs up well'. Yet to Charles that huge red handbag now appears to be weighing her down, alongside what he can only imagine are her thoughts.

He notices instantly the tension that is clenching her face and indeed her whole frame, wound tight – as she surely must be – by an anxiety that a fresh and spacious chain-hotel bedroom and fine Texas plumbing have so far failed to alleviate.

"*The title!*" he almost yells. "To my book."

"Excuse me?"

She is taken aback, as if some strange man has suddenly begun ranting in public and there is nothing she can do to stop him. And he does currently look just on the wrong side of demented.

"*It was yours!* From a poem you wrote way back. A poem about us. I only just rem—"

"I really don't think so. Where did you want to eat?"

Charles realises that it is time to move on, although he does still feel slightly chilled by this recent, wholly unappreciated revelation. "No idea. Let's just walk and find a place. Check out the city."

"*I'm not on fucking holiday!*" She feels his stare – indeed, she feels more than one shocked stare – but has no plans to apologise. "I'm quite tired, Charlie. And know what – tomorrow is a pretty big day. For me."

"I know. I do know, Laura," he says, contritely yet wanting desperately to change the mood, ease her anguish, if only for a moment. "But I only got to that month in 1987," he says, lightly. "Y'know, when I was asked to leave my law firm."

"Are the ensuing months and years just as life-enhancing?"

"An author never reveals his plots."

He offers her what he considers one of his most disarming smiles. It hits the small of her back as she exits through the hotel's revolving doors.

FORTY-FOUR

After some minutes of stilted and relatively aimless walking, Charles Dickens and Laura Griffin, briefly lovers, biologically parents and now barely even acquainted, find themselves at what they take to be the bank of a wide river, a strip of water which they soon discover is known in this part of town as Lady Bird Lake. Charles wonders if this might be named after the former First Lady. After all, weren't she and her husband, the late President Johnson, both Texans?

It is a while before he and Laura converse again, although Charles can tell that she is searching almost desperately for some adequate and not-too-fancy, get-this-evening-over-with nourishment. So it comes as some surprise that it is she who asks the first question, one which is far from sustenance-related.

"The name of your character. The woman – well, girl – in your book."

Charles has just seen his first guy in a white Stetson, so is slightly late in responding. "Estella?" he says, finally.

"Uh huh. From *Great Expectations*, right? Did you select it because she was callous and manipulative?"

Charles says nothing. When she turns to look at him, he appears unexpectedly sad.

"…Charlie? I'm not taking offence or anything. Hey, like you keep saying, it's just a novel."

He lowers his voice, although he suspects that his accent might make him impenetrable here anyway. "It's the name… the name we were going to call our daughter. Had she been born. Estella comes out good, you know, Laura. In the end."

Laura stops walking. For a moment, she thinks that she stops breathing. "Oh, Charlie. What happened?"

He leans against the balustrade and looks over onto the lake. Some people are kayaking, others enjoying stand-up paddle boards. The occasional tourist steamboat passes by. There appears to be some flurry of activity further up by a bridge, but he can't quite make it out.

"My wife – my ex-wife – was into her seventh month of pregnancy. And she was doing fine. More than fine. Textbook. Then the baby – a wee girl, apparently – just sort of, well… stopped."

He feels a hand rest gently on the arm of his light summer jacket.

"Ohh, Charlie. I don't know what to… why didn't you tell me?"

He shakes his head. "I did sort of want to tell you, Laura, I really did somewhere – but we were only up to July '87." He hears her soft sigh float past him onto the water. "It's something I try not to dwell on."

"*YOU?*" says Laura, far louder than intended. People

317

nearby turn to stare. "You?" she repeats more quietly, although he probably got the first one. "Someone who's been so invested in the what-coulda-shoulda-woulda-beens damn near all his adult life!"

She is correct, of course, so he can only shrug. Perhaps he should have said that it was something he hadn't wanted to talk about too much in these tricky circumstances, and still doesn't, as if he might be accused of using that poor little unborn girl's fate to seek some sort of sympathy and special treatment this time round. I'll see your trauma and raise you.

"Did you... you and your wife... try again? After..."

He shakes his head and looks towards the bridge. There is definitely something curious going on up there. "We were hoping it... she... Estella... would save or at least prop up for some while longer a pretty shaky marriage. I truly doubt this would have been the case. Is it ever? And without her, well, things took their pretty inevitable course. Ironic, isn't it, after that wee story I sent you, so long ago. Art and life! Maybe we should've bought a dog." He turns back to Laura with a smile he doesn't feel and continues in a cheerier voice that isn't quite his. "Laura, I've been driving like a maniac all day. I have got to get something vast and American to eat. But first, do you mind if we check out that bridge?"

"The bridge?"

"Aye, look." He points along the water, where some sort of black dust or mist appears to be rising into the twilight, blocking the view. "There's something very curious going on down there. A load of birds, or something."

"*They ain't birds, hon.*"

They turn around to find a smartly dressed, elderly lady, in a wheelchair.

"No? What are they then?" asks Charles.

"They's bats."

"*BATS!*" they both exclaim at once, as they turn to watch the black swarm hovering in what looks like their thousands.

"They come right on in from Mexico, like me. Exceptin' I took a bus." The old lady laughs at this, showing a set of gleaming off-white teeth. "Come out at night, to feed on bugs. Don't usually stay this late in the year, but it's been extra warm."

"Well, thanks for… all the information," says Charles.

"You two kids ever seen a bat before?" asks the woman.

Charles and Laura look at each other, as they both suddenly remember.

"Possibly," says Charles.

"Maybe," says Laura.

"Say, ma'am," says Charles, who never usually employs a 'say', or a 'ma'am', "do you happen to know a really decent Tex-Mex restaurant around here?"

"This is Texas, I'm Mexican, what do you think?" Charles and Laura wait her out. "Rosario's, by the bridge. Tell them Jesenia sent you." Charles and Laura nod their thanks and move on, as Jesenia offers one final local tip. "*Their bat wings are delicious!*"

"Do you think she means that?" asks Charles. He receives only a stare.

They walk on a bit further, in silence, intrigued by the natural attraction up ahead, yet still disturbed by what just went before. "Laura, did you truly want to get right away from me this morning?"

"I truly did, Charles."

"Oh. Okay." He wants to ask if she still does but senses that he might not appreciate the answer.

FORTY-FIVE

Whilst he doubts that the mention of Jesenia's revered name has changed anything much by way of seating or service, Charles has no complaints about the meal.

Yet curiously, despite having been ravenous all evening, he now finds that he has less stomach than he thought for the rather exotic food set before him and is perhaps possessed of a far less accommodating belly than those sported by those enthusiastic patrons he can spot happily guzzling nearby.

It is as if the bats – and there seemed to be millions of them out there, all scouring the air for their evening meal – have summoned up not simply memories but some sort of reckoning. He can't even find sustenance in the flowing conversation, because so far there isn't any. Whilst he is deep into his own thoughts, Laura is also clearly miles away. Not miles from Austin, he suspects, but most certainly leagues from him.

When she does finally speak, Charles feels an almost bodily shock, as if someone who has observed a vow of silence for decades suddenly asks a stranger to pass the mustard. Yet, from the casual way Laura is talking, an outside listener would assume that the topic under discussion had already begun its journey some good time before.

"...So she told me on the phone... that her dad had died a couple of years ago. She loved him very much. Still in Ohio, go figure." Laura shakes her head sadly. "It's just her and her mom now. She – Erin – is at the university here in town. It's an excellent school, she must be very bright, Charlie." Charles nods in agreement; he can't argue with inevitability. "Her mom is okay with, y'know, her little girl reaching out to me. Kinda okay."

"Good woman. Decent. Has to be hard for her."

Laura gulps her wine. It's her third glass. Charles suddenly wonders if she has a problem and then just as suddenly wonders if the problem she has is Charles.

"Sometimes these kids," she says, almost to herself, "y'know, like adopted kids – they just want to know like who you are. Jeez, I'm channelling Jess! '*Like*'! Just to discover who you are – and why in God's name you didn't want them to stay a part of your life forever. Didn't *need* them to be part of your life. Then they can scoot back home and get on with their own. Life. Without you. Like forever."

"How are you with that?" asks Charles, gently.

She shrugs. "Hey, if she's happy. Who am I to...?" He notices the tears just starting to form. "She sounded okay, y'know, on the phone. A deal less shaky than me, that's for sure."

With this, they return to silence.

Despite being lost in her own thoughts and fears, Laura notices that Charles is looking increasingly uncomfortable, as if he doesn't know exactly how to behave or what to say.

Yet, in truth, Charles is clearer and more certain about what he wants to tell her, how he believes this whole thing should play out, than he has been for some while.

"Laura, I'm going back home," he announces quietly. "Tomorrow, first thing. Back to London. I'll leave the car at the airport here."

Charles can't be certain whether the anxious and visibly tormented woman across the table from him is staring over her half-devoured food in relief or surprise, although he suspects that it is a comforting blend of both. For some reason she takes off her glasses.

"*Seriously?* Before I even meet…?"

He nods swiftly, trying to ignore how this first, unexpected glimpse of a spectacle-free Laura makes her look.

"I've… well, I've barged back into your life," he reminds her. "Steamrollered, more like. Just at the very time you needed peace. Space. *Breathing* space. You made that clear this morning, at the motel, when you buggered off. All too clear. And I should have taken this for an answer, of course I should, instead of… Okay, maybe I helped you come to a decision about meeting Erin, and if so, I'm truly glad I did, but it's one I'm pretty certain you would have to come to in your own time. So, you were right, Laura. You were right all along. You *should* be here on your own."

He shakes his head and tries to offer a smile. Something inside him doesn't want to make this too heavy or drawn out, for her sake as much as his. "You've been her mother for twenty-one years, Laura. I can only imagine how those years were for you – the pain that won't ever have gone away, despite the life you built for yourself. No, I can't imagine. But compared to that, I'm what? A... a distant relative. At best."

"O-kay," says Laura, quietly, "so what do I tell her, Charlie – about you?" She knows that she is still in shock from the abrupt reversal but has to take him at his word. A word she clearly knows that she has encouraged.

Charles might have hoped for at least a sliver of protest at his self-deprecation, a token rebuttal or a vain attempt to dissuade, but he understands how pressing this particular question has to be for her and must always have been.

"Whatever works for you," he says. "Erin's bound to want to learn how she, y'know, happened. And at least she'll know now that it was an act of love. Well, I *hope* it was." When Laura continues to keep her own counsel, Charles ploughs on. He knows that this was something he had thought of earlier, when they passed the old bookstore near the station, but hadn't yet found the right time to broach. With an attempt at half a smile, he says, "Shame you didn't bring my book with you."

"Thank you, Charlie," she says, softly. "For... your understanding. And yeah, I can't disagree, it's probably for the best. But know what, I did—"

"There's another reason why I should get out of your life," he says, interrupting her, because he realises that this is what he has to say, what he *needs* to say. "Something I'm less proud of."

Laura, who has been keeping a tally of things of which this man shouldn't be proud, is disappointed but not totally surprised that there's more. "You're a criminal."

"What? *No!* Of course I'm not a criminal. What sort of books do you read, Laura?"

"Sorry." They find themselves both smiling. Not huge grins but clearly identifiable. And this time he can really see her unframed eyes. "I'm so sorry."

Charles says nothing but attempts another sally at whatever is on his plate. He can't quite remember what he had ordered from one of Jesenia's pals, but naturally it had arrived trucker-size. "Lost my thread now. Oh. Aye." He takes an audible breath. Laura has no idea what's coming this time but already finds herself apprehensive. "When I said… some time in all this madness… that I'm over you." He stops here, so she is not certain whether this was a complete thought. Didn't sound much like one, but who knows with this person? And now he seems to be taking out his wallet.

"Okay," she says, almost relieved. "You want to get the check? Great. Let's split it. After all you've spent, what with the car hire…"

Charles shakes his head. It isn't one of his credit cards that he pulls out. It looks like a photo of some sort. From another era. One that has clearly seen better days.

"I can't seem to let this go," says Charles, the sadness in his voice overlaid with what sounds to Laura surprisingly like guilt. Or, at least, contrition.

She takes the crumpled snapshot from him and examines it with extreme delicacy, as if it is some sort of precious heirloom, a relic of a different time, one that she is expertly assessing for authenticity. "Looks like you had a damn good try," she says, thoughtfully. "That was Raven Run Park. It was our last day, as I recall. Together, I mean."

"It was." He is finding it strangely difficult to look into her face, so he addresses the rest of his conversation, which is slowly resembling a confession, towards his still-heaving plate. "I don't think I am 'over you', Laura. Or, at least, the you I loved way back when. Okay – call me immature, fixated, I dunno, locked into some sort of idealised past. Compounded, of course, and most probably magnified, by the decades of inexplicable silence. Well, inexplicable until now. Nobody real can be *that* perfect, can they? Not even you."

"No, Charlie—"

"You were like my emotional gold standard, and anyone else who came along was – how can I put it – base metal. Bonkers, I know. And unfair. To them. Unkind." He realises that he is almost giving a reading, or a lecture, yet he can't seem to stop. "But the only way I can explain it is, well, it's like a… a condition. An obsession. Something I can't fully move past or get around. Ha, I'm *stuck*, Laura. On you. Lord knows I've tried. But I'm not sure I'll ever completely, y'know, manage." He raises his head and smiles sadly at her. "Pathetic, isn't it? Britain's oldest schoolboy."

Laura doesn't respond, although she has clearly been listening with some intensity. She turns round in her chair and reaches down into her extra-large bag. As Charles watches in some bemusement, with no idea how she is reacting to his words and now fervently wishing that he could have just kept them to himself, she lifts out her copy of his latest book.

He shakes his head quite vehemently. "Oh God! *Please don't quote my own bloody book at me!* I know my guy finally moves on. Thanks to the love of a good woman. People yearn for happy endings. Give the people what they want, I say. But I didn't find that woman – not for the want of trying! And each time that I failed, I swung right back to my default state. *You!* Maybe that's why I kept failing. You did quite a job on me, Ms Sherman!" He taps her hand very gently, nothing too provocative, then takes it away before she can react or withdraw. "Sorry, Laura, I'm not good old Oliver, that well-bred English guy from my novel. I wish I was. I truly wish I was someone who could finally, y'know, move on and just… fly!"

Laura is still silent. He is starting to feel that he has humiliated himself with his honesty. If this is what it is. And maybe her too. Demeaned himself to a person he no longer knows and perhaps never really did. He can almost see his guts spilled helplessly all over his half-eaten enchiladas.

After some moments of reflection, Laura turns to the back of the book. The well-read and forensically examined adoption letter is still there, protected by the world's most uninformative dust jacket.

Laura lifts it out, provoking Charles's curiosity. Surely she is not going to read it aloud to him and to the assembled Tex-Mexes? Yet she simply sets it aside to reveal the smaller piece of paper behind it. She takes hold of this item very carefully, turns it around for Charles to see and gently sets it down on the still food-heavy table. Right next to his distressed memento of that last day in Raven Run Park.

Charles needs no explanation as to what she is offering him. It is the faded photo of himself, taken that same day, at almost the same time. A kilted Norman Gemmell is still gurning in the background. The twenty-two-year-old artefact is a little faded, perhaps, a tiny bit frayed, yet very far from crumpled.

"I fear that might just make two of us, Charlie Dickens," admits Laura Griffin, formerly Laura Sherman, in a voice far softer and more tender than he has experienced in all these past days and months. A voice he recalls now, with some yearning, from a time that quite suddenly doesn't seem nearly so far away.

The two travelling companions, fleetingly lovers, now unexpectedly and uncomfortably parents, still strangers – only maybe now not so much – just stare at each other. In shock, perhaps, and with some forgivable unease.

Yet this time it's also a far more familiar gaze, one they both seem to recall, from a time of innocence and rapture and just the occasional bat.

"Or three of us," says Charles. "With Norman."

FORTY-SIX

Charles is sensing that to mention condoms right now, or more specifically his lack of them, might immediately spoil the mood.

A mood that had been sustained throughout the slightly hurried walk back to their hotel, this time hand in hand and occasionally lip to lip. He is still marvelling at how normal it had felt to be close to her, for the first time in twenty-two years, and even how familiar her touch and scent have been, despite the inevitable changes the decades have wrought on them both.

He doesn't recall a demanding of the universe, that first time – *what the hell is happening?* – even though the experience wasn't even remotely close to anything in his previous history. In those far-off glory days, he was with the moment and he simply knew.

This time round, older if not wiser, he has been finding it just a bit more tricky, because he is far from certain what the moment actually is and where the hell they are going with it. He is also musing on what exactly he just did or said this evening that has totally reversed the dynamics of the day – or was he simply missing something that was always there, bubbling under the sometimes glacial surface? An undercurrent that he, as an acknowledged observer and chronicler of human interaction, should have bloody well noticed.

Where they did go with this was in the direction of Laura's anonymous hotel room, clutching on to each other for dear life, arms gliding and patting and grasping like an overzealous body search, as they both tried to bang open the door with their almost locked hips, hopefully without falling over into an indelicate heap for the Austin-visitor world to pass by and see. Charles could already feel her soft but purposeful hands moving hungrily inside his shirt, as he wondered whether his pulling her flimsy blouse over her head would serve to stimulate or strangle.

When they finally ended up still clasped but naked in her bed, he had broached the obvious question. The latex elephant in the room.

"Er, Laura. I don't have any… I only expected supper."

"And you didn't even finish that. Don't worry, hon," she says, between kisses. "This time the precautions are on me. You just carry on with what all you're doin' and forget about 'jimmys.'"

"'Johnnies,'" corrects Charles, kissing the little mole he still remembers, even from the darkness, just below her left breast.

"Pedant," says Laura, but only softly, as she also recalls that kiss.

Austin, Charles and Laura are slowly waking up.

"Well, it surely was more comfortable than a cave," murmurs Laura dozily, turning to look at him in a way they both know they never did on their only previous encounter, frenzied and dank and Homeric as it was. Although they would probably both admit to a similar sense of shell-shock as to what has just occurred.

"And a damn sight more expensive," says Charles, knowing in an instant that this has never made any list of the ten most romantic post-coital things to say. Nor, as even he would later admit, has his follow-up. "Laura, can I tell you something?"

"Charlie, please," she says, in some concern, "you really don't have to say anything."

"I really do."

He has turned to her now in the semi-darkness, feeling the warmth of her still achingly familiar, though admittedly far from identical, body. She herself had acknowledged this painful evolution several times during their passionate encounter, meeting his gentle denials every time, always accompanied by his own gracious admissions of inevitable age-related wear and tear. (Which, of course, gave immediate lie to his own gallant reassurances, but at least he tried.)

Charles knows, with a sudden jolt, that he must face Laura Griffin, eye to languorous eye, and say what he now realises has to be said. What this unexpected night has obliged him to say.

"I really think I'm over you now, Laura."

Laura pulls sharply away from him, languor vanishing like the setting sun. She flicks on the room light from her bedside. They both blink in the sudden glare, before she turns back to him, horrified.

"You're over me! You are *OVER* me?" She scrapes a hand hard through her hair, waking up fast. "O-kay. So last night, that was all… what, to get to some sort of completion? Like a friggin' exorcism! Or even… Jeez, no – revenge?"

"Perhaps I didn't express myself too well."

"*You're a writer!* It's what you do."

"Aye. Okay. You got me. But what I meant was… well, last night… when we were, y'know…"

"I was there, Charles."

"Exactly!" He can see that he has totally lost her now, but still he ploughs on hopefully. "*So was I!* There! Right there with you. Laura Griffin. Aged thirty-nine."

"Appreciate the age check."

"Not with Laura Sherman, aged seventeen. Or with any of the women I chose – because, perhaps subconsciously, they reminded me of you but clearly couldn't be. Not with Abi Chadwick either. That young woman who…" She winces. "Okay, forget Abi Chadwick. *I was right there!* Right here. In the now. In… the moment."

"Sounding a bit new-agey, but that's Austin for you."

He moves away from her and slips his feet out of the bed, so that he can sit upright on the side, above the sheets, and talk directly to the curtains, through which some morning light is already beginning to seep. To Laura it seems as if he is trying to centre himself, prior, perhaps, to a further confession. God knows what is coming down the pipe now. Although she does wonder if he is talking more to himself than to her.

"For over twenty years I've been *blaming* you," he admits, to an unfeeling Austin, shaking his head slightly as he talks, as if he can't quite believe it himself. "That was my... narrative. Twenty sodding years. For every failed relationship, every demolished dream, every fuck-up. Because it was so much easier to make *you* the scapegoat – the first love, who so cruelly dumped me, who prevented the perfect story from ending the way it was supposed to. Easier to harbour this 'grudge', nurture this... betrayal, than to just face up to myself and my own inability to, I dunno... aye, I do know – to *commit*. Fully. To grow up. Fully. Even in my marriages, I don't think I was really there, Laura. I was in a world of bloody fiction. The realm of 'what if?'. And you were part of my forever unfinished story."

He laughs to himself. "Y'know, I sometimes wonder if you and I had kept on writing, if you hadn't suddenly stopped, whether we wouldn't have just petered out anyway, because of me. Because of who I truly was. Yet in my head I was always the loyal one, the steadfast, stolid one – even when I was totally fucking up. I did begin to move on, y'know, with this last book – or I fooled myself that I had. But even then..."

He feels a warm hand rest lightly on the already chilled skin of his shoulder. As if it wants to intervene in the self-flagellation.

"So all you needed to get over me..." she murmurs.

"...*was you!*" Charles manages to laugh at this. "The

new, and dare I say tastefully improved, Laura. Who I'm just starting to get to know. And, despite some pretty massive bumps along the way, to like." He pauses for a moment, as if scared of going too far or at least preparing himself for how far he fully intends to go. "And – I've said it once and I'll say it again – starting to fall in love with."

He hears a tinkling yet throaty laugh from behind him. Not something he has heard much of recently, except perhaps in his head.

"Well, Mister Dickens," she says, in her most southern drawl, "as ah believe ah may have told you on a previous occasion, you suh are one of the last true romantics." She stands up and joins him at his side of the bed. "But y'know, Charlie, just maybe I am too. Lordy! Who knew?" Laura can't look at him, not just yet. She can suddenly see the advantages of talking to a hotel curtain. "Funny, I guess, somewhere, it was always you. I just didn't know it until you turned up again in my life – and right then, well it was all too much for me. My world is small, Charlie. It can't take earthquakes. But a few just happened all at once, still happening, and it has thoroughly floored me. So… okay – where do we go from here? More letters – or is it email now?"

Charles turns back to her. "I'm not sure, Laura. Not sure of anything anymore. But you… well, don't you have a daughter to meet?"

Laura Griffin closes her eyes. As the fear rushes straight back in.

FORTY-SEVEN

Austin is acting as if it doesn't know or even care that this is the most important day in the history of the world. Whilst its two better-informed visitors, the pair exiting through the hotel's revolving doors, are under no such illusions.

Charles reckons that they must look to passers-by like a couple who are going through a very bad patch and had felt, in some misguided way, that a break in such a splendid, historic city on Thanksgiving weekend might just make things right again. He also wonders when he will stop acting like an observer of his own life and suddenly realises that for one night at least, the quite beautiful night just passed, he might magically have done just that.

"You okay?" he asks Laura, clasping her hand once more, a clasp that has barely been released for the past hour, save for risk of accident in the revolving door.

"No."

"She asked to meet you, Laura. Erin wants to meet you."

Laura turns to Charles, seeking only truth in his expressive, lopsided and once again so familiar face. "What if... what if she's built up this picture of me? Maybe for her whole life. Like in *Annie*." She watches a look of bewilderment cloud his already concerned face. "The *musical*? Oh, come on! And what if... Charlie, what if she's bitterly disappointed? It's not as if I'm anything special."

Charles feels on safer ground now. "Actually, you are, Laura. You're a very special person. Take a walk now. Go – clear your head. She'll be every bit as nervous as you. Trust me."

Laura nods, taps his hand gratefully and starts to walk away.

She tries to remember the directions given to her by the concierge. The route to the small café where she and her grown-up daughter will finally meet. Fortunately, it is not too far, as she doesn't believe she has the strength to take her yearning, aching and, after last night, quite exhausted body right across a city.

"And Laura," he calls to her, before she strays out of earshot, "if all your daughter needs is to see you just this one time, then you're giving her all that she needs."

She suddenly skips back and kisses him.

"Thank you for being here, Charlie Dickens. Really here."

"I'll be really here in the lobby. When you're done."

She walks more resolutely away, turning after a few steps to see her very first love, now fully grown into someone not a million miles away from the guy she had always expected him to be, only possibly a bit weirder and a tad more wayward, and maybe still a little lost, watching her from outside the hotel. Then, turning just once more, as she realises that she is walking in totally the wrong direction.

*

Until he began mapping out this journey, Charles had never fully taken on board that Austin, a city that he is growing rather to like and admire, is the state capital of Texas. But then again, he reasons, as he begins his solitary stroll, how many Texans know that Edinburgh is the capital of his own tiny and distant realm?

His saunter this morning – although the casualness of this word belies his mental state – is relatively aimless. Downtown Austin may be appealing and its flagship building, the sunset-red granite State Capitol, eye-catchingly Texan-huge, but he is somewhere else entirely in his head.

Being mentally elsewhere, Charles knows only too well, is practically his default state. He has always assumed, often in his own defence, that this is probably also the case for a majority of his fellow writers and indeed for most people whose work and life is predominantly creating something where nothing was before. It sounds almost God-like, as he mulls it to himself. He wonders if this accounts for what even he recognises in himself as a certain arrogance, a posture that can often mask the permanent, existential dread.

Yet today, the elsewhere-ness and the churning rush inside of him have taken a seismic leap and seem even

337

more overwhelming. The thoughts screaming inside his brain feel like they're going to blow his head wide open.

It is only when he receives a particularly stern look from a young woman passing by and watches another deliberately carving a path away from him, that he realises he has been carefully scrutinising every Caucasian female of a certain age and speculating if she could be his daughter.

He wishes that he could explain and apologise to them all but knows that this would be just plain creepy.

After puzzling over a signpost directing him to The Museum of the Weird, and resisting the temptation (his life is weird enough right now, thank you), he decides to return to the hotel and wait it out in caffeine-fuelled, and possibly even alcohol-enhanced, agony.

As with juries, so he has heard, the longer the wait, the better the outcome.

Or was it the worse?

FORTY-EIGHT

The staff at the smart but clinical Austin hotel are starting to take bets as to whom the Brit with the accent like Sean Connery is waiting for so restlessly. He is clearly not reading the local newspaper in his hand, as nobody outside of Austin could be that interested in what's going down within. Nor does it appear that his manically jotting down random stuff on a notepad can afford him the peace and distraction he needs.

And how much coffee can one man drink?

They wonder if someone especially important to him is keeping him on edge, as he is forever checking his watch and the clocks above the reception desk, most of which are telling him the time in countries he doesn't actually happen to be in. Whoever it is, they must be incredibly late by now or indeed, sorry to say this, sir, perhaps not coming at all. It looks very like the poor man has been stood up. Perhaps this is why at least every five minutes he is leaping up from his seat in the lobby and pacing the short distance to the exit, in order to take a good and forever frustrated look both up and down the teeming block.

It is when he is checking his phone yet again for any signs of an update, that he hears her voice almost next to him. How did he fail to spot her, he wonders, as do the relieved hotel staff, who have been keenly watching her since she had hurried in through the revolving doors, looking quite flushed and anxious.

"Charlie?"

He looks up in shock, despite her return being the one thing on his mind. Charles can tell immediately that Laura has been crying. He realises that he has absolutely no idea whether this is due to joy or despair or an unsettling cocktail of both, with a few other emotions shaken in.

He gets up too swiftly, almost banging his head on her chin. To his surprise, he can't speak, although vomiting could well be an option. So he just looks at her. Waiting. This continues for some time as she can't speak either. She can only shake, which she does with such vigour and lack of control that he has to hold her and squeeze her tight, until she settles. She is like a child's spinning top that could suddenly reel away if unconfined.

Well?

She holds her hand out to him. He reaches for it. But as he does, she turns, inclining her head and body back in a disconcerting way towards the entrance.

"*Well?*" says Charles, this time out loud, because somebody has to say something and it doesn't look like it is going to be Laura Griffin any time soon.

Instead of talking, Laura – still shaking, only not quite so much – pulls away from him. She points rather unsteadily to the doorway. All Charles can see, standing with her back towards him, is a tall young woman in a sort of hoody, leaning against a glass panel.

"Charlie," says Laura Griffin, once known to him as Laura Sherman, "would you like to meet Erin? Would you like to meet our daughter?"

THE READING

FORTY-NINE

Lexington, Kentucky. July 2016

The owner of the BlueGrass Bookstore is less sprightly now but even better read.

He appears content simply to sit in his wheelchair, discreetly parked to the side of the lectern, watchfully observing his family, as they cater with aplomb to this evening's enthusiastic patrons.

There is more adequate seating tonight than when Charles first appeared here, twelve years ago, on his momentous, short-notice visit. In fact, so far as he can recall, there was no seating at all. But the bookstore was smaller at that time, and didn't have a smart little café attached. Thankfully, the air-conditioning is on full blast this mid-summer evening, so there is a good chance that most of the audience will manage to stay awake and that his prose will be all that is glistening.

The window poster and store cards announce '07.24.2016. *C.D. MacNaughtan. Bestselling author of*

Moments Later'. Stripped across all these items is news so exciting it can only be in day-glo red: '*TONIGHT!!*' And it must have worked, as the place is filled to capacity, with some devotees even standing at the rear. The piles of books to be signed occupy two quite large tables. There is no *Da Vinci Code* to be seen.

Charles smiles at the assembled throng, as he begins his preamble.

In his early fifties, he is greying now but to his huge relief still has all or at least most of his hair. He would admit that he is showing more brow than at his first reading, but if this is the worst recession in his life, he will regard himself as a very lucky man.

"Hi there," he greets them. "And thank you all for coming, on this steamy evening. Goodness, what a turnout. As many of you know, or will do if you choose to read the new book – my first and probably last foray into memoir – I came here on a visit as a very young man. And left an important bit of myself behind."

He pauses for the laughter, which he is certain will be forthcoming. So many people here know the story. Many of them also know Laura, who is sitting near the front with Jess and Henry, now in their twenties and both home on visits. Some of these locals knew her as Laura Sherman; colleagues such as Kyra, sitting behind her and stroking her shoulder, knew her as Laura Griffin; and now her friends and students know her as Laura – or Mrs – Dickens, because Charles's age-old secret is out and he didn't die of shame.

Seated next to her daughter and grandchildren is an elderly and rather frail Mrs Audrey Sherman, who has just about forgiven her singular son-in-law for his earlier unbridled lust, because at least he didn't deceive her about his writing ambitions. And it has to be said that she can't fault him as yet on the husband/step-father front.

"I'm delighted to say," continues Charles, with a warm smile to his family and beyond, "that I'm now here a bit more permanently. I hope! And writing no doubt in a unique Kentuckian/Glaswegian rhythm. Bagpipes and banjo, as I recall, from that first 'braw' welcome you gave all of us wee Bravehearts."

He notices Laura turning round, sparked by some maternal instinct which he knows he will never fathom, just as the door of the bookstore starts very gingerly to open.

Charles follows her eyeline to see a tall, smartly dressed woman in her early thirties, accompanied by a man of similar age, who holds a small and very sleepy toddler. They both shrug apologies, as they wave to Charles and Laura.

The author smiles warmly back. "So, thank you so much for coming to this truly 'family' event." He opens the book. "Don't worry, I'm no' going to read it all." He is gratified to hear a few disappointed 'ahh's from those Lexingtonians whom he now regards as his friends.

Charles, or Charlie, looks over the book in his hand towards those same crinkling, almond-shaped eyes that first caught his attention and reeled him in so willingly, on a warm spring day, in a 'hoaching' airport, some thirty-four years earlier. And never let him go.

"But I'd like to start, if I may, where it all began…"

*

Raven Run Nature Sanctuary, Kentucky. May 1982

Now that the necessary photos have been taken and Norman 'spoiler' Gemmell has disappeared back into the undergrowth, the two young lovers can simply hold each other ribcrackingly close and contemplate the future, with a youthful confidence that right now brooks no uncertainty.

"Charlie, how many people, do you think," asks the young woman, in all seriousness, as if this is the boy's specialist subject, "who get together pretty young, are still together in their fifties?"

"Three," says the Scotsman, with some authority.

"Three!"

"Aye," he says, counting on his fingers. " Athos, Porthos and Aramis."

"Excuse me? Who the H are they?"

"The Three Musketeers. They met awful young and stayed together for years and years. Of course, they fought from time to time."

The young woman walks briskly off, shaking her head and laughing. That tinkling, gutsily musical laugh he already loves.

"You are weird, suh. See y'all!"

The visitor from a small country runs after her. Secure in the knowledge that nothing could or will ever stop them from being together.

Knowing already, as a writer, that the best stories have to be those that resolve themselves to the satisfaction of all.

IN THE END

Acknowledgements

It has to be unusual to cite a television programme as the inspiration for a novel. But it was whilst watching the superb *Queen's Gambit* on Netflix that the notion for this book occurred. Some pivotal scenes were set in the Henry Clay High School, Lexington, Kentucky, during the sixties, which was exactly when I, along with several other Glasgow teenagers, was briefly a pupil there. This was on an English Speaking Union exchange visit from state schools in Scotland. I stayed with a very hospitable family at the Veterans Administration Hospital, where my host's father was the chief medical practitioner.

The rest, as I must assure my wife and family, is pure fiction.

Paul A. Mendelson graduated from Cambridge with a first in Law, which did him little good as he very swiftly left legal practice to create award-winning advertising campaigns. He then moved from 30-seconds to 30-minutes to create several hit BBC comedy series, including BAFTA-nominated '*May to December*', '*So Haunt Me*' and the hugely popular '*My Hero*', then back to ITV for the much acclaimed Martin Clunes cancer drama '*Losing It*'. He also co-created '*Neighbors From Hell*' for DreamWorks Animation and writes regularly for BBC Radio 4 Drama.

The Forever Moment is Paul's eighth book, all of which he has scripted. Three have already been optioned for movies. Two of his novels *Losing Arthur* and *The Funnies* are for children (9+), although adults confess they enjoy them too.

Paul is married with two daughters and lives in North London.